Kathy —

Thank you for your
interest in Happy Ranch.
A new and different part
of California for you.

Enjoy,
Terry W.
(oops)

~

One dollar from each sale of this book
reported to the author will be donated to *La Casa Hogar*,
a non-profit advocacy and educational agency
for farmworker families in Yakima, Washington.

~

BELAGANA
BELAZANA

(Bilagáana-Bilasáana)

An Outsider's Quest in the Navajo Nation

T. LLOYD WINETSKY

T. Lloyd Winetsky

℗

Pen-L Publishing
Fayetteville, Arkansas
Pen-L.com

1-1

PREFACE

Not just a few outsiders have spent time in the Navajo Nation, researched tribal customs, or both, before finding the hubris to write a story from a Navajo's point of view. The author of this work does not profess a deep understanding of Navajo culture and is suspicious of non-Navajos who claim that they do. The setting and characterizations here are portrayed from the author's perspective as a self-described intruder in their land for several years. "Diné" (*Diné'é*) means the Navajo people, and "Belagana" (*Bilagáana*) means the white man—this novel supposes more about the latter than the former.

Belagana-Belazana takes place during the second half of the last century and was first drafted two years before the water crisis in Flint, Michigan, made headlines. Not written as a "topical response" to that fiasco, this book demonstrates instead that lead poisoning and other water contamination problems have been long-standing issues in the U.S., especially in low-income communities. The fictional account of lead contamination here is derived from an incident in a school, decades ago. Also, many other scenes are derived from actual circumstances.

Many states, parks, monuments, and some larger cities or towns are referred to by real names. Navajo surnames in the novel such as Benally, Nez, and many others, do not pertain to actual families or their clans. Any similarities between characters and real persons are coincidental. The poems at the beginning of some chapters are revised from the author's collection, *Belagana*.

)-)

To children who just want to trust adults—especially to those whose trust we have compromised.

)-)

1

A long-forgotten Raven Point Boarding School principal had once arranged for Jon Begay, the school maintenance man and custodian for over thirty years, to rig up a one-way buzzer from the dormitory office to the counselor's trailer. My assistant in the dorms, Leonard, told me he hadn't used the buzzer for an emergency since the previous winter.

The first time it went off at night it seemed extra loud, waking me from a sound sleep. Several hours had passed since the end of Wednesday afternoon's festivities, which had included the year's second basketball game followed by a Thanksgiving dinner with our kids and many of their relatives. We wound things up with a movie for the boarding students who hadn't been checked out of the dorm for the holiday weekend.

There was no sense trying to call Leonard on our crappy walkie-talkies, so, moving groggily, I dressed in jeans, T-shirt and an old wool sweater. My keys and flashlight stuffed into my back pockets, I put on my baseball cap and boots, expecting the emergency to be something related to our decrepit facility, maybe frozen pipes in one of the dorm bathrooms, which made me envision mopping up rusty water until dawn. The one bit of good news was that this 1:30 a.m. summons would at least give me a chance to finish the serious conversation I'd started with Leonard earlier that day.

I tossed aside the old bath towel that poorly blocked the draft under my door, pulled the handle, and stepped carefully down the wobbly, icy stairs before zipping and buttoning my navy-blue arctic parka. My mother gave it to me in Tucson before I left for the Navajo Reservation, but I didn't tell her I thought the bulging goose-down coat was overkill. Now I was grateful to have it on a frigid moonless night that would've been perfect for Halloween.

Yawning, I took out my flashlight, flicked it on, and aimed it at the thermometer on the side of the trailer—twenty-two degrees with a light breeze on my face. I wouldn't be outside long enough to need my hood, but I buried my left hand in the parka's pocket and found my gloves. I put one of them on the hand that held the flashlight and walked off, looking up at the sky. The Big Dipper's lip pointed reliably north, but scattered clouds were passing over the polestar.

On an inch or two of well-trampled snow I crunched past the dark playground, the flashlight beam ahead of me. Still drowsy, I took out my wad of keys, crossed the boardwalk to the rec room door, unlocked it, and walked in. As usual, the lights were off for the night, except in the small office, where Leonard blared unintelligibly into the phone as if speaking to Antarctica.

Walking across the stifling rec room, I unbuttoned my parka right away. As I fingered some sleep out of one eye, Marla, a night aide, came out of the boys' dorm and stood in the doorway, directing the boys—in Navajo—to get back to bed. The door at the far end of their dorm was shut, and the sleeping girls beyond were apparently unaware of the excitement as Marla killed the lights over the boys' bunks.

Leonard left the office, speaking in Navajo to Marla and handing her a note. He wore a military-surplus peacoat, showing the collars of three layers of clothes beneath. As I approached him, Leonard lugged a frame pack half as tall as his below-average height. All business, no sign of his usual cheerfulness, he stopped to secure one of the straps, and then looked up at me. "Well,

Mr. Noland," he said formally for Marla's benefit, "here we go. Your first runaways." One of his older dogs, half-crippled Marie, waited right beside him, panting eagerly as she watched Marla return to the dorms.

"I was hoping for a busted pipe." I shook off another yawn.

"No such luck. We searched everywhere around here before I buzzed you."

"Were you just calling now for some help?"

"Yeah, nobody's around. I also woke up my sister so they'd know we probably won't make it for Thanksgiving."

"Maybe this won't take that long."

"I doubt it."

"How many are missing?"

"Two, Hawthorne Shepard and—"

"His little brother?" Now fully awake, I was alarmed that Peter Shepard, a second-grader, might be out there in the elements.

"No, it's Billy."

"Good God, that's worse."

The endless Navajo sky
On a calm day
Glides the mind
Into flight,
Where horizon clouds
Are islands
And distant airplanes ships
On a bluebottle sea
That the Spaniards
And the rest
Somehow overlooked.

2

Threes have recently been wild in my life. After working on the Navajo for three years, I left three months ago like a distant cousin in the saying about relatives or fish stinking after three days—both welcome and unwelcome. That paradox will probably always be a part of me—for three main reasons, I think.

First, like so many other outsiders, I remain enchanted by the Navajos' land—its striking blend of desolation and beauty will always lure me back. In contrast, I was unprepared for the conflicts I encountered on the Navajo and now see many cultural, societal, and educational issues in a whole different light. Thirdly, I am bound to a friendship that developed out there during a manhunt in a blizzard for two boys.

Our pursuit of Hawthorne Shepard and Billy Benally took place during my first year in what is sometimes called the Navajo Reservation, the Navajo, Navajo Nation, *Dine'é bi zhaad*, the Rez, the Big Rez, and even Navajoland, which sounds like a Disney attraction. While the name changes with the predilection of the speaker, I believe the Navajo is a place that remains relatively timeless. In fact, I think these events could have occurred last fall or many autumns ago—any time of boarding schools and pickup trucks, but before what seems to be the rapidly approaching era of computers as common as both televisions and telephones in our homes.

The most useful twentieth century technology that I brought with me to the Navajo turned out to be the old red F-100 pickup that I bought years before to help with odd jobs on our suburban acre near Phoenix. After the Ford baked in the desert sun to the color of tomato soup, our daughter, Rebecca, dubbed it "Campbell," a nickname I readily adopted, although our pre-teenager became even more embarrassed by the faded old beater in our driveway.

During my three years on the Navajo, Campbell's four-wheel drive saved me from the mud and snow several times, and the kids there had their own name for my pickup soon after I showed up. "That's Father's Ol' Red Donkey," a twelve-year-old boy who spoke more English than most of the kids told me. "An' I bet your wife drives a Grandmother's Car," which stood for any GMC vehicle.

When I first ventured into Raven Point from Tsosie, on a dirt-and-rock path undeserving of the word "road," I had no wife or anyone else along to point out the obvious—that I'd likely made a mistake to take the job and would be well-advised to turn around. Forty-six at the time, I had lived in southern Arizona for most of my life, usually on my own terms.

I was an only but not a lonely child. My L.A.-born parents were tenured in the fine arts and often included me in their projects and activities. By the time my dad died during my junior year in high school, I had an iconoclastic worldview, but I generally kept it to myself. At age twenty, I wasn't as obnoxious as Holden Caulfield, as revolutionary as Eugene Debs, nor as idealistic as John Dewey, but my parents' example led me to give teaching a try.

In my first job, teaching eighth-grade English to kids mostly from settled Mexican-American families in Tucson, I discovered after a few months that I often trusted and believed young people more than I did adults. That attitude earned scorn right away from the proverbial "girl next door," whom I had naively married in my senior year of college. After our divorce, I taught in Tucson for three more years before I fell for a tall, thin, fledgling social worker from Scottsdale.

To be with her, I took a job teaching drama, speech, journalism, and creative writing to middle-income high school kids near Phoenix. Though I believed that I ran a strict classroom, I tried to offer my students new experiences in the oral and written arts. Many of them proved to be inquisitive and genuine, so my approach, as before, was usually to encourage kids and avoid adults.

Several years into the second marriage I think it was my agnosticism that drove my wife to switch to a gloomy fear-mongering version of Christianity, paired with an astrology chart she actually paid for, to guide her life and our marriage. That was the beginning of the end, capped off when our only child, at age thirteen, rejected her mother's church. I, of course, was pleased to support Rebecca's rebellion.

By the time I was forty I spoke my mind with less regard for the consequences and bid good riddance to most of my childhood friends. For a few more years, my wife and I took separate rooms under the same roof "for Rebecca's sake," until our daughter eagerly escaped our unraveled nest for a state university in California.

In the summers before Rebecca left, I enjoyed traveling alone to Oregon and Mexico, the latter so many times that I began to shun the larger Mexican cities as they became more like the rat races in L.A. and Phoenix. About the same time as the marriage reached its inevitable end, my school started a back-to-basics reform, a plan that would eliminate my "impractical" subjects until I would be left only with six periods of sophomore English.

Before we signed the divorce papers I registered with my college placement center to begin a search for a new teaching position not too far from my elderly mother in Tucson, but in a place that might encourage me to develop more of the self-sufficiency I'd come to idealize from my frequent visits to rural Mexico.

It was late June when two Federal Indian Commission administrators hired me on the spot in Tucson to teach fifth and sixth grade on the Navajo Reservation, although I had no experience with kids that young. Until then, my exposure to Native Americans consisted of little more than driving past the San Xavier and Gila River Reservations, and once attending a Yaqui Easter ritual to get credit for an anthropology class.

ꞁ-ꞁ

So, in mid-August I set out for the Navajo Reservation in Campbell, driving past Phoenix without stopping to see my ex-wife. After abandoning social work years before to become a tax accountant, she had hidden the fact that everything we owned, except my truck, was in her name, including both our cars and the house. During the divorce I had agreed to accept a fourth of the disposable cash, and said to hell with the rest of it. I headed north with camping gear, clothes, boxes of books, a few cartons of packaged and canned food, plus some other basic household necessities, leaving the rest of my scant possessions in my mother's basement in Tucson.

It had never bothered me before to leave the familiar Sonoran Desert. I always intended to "Come Back Soon" as if beholden to a Chamber billboard on the outskirts of town. As the saguaros gave way to sage then ponderosa pine, I fought off an unexpected sense of detachment and tried to focus on the experiences ahead. My mixed emotions leveled off a couple of hours later on my return visit to the red rock country south of Flagstaff, where I turned off into a picnic area under rouge-colored cliffs and enjoyed a sandwich and a cold beer.

As much as I wanted to see Grand Canyon again, it was still tourist season, and a map search showed my new school was only about four hours away. I hoped for some fall excursions to the Canyon with the idea that I would have the amazing gorges mostly to myself.

East of Flagstaff was all new country to me. Not an hour past the tree line, I took a bypass onto old Route 66 through desolate high desert terrain—scrub vegetation interrupted only by a few dusty highway towns. I checked the map before sunset and saw that I'd be skirting the southern border of the Navajo Reservation almost all the way to Gallup, New Mexico. One road sign piqued my interest during the long drive in the dark—a turn-off for Petrified Forest National Park, a detour that would have to wait for another day.

It grew late and I saw no obvious place to camp before Gallup, so I splurged for a room in one of several cheap one-story motels with neon VACANCY signs. After a restless night in the noisy accommodations, I slept in that Monday morning, knowing I had until one o'clock to make it a few more miles to "New Teacher Orientation" in the outskirts of Gallup.

Breakfast was cold eggs and hot watery coffee in a grungy café near four somber dark-skinned men, seemingly hung over. Their worn-out work clothes gave me no hint if they were Mexican, Navajo, or from some other tribe. After my dull repast, Gallup at midday was still half asleep as I drove by idle pawnshops, taverns, drab stores, and a sign that read, GALLUP—INDIAN CAPITAL OF THE WORLD. I left city limits, following my FIC directions to a large school where we would board in student dorms for the rest of the week.

After orientation began in the auditorium, our second speaker made it clear that I was getting into something I hadn't quite expected. Not only is the Navajo tribe the largest in the U.S., the majority of its people live in small family clusters across a reservation larger than West Virginia, their land spilling over from Arizona into Utah and New Mexico. The Navajo, unlike most other tribes, have managed to hold onto much of what had always been their sacred ground—what latecomers decided to call the Four Corners area, an arbitrary spot in the high desert where "a fella can actually put his hands in Utah and Colorado and his feet in Arizona and New Mexico," as I once heard a tourist gush in Phoenix.

Another FIC presenter told us in a supercilious tone that the Navajos were among the least "acculturated" of the native peoples. As if describing a deficit, he explained that the majority of Navajos had clung to their native religion, culture, and language regardless of "untiring efforts" by teachers and preachers. Indeed, I was hired to teach English to kids like Billy Benally, raised in a traditional hogan miles from the nearest neighbor and rounded up every school year to be confined and sheared, not unlike the ubiquitous Navajo sheep.

I didn't know what to make of the mostly reticent Navajos at orientation who worked for the Commission. They quietly ran the meetings along with talkative short-haired, light-skinned guys in suits, some of whom were "white" while others turned out to be part Cherokee, Shawnee or Ute. None of those administrators, Navajo or not, wore symbols of indigenous culture, unless you counted cuff links or bolo ties with polished stones of turquoise or petrified wood.

A ridiculous anthropologist from Tempe spoke to us in beads and a fringy leather outfit, but one presenter, a Mrs. Joe, appeared in what I took to be genuine Navajo garb—a long cotton skirt, blue satin blouse, and a resplendent silver and turquoise necklace. Her black hair was tied with white wool yarn, gathered into a heavy bun at the back of her head. Obviously uncomfortable, she lectured for an hour in clear but monotonous English on *Dine'é*, the People, and The Navajo Way. By the end of the day she had changed into a business suit and wore poufy hair, busily attending to the male bureaucrats' whims.

That first day was followed by three and a half more to indoctrinate us on the textbook we were to use for English as a Second Language. The book's pedantic co-author, an Austrian woman older than me from some college in Texas, adamantly told us that her "scientifically proven" method to teach English was the "only" one that worked, but her own barely understandable speech cast serious doubts on that claim. Less than zealous about being a missionary for Standard American English, I managed to keep my opinions to myself.

On the last day of orientation, a teacher on her way to a small school in a different agency said she'd been warned to stock up on perishables before leaving Gallup. I just wanted to get out of there, so I took off late that Friday afternoon and followed my road map to Window Rock, Arizona—the home of Navajo tribal government. It was after dark by then, and I pressed on, missing any chance to see the town or the countryside but determined to make it to Tsosie—which, according to my map, was the closest highway town to Raven Point.

About fifty more miles in sparse traffic finally brought me to another town, Old Mission, where just a handful of businesses—a gas station, café, and a log trading post—had closed for the night. I passed a church, then a well-lit but deserted government compound consisting of an FIC school and Old Mission Agency, the office in charge of my school in Raven Point, somewhere off to the south of this town.

In the next two hours I saw a few dirt side roads and an occasional electric light to the east, but all was pitch black to the west. Not one car passed me, and when I finally met the first pair of headlights it dawned on me that one of Campbell's not-so-rare breakdowns would leave me in one hell of a predicament. I'd followed the advice of a friend who warned me to bring along extra fuses, oil, brake fluid, antifreeze, filters, belts, and spark plugs, although I didn't know what to do with half of them.

When Campbell's temperature gauge leaned toward to the "H" side, I downshifted and slowed to a steady forty-five, constantly checking the dashboard. It was nearly eleven when I finally saw the lights of a small town to the east. A bent sign at the crossroads said TSOSIE, an arrow pointing to the right. Making the turn, I drove toward a singular concentration of streetlights, then entered the Tsosie Boarding School compound. I parked in a mostly vacant lot, retrieved some gear from the truck bed, locked up, and then dozed fitfully through that warm night atop my sleeping bag on Campbell's front seat.

)-|

When I woke the next morning I didn't see any school buildings, just rows of yellow, pink, baby-blue, peach, and pastel-green stucco duplexes and bungalows, the larger ones with garages—government housing, just like near Gallup. I put on my baseball cap, got out, stretched my stiff bones, and stowed the sleeping bag in back. Several kids were messing around on bikes near their homes on that mild late-August morning. Two of them were white, the rest Native American, likely a mixture of Navajo and other tribes. A mature poplar grew in each dirt yard, their verdant leaves yet to show signs of autumn.

The kids' banter was the only noise until a car started up over in the next row of houses. Aware of something different about the horizon, I climbed up into the truck bed to get a better look, first noticing that all the TV antennae were secured to the rooftops with industrial guy wire that augured some stiff winds.

The inviting green mountains to the east had sufficient altitude to grow stands of pine—the source, we were told at orientation, for a Navajo lumber industry. A young and very tan teacher, perhaps Navajo herself, had asked politely if the tribe was re-seeding those forests. A middle-aged Navajo official told her gruffly, "That's up to Mother Nature." A younger man on the tribal panel said nothing and just shook his head.

The cloudless blue sky above me was almost royal—no smoke, smog, steam, or even dust in the air. To the north, west, and south, the horizon seemed endless, as if you could see beyond the curvature of the earth. After a raven squawked its brief complaint overhead I could hear the drafts of its beating wings before it disappeared. Temporarily mesmerized, I finally climbed down and got into the cab to dig out a spiral notebook from my backpack. Hoping to do justice to that amazing sky, I found myself writing and revising a poem for the first time in months.

When I pulled out of the housing area about a half hour later, I passed two yellowish, block-long school buildings—not a person in sight. Beyond the compound, I came to the main street through Tsosie, where there was no traffic at all. A sign read, STATE ROAD to the left, TSOSIE CREEK to the right. Taking neither turn, I drove across to a dirt lot cut out of the high desert scrub for a small shopping center. It housed a coin laundry, a closed café, and a gas pump in front of a market with dirty white walls, where scabs and chips revealed a previous orange paint job. The grocery displayed a large Coca-Cola placard with the words, TSOSIE STORE and YA-TA-HEY—a word I had seen on signs in Gallup. We were told at orientation that it was the Anglicization of *Yá'át'ééh*, a Navajo greeting apparently closer to "All is well" than to "Hello."

I parked by a sedan that had a flat tire. Beyond it were two pickups, one as old as mine, the other a new blue Chevy. I locked my truck and looked to the storefront, where a dark-skinned man with short hair, probably in his fifties, dozed while sitting straight up on a bench, a lit cigarette in hand. In scuffed shoes, ragged khakis, and a buttoned overcoat, he wore what looked like a military medal pinned to his lapel. His only other adornment was a silver band around the crown of his tan cowboy hat. Maybe I was about to meet my first "real" Navajo.

3

Not two hours into Thanksgiving, Leonard and I, both silent, set out in the dorm's panel truck to find Hawthorne and Billy. I wondered why he'd brought along his lame mutt, Marie, on a search like this while leaving his young Weimaraner behind.

We entered the mouth of the canyon slowly, our high beams spotlighting barren cottonwoods to the sides and a crust of old snow on rounded stones ahead in a creek bed that served as the primitive road. The truck's clock was busted, but Leonard had a small black one secured atop the dashboard. His radio was on just loud enough to receive calls, though I had no idea whom he expected to hear at a quarter to two in the morning.

"At least I finally get a minute to talk to you," I told him. "This is a hell of a way to do it. Anyway, Jeannie told me she'd help us with a community meeting about the water."

Driving about ten miles per hour, he searched the icy trail ahead as if it were possible to spot footprints. "Right. I left her a note to start calling people to come to the gym on Monday."

"The same time the agency's here?"

"Yeah." He held his concentration on the beams ahead. "You're the one they'll be gunning for, so they need to face the community, not just you."

"Okay, good." I sighed. "Something else—Jennings referred to you with, um, an insult."

"Only one?" He showed his first full smile of the night.

"Two, actually—but I don't think it's funny."

"Sean, if I worried about that, I wouldn't get anything done."

"Doesn't mean I have to put up with it."

"We need to focus on exposing their negligence. I'm not sure yet, but I think I can bring in some help."

"How's that?"

"First let's find these boys; we'll talk about the meeting later." He extended his neck forward to peer through the winch frame on the front of the truck.

"How much of a head start you think they have?"

"Not sure. Hawthorne took advantage of the busy night and put both their names on the checkout list. Marla's close with the Benallys, and when she did her first bed check around one a.m., she knew those two didn't actually go home. So we started searching the compound."

"I'll be—" I stopped when two distant headlights appeared from the void. As their glare grew brighter, Leonard dimmed our lights, but then the other vehicle made a left turn, so Leonard switched back to high beams. We soon came to the same turn-off the other driver had taken, his taillights still visible on the dirt road to Tsosie.

Leonard drove straight ahead, detaching the radio mike. "Maybe they saw the boys." He pressed the mike's button with his thumb. "Raven Point three to driver on Tsosie road," he said twice and waited, then repeated calls on two other channels before hanging up. "Hm, can't imagine the Etcittys out here this time of night."

"Why aren't we heading that way?"

"We're going on by the Etcittys' place and past the canyon— the Benallys' cabin is just a few miles, but the Shepards' house is way out there."

I watched the creek bed narrow even more. "This is their only way in and out?"

"No, just to and from the school. They have a better road from the west."

I unbuttoned and unzipped my parka but left it on. "How far could we be going?"

"We'll check in at Benallys' and probably find Billy—maybe both of them. Remember Walter at registration?"

"Yeah, out in that old Buick, but I didn't actually meet him."

"He and May are great-uncle and aunt to both boys, not just Billy."

"Hawthorne's very protective of him in basketball practice."

"They're more like brothers than second cousins," he said, eyes still searching the road. "But Hawthorne doesn't like anybody getting bullied."

"Yeah, I've noticed that."

"My guess is he took Billy along because Walter didn't come in for him as usual. If Hawthorne's not at Benallys', Samson's is about ten more miles, just before the highway."

"Hell of a long way for a kid in a secondhand coat."

"Hawthorne probably wore long johns and a couple of shirts." Leonard was even more fixated on the road. "He might even have a flashlight—something to look for out there."

"Right." His intensity reminded me to watch more carefully myself. "You think he can make it all the way home?"

"If anyone can—especially if he warms up at Billy's."

After we passed the side road to the Etcittys' place, Leonard glanced back to check on Marie, so I did the same and saw the dog curled up asleep on a blanket. With the other seats folded down, I could see a few objects in silhouette near the back doors—a toolbox, a storage trunk, some long poles, and Leonard's compact sleeping bag atop his frame pack.

I faced front. "Leonard, I left my place so fast all I have is my coat and flashlight."

Sounding like an Eagle Scout, he reassured me that his pack contained all the basic necessities. ". . . compass, the whole deal. You wearing a watch?"

"No, got out of the habit in Mexico."

"Mine will do."

"For what?"

"In case we end up tracking them for a while."

Out there? Good God.

"You been down to Mexico a lot?" Leonard asked, speeding up a little, his gaze still locked on the beams ahead.

"Just some summer jaunts south of the border." The heater had completely kicked in, so I removed my parka to stuff it between my right side and the drafty door. I looked ahead; the trees on both sides and darkness above made the desolate road seem like an endless tunnel. "So how bad does this road get?"

"Not much worse than most, but a couple of steep spots could be getting a bit icy 'n dicey. We're not far from the first one, but we should be okay."

How reassuring. "What options do we have if Hawthorne's not with the Benallys?"

"Everything's shut tight, but I might catch someone in Old Mission or Tsosie." He mulled that over. "If that doesn't work, we'll radio the Navajo Police, ask them to drive in from the highway, check the Shepard place, then start in for Benallys' until they meet us—or Hawthorne."

I imagined the two boys trudging along in the dark. "Man." I shook my head.

"What's wrong?" he asked, his attention still on the road.

"Hawthorne and Billy. I thought basketball practice would keep the kids fired up until Christmas vacation."

"'Fired up' isn't going to happen, but basketball does help. You just don't know—I was worried about Martin taking off, not those two. I messed up with Hawthorne."

"How?"

"It's been fairly quiet out at his place recently, and Hawthorne hasn't taken off since fourth grade. Yesterday at dinner, when Hosteen was talking seriously with the other Shepards, I should've figured something was going on with Samson. He wasn't even there—and Samson doesn't usually miss a free meal."

"Hosteen and Samson sure don't seem like brothers, even stepbrothers."

"Samson's church bribes him to stay on the wagon, but he's probably on a new bender. For Hawthorne to pull something like this, I think he's worried Samson might hurt someone at home."

"That's a lot for a kid to have on his shoulders."

He nodded solemnly and accelerated, but several seconds later the truck slid slightly on a curve. Leonard slowed down. "Discretion is the better part of valor, or we won't be finding anybody tonight."

"No argument from me, Shakespeare."

"Okay, English teacher, which play was that?"

"One of the King Henrys, I think." We watched the road for a few moments. "Leonard, after Samson's little show at the Council meeting, I take it you've had other problems with him."

He nodded. "If we end up going all the way out there tonight you'll have to go to the door." Leonard downshifted, slowing the truck even more. "Samson won't even talk to me."

"So what happened before?"

"Plenty of time for that—right now we need to get ready for this hill. The road dips sharply not far from here, probably an ancient waterfall. While we're still on level ground, we have to chain up."

"What about the four-wheel drive?"

"It's on, but it won't help much unless we're off the road." He switched to low beams, shifted into neutral, and pulled the hand brake. "Look ahead." Since the brief snowstorm several days before, enough vehicles had driven by to compress the surface to solid ice, its sheen reflecting our headlights to the point where the road dropped from our view.

"It'll only take us a few minutes," he said, removing his peacoat, revealing a thick army-green belt with a sheath, a water flask, and a compass case. Leonard jumped down with Marie to go back for the chains; I got out in just my sweater and hurried to join him.

The dog and I watched Leonard lay the first chain in front of a back tire. Shivering, I placed the other back chain while he did the two in front. He got behind the wheel and let the van roll forward a couple of feet. I'd left my gloves in my parka, so my fingers were frozen by the time we clipped the chains and stretched on the tighteners.

When we got back in, I grabbed my parka and huddled into it, stuffing both hands into the pockets. With the heater blasting, Leonard inched ahead in first gear, lightly tapping the brakes to test the chains until he came to a gradual stop at the edge of the gleaming radical downslope.

My God. My only sliding experiences as a kid were butt-on-cardboard thrills down the sides of arroyos after a rare Tucson snowfall. Then, as an adult, I'd convinced myself that standing up while skiing straight downhill wasn't fun, just plain foolhardy. Now, the sight of the road disappearing over a precipice exceeded my imagination's most daunting image of what it must look like to stand at the top of a ski run.

Don't ask
An old Navajo
Which way to Piñon
Unless
You want to visit
The Grand Canyon.

4

At the Tsosie store I walked directly toward the man on the bench, thinking he might be hung over. The previous Wednesday night in Gallup, I'd driven by scores of drunks hanging out by the bars, almost all men, including a few white guys. Since I'd learned that the Navajo tribe was by far the most populous, I surmised that the most of those drunks in Gallup were Navajos.

"Morning," I said, too cheerfully, to the man in front of the store. He raised his head and took a puff from the cigarette, glancing at me dismissively before closing his eyes. A CLOSED sign hung inside the store's barred window, but the door was ajar, so I entered anyway. The two aisles inside—mostly candy, chips, and grocery staples—led back to three tall coolers and a long meat counter. Behind that, at an oversized chopping block, a white guy in a red stocking hat sawed away at a side of meat, a blood-streaked white apron over his flannel shirt. About my age and size, he had a half spare tire like mine that made us both about twenty pounds over "ideal" weight on a medical chart.

He faced me and seemed to sneer at my denim shirt and old jeans, then at my face and the inch or so of light auburn hair below the sides of the cap that covered my beginning-to-recede forehead. "We're still closed, Red," he said.

Since most of my freckles were gone and I hadn't heard that nickname for years, I glared at him. "So I have to come back later to buy something?"

"Whaddya need?"

"Just a few things." I glanced back at the parking lot. "Is it always this quiet here on Saturday mornings?"

"Payday yesterday—everybody's sleeping it off."

"I see." I studied the meat in his display case, the prices double of what I noticed in Tucson, and I was down to forty dollars in traveler's checks plus a couple of bucks and change.

"Something wrong?"

"Prices seem pretty steep."

"You can always go to the trading post—even higher."

"Those big Canadian hot dogs look good—take a personal check from Phoenix?"

"Nope."

"Traveler's check?"

"That I can do. How many pounds?"

"Three, I guess."

"Having a picnic up on the creek?" He reached into the back of the meat case.

"No. Is there really a creek around here?"

"Yup, runs all year. East, ten hard miles—real nice from there to the mountains."

"Sounds great. Um, I'm heading into Raven Point."

"On purpose? Must be a teacher."

"Yeah, you know where the road is?"

He laughed as he wrapped the chubby franks in white paper. "Look pretty old to be new out here. Tell ya what, I'll give the directions after ya pay for your stuff—might change your mind about Raven Point." The butcher shook his head, sniggering as he wrote in black grease pen on the package and put it on top of the meat case. "What else you need?"

"Milk, bread, fresh fruit."

"Got regular milk and bread—with limits. This ain't a super-market."

After he brought out two quarts of whole milk and a loaf of white bread, I chose a few cans of fruit and vegetables to add to what I already had in the truck. "That's about it," I said, signing the check and handing it over. "What about those directions?"

"Okay, your funeral. It's the second unmarked dirt road after the FIC compound—turn left. You'd be better off driving all the way back around on the highway."

I wanted to know what he meant, but this jerk was getting to me. "I have a pickup. I think I'll take the direct road."

"Direct, huh, ya mean like a crow? Except *you* can't fly." Enjoying his quips, he laughed again as he gave me my change.

Not thanking him, I took everything outside and put the perishables in the Styrofoam chest I kept in the cab. I soon realized that I had to break the other check for gas, so I trudged back in to hear Mr. YA-TA-HEY mock me again.

}-{

Heading toward the state highway with about ten dollars in my pocket, I found the spot he'd mentioned and turned onto a dirt track into the desert. The road had no bar ditches or furrows—no sign of maintenance at all, but the first hundred yards were surprisingly smooth, better than the two-lane paved state road and Tsosie's badly pocked main street. I drove through flat, drab-brown terrain punctuated only by desiccated stalks of grass, grey brush, sage, greasewood and an occasional stunted piñon—a common high desert pine and the source of piñon nuts, a Navajo staple, they'd told us in Gallup.

The road stayed like that for about fifteen minutes, and I was moving right along at about thirty-five, dust billowing behind, until I came to a rise in the terrain and clumps of taller, bushier piñons. A side road, little more than a path, went off to the west toward what Mexicans would call a *ranchito*—a few distant squat buildings, crude corrals, and a couple of pickups.

Beyond the pines I picked up downhill speed before going up again, where the road itself and the land around it changed to a hard moonscape. I had to slow down for crevices and undulations in the rock, then follow the barely discernible road for about a mile to a modest summit where I stopped and got out.

I was standing near the center of a group of rounded sandstone hills hundreds of yards across, resembling swirled rust-colored cake batter, bringing to mind Mars more than the moon. Perched on the undisturbed expanse, Campbell and I were the only signs of humanity in any direction. Although I knew from an orientation slide show that these petrified sand dune formations were common on the Navajo in places like Canyon de Chelly and Window Rock, I wasn't expecting to drive right onto one of them.

The only flora there was random green, grey, or white grasses and a few small bushes struggling to escape from fractures in the hard earth. Though it couldn't have rained that morning, indentations here and there in the sandstone held shallow pools of standing water. Other than a few bugs, it seemed doubtful that animals would frequent such a desolate place, but then a bird appeared at one of the pools for a drink. A piñon jay, I'd learn later, it was shorter than the mountain jays I knew but just as chesty. When the bluish-grey bird flew off, I imagined a midnight convergence of coyotes, mule deer, rodents, and reptiles at the spot, slaking their thirst under the cover of darkness.

The cobalt sky remained clear overhead and back toward Tsosie, but a disturbance was mounting to the south with grey and white thunderheads billowing far up into the atmosphere. That portent of a summer monsoon was a sight I knew well from Tucson and Phoenix, but seeing such a storm this far north surprised me.

I'd already driven across one wide arroyo—called a "wash" in Tucson—and I expected more of them ahead. Not alarmed or even in a hurry, I was ready to enjoy the thunderstorm. Though the washes would likely run deep, all I had to do was park on high ground in the safety of my truck, watch the downpour for a half hour or so, then wait for branches and other flotsam to rush by until the current petered out.

Taking time to explore the sandstone, I accidentally startled a black-tailed jackrabbit out of a dry-looking juniper, the only good-sized bush around. After it dashed away, I got back in the cab and checked the odometer—I'd driven nine miles since gassing up in Tsosie. Deciding a cold beer wouldn't hurt anything, I cracked open one of three cans remaining in the cooler and sipped while I scanned the red rock and approaching storm. After the first rumbles of thunder I started the motor and drove along the hard road, defined only by a hint of wear in its surface.

The downhill side of the bluff was much steeper and the rock far more fractured, so I had to ride my brakes at times to keep my head from hitting the roof and to save my springs and shocks for another day. When Campbell began to level off, the ground became a loam of red sand mixed with lead-colored dirt. Ahead of me, the road deteriorated into swerving dry ruts, but at least I was sure of my direction. Driving between the ruts where it was relatively smooth, I looked down at the old tread marks preserved in molds of grey sunbaked clay.

As I moved at a fair clip straight for the bruise-colored clouds, lightning struck in the distance and thunder followed in seconds. I sped up, but when my right front wheel fell into a deep rut everything in the cab and truck bed jumped. My head hit the sun visor and knocked off my cap, and when the Styrofoam chest tumbled over, I stopped to put it right.

I got out to secure a tarp over my boxes and gear in back. A lightning bolt flashed nearby, followed a couple of seconds later by a rumble and a swirling wind strong enough to wobble the truck. As I finished struggling with the tarp, intermittent splats began to pelt the dry road. Seeing that I was about equidistant from rises in the terrain ahead and behind, I decided to go on.

Lightning and thunder cracked simultaneously as I hauled my knapsack with me into the cab. The deluge began, so I rolled up the windows, driving for higher ground at less than ten miles per hour, the wipers at full speed but useless in the squall. Though I had forgotten to engage the four-wheel drive on the front hubs,

Campbell was holding the road. When I felt the truck dip, I thought it must be in a wash, so I shifted to third and accelerated, hoping that I was headed for the incline and not into some boulder.

When the motor strained, I shifted down to second and accelerated—now going uphill for sure. Once the truck came to level ground, I stopped, killed the motor, and let out a sigh of relief. Although Campbell was stationary, the way ahead looked like the inside of a carwash minus the giant brushes. I picked up my cap, put it on, then just sat back as the gullywasher pounded the roof and rocked the whole truck.

Minutes later the rain slowed some, but I still couldn't see far beyond my windows. When it finally eased to a steady drizzle, I got out on wet but hard ground and inspected my gear under the tarp. Some of it was damp, but there seemed to be no real harm done. My surroundings visible again, I checked out the rocky bluff nearby. It wasn't sandstone, and growing next to the road were bitterbrush, yarrow, and ragweed that I recognized from Tucson and Phoenix, along with some piñons that were more like trees than bushes. Wherever there was soil between the hardpan, sopping green undergrowth drooped to the ground.

Looking back, I saw that I had not crossed a wash, but a small valley. Ahead, before the next piñon-covered ridge, lay another valley, the road dark-grey again, probably that same rutted clay as before. I retrieved the binoculars from my pack to inspect the road ahead for ruts. If they'd been there before, the downpour had washed them away.

Now that the drizzle had stopped, brilliant sunshine broke through the scattering clouds, and steam began to rise from the firm ground. I decided to wait while the excess water drained off the clay ahead. Inhaling the fresh sweet smell of wet dirt and pinesap, I picked up my binoculars and focused on three airborne ravens not fifty yards away. One of the big corvids, probably a fledgling with its ruffled black feathers, blundered a landing into some bushes while the larger parents fluttered gracefully close by, scolding their offspring. A second bedraggled juvenile appeared, and I enjoyed the flying lessons until they were gone.

This time I remembered to set the hubs on Campbell's front wheels. I got in, started the motor and engaged the four-wheel drive. Still on a hard surface, I descended slowly in second gear, rolling down the windows to enjoy the air. I picked up speed, then decided to downshift just before I came to the clay, but the truck lost traction a few seconds later, swerving a quarter turn to leave me gazing through the passenger window at the mud ahead.

I remembered to turn the wheel in the same direction I was sliding. The frame righted itself briefly before it rotated the opposite way, and then I was looking ahead through my driver's side window. "Shit," I mumbled as I swung the steering wheel in that direction, but this time the truck twisted more than halfway around to just ooze off the road, listing to the left and settling into a gulley, where my door wouldn't open.

"I'll be damned." I crawled up the bench seat to push the passenger door up in order to get out. I took a pratfall into the water and mud, then pulled myself up by grabbing the rail of the truck bed. The right-side wheels were only inches above the muck, but Campbell's frame was high-centered and the grey slime had swallowed the whole left side.

I did my best to scrape the muddy slop off the legs and ass of my jeans, then climbed onto the back bumper to scan the barren valley. About a hundred yards ahead the road ascended to another stand of piñons, but I wouldn't be able reach that or anywhere else for quite a while, not even on foot.

From the truck bed, I took out my small army-surplus shovel and flipped down the blade so it would work like a hoe and began to scrape out mud from under the truck's right side. I worked for about fifteen minutes and fell a few times, but the ooze from the other side replaced every glop of mud I'd shoveled out.

Hopeless. Out of breath, I straightened up and scanned the sky, already a clear blue, the sun more than halfway to its zenith. And then, on the high ground ahead, I caught sight of a large object moving slowly from the east through the piñons and out to the main road. Two horses, a wagon, and a driver wearing a large flat-brimmed hat came to a stop.

The man seemed to be considering whether to go left or right. "Hey, right here!" I shouted in my yell-at-the-kids-in-the-hall voice. At first, the wagon didn't budge, but then it turned my way and began to inch down the slope. I straightened the blade and used the shovel for support to make my way to Campbell's tailgate.

When my potential rescuer reached the fluid mud and shook the reins, his horses moved steadily forward into the sludge. The wagon appeared to be a unique contraption, its wooden bed jury-rigged over a truck frame atop four huge farm tractor tires. The sinewy dark-brown horses slogged on through the clay, barely straining as they made headway. A grizzled white-and-brown dog struggled behind, cowering in the wagon's wide tracks before they turned back to mud.

When the wagon came close, I got my first good look at the driver. He wore black trousers and a red flannel shirt, an odd grin on his brown face beneath the brim of an Amish-like black hat. He had a red bandanna around his forehead and wore his long hair almost like the lady at orientation, a thick dark-grey knot behind his head. His face had few wrinkles, and he looked fit; I guessed that he was somewhere in his mid-fifties. He gazed ahead as if he intended to pass right by; wisps of steam rose skyward from the arched backs of his snorting horses.

Fortunately, the driver finally pulled on the reins to stop his team. After coming to a halt, the horses shook, and the dog caught up but stayed a few cautious feet behind. The man sized up my half-swamped truck, then me, and his grin changed to a neutral stare. He uttered two low guttural sounds that I assumed was some kind of greeting.

"Um, hi, I'm a teacher—going to Raven Point."

When the man puckered his mouth and twisted it back toward the ridge he'd descended, it was my first experience with the traditional but common Navajo habit of indicating a direction with the lips. The same time as he pointed, my rescuer mumbled something like, "*Ni-lady.*" I took those three syllables to mean, "It's that way."

"Can I ride in with you?"

He said, "*Aoó*" with a hint of a nod, so I took that as an affirmative.

"Can I bring a few things?"

He glared at me, then looked away, his body language telling me, "I'm waiting for you, aren't I?" I didn't mess with the stuff under the tarp. Instead, I made my way carefully around to the truck's passenger side and tossed the shovel in back. I opened the door and put on my knapsack, bulging with basic necessities. I picked up the small cooler under one arm and started off, bracing myself on the truck with the other hand.

By then, the man had turned the wagon around and pulled closer, but I still would need to cross several feet of mud to grab his sideboard. I lost my footing with my third or fourth step and fell straight back into the slop again, losing grip of the cooler. The knapsack broke my fall, but I sat up and saw the chest's lid partway open—a can of beer had plopped into the muck.

The man was staring straight at the beer. "Pour it out," he said in a throaty voice.

"What for?"

"How much you got?"

"Two cans, but—"

"You got any hard liquor?"

"No."

"You want a ride, pour it out."

"All right," I said just as bluntly. I opened and drained the cans, leaving the empties in the cooler. I finally made it to the wagon and set the cooler and knapsack in the bed among snags of dry piñon.

I hoisted myself up beside him on the bench. "I'm Sean Noland." I didn't offer my hand, but not to be unfriendly. He was holding the reins anyway, and I also didn't want to make an awk-ward gesture.

"Hosteen Shepard," he grumbled, shaking the traces to get the horses moving.

"I appreciate the help."

Eyes forward, he didn't answer, but the strange partial grin came back to his face as we rode on in silence and the jolting wagon stirred an old memory of a college hayride through the saguaros. After the horses pulled out of the worst of the mud, we made better time up to the knoll, passing a narrow crossroad to the left. I figured it to be the way out to his place, as there were tire tracks but no ruts in a firmer surface.

"Um, Mr. Shepard, can you tell me why you wanted me to get rid of that beer?"

"*Ndaga'*," he said louder, an obvious negative.

He drove on, and I asked two questions—if the school was very far and if the road always turned to mud so quickly. I got that same negative both times before I gave up and just watched the landscape, wondering what to expect in Raven Point.

Here,
After a sudden breeze
And summer rain,
Mother Earth allows a few moments
When even alkaline acres
Go wild with flowers.

5

Shepard's wagon passed slowly through the mud in the next two valleys and then climbed up onto a mesa, where the piñons thickened again. A small cottontail burst from the undergrowth and retreated just as quickly. The green plants here had recovered from the drenching to reach for the sun with familiar blossoms of purple lupine, red paintbrush, golden sunflowers, plus some kind of white composite I didn't know.

"Man, beautiful," I said.

Shepard kept his eyes ahead but his curious grin widened as if to say, "Of course it's beautiful." After two or three miles of silence broken only by occasional creaks in the wagon, the horses' heaves, and a cranky call from a distant jay—we came to the end of the mesa. Shepard guided his team into a gradual descent through a rocky, dun-brown canyon, no longer the red sandstone I had seen earlier, so that meant less iron, if my one geology class served me well.

On the way to the canyon floor we rolled through mature stands of healthy cottonwood and occasional clumps of quaking aspen. White seed puffs floated all around us, settling like gentle snow on the dark horses' backs. Shepard drove his team straight into a shallow pebbled creek that probably ran with a couple feet of water during the storm—now it served as the road. I looked back to see the scrawny old dog still behind us, lapping up water from the silty stream. On the left bank, more wildflowers waved through the rusted skeleton of a Studebaker, while tawny-colored rock on the canyon's other side loomed upward for about fifty yards.

Halfway up that sheer wall, behind a slight outcropping, piles of stone rubble filled a concavity some thirty feet wide. Some of the debris resembled straight-sided bricks, so it could have been a small pueblo ruin like the major digs at Mesa Verde or Chaco Canyon. As the wagon rumbled on, I stared back at those possible remnants of ancient civilization, trying to imagine everyday human activity in such a precarious spot.

I faced forward again as Shepard left the creek for a dirt lane leading out of the canyon into another stand of modest pines. In the distance, I spotted more red sandstone and the first sign of civilization, an elevated water tank. Regardless of the trip's difficulties, I was so taken by the wilderness that I felt a sense of dread for what awaited me.

The road soon led us into a clearing for a compound with four good-sized buildings, a few sheds, and four small pink trailers nestled against a vermillion bluff scattered with dwarfed piñons. The water tank, on tall steel poles above the trailers, had RAVEN POINT on its side in tall fading black letters.

I kept myself from saying *My God* as Shepard coaxed the horses off of the road, which continued on past two structures outside the compound. The first, a small wood-framed store, had two pickups parked outside. I squinted through the sunlight at the last building, not twenty feet down the road. Similar in size to the store, it was connected by overhead wires to the most obvious evidence of the twentieth century—a line of utility poles that seemed to march off to the south, away from Raven Point.

I lowered the brim of my cap against the warm sunshine as Shepard drove by a sturdy wooden sign. RAVEN POINT BOARDING SCHOOL, it said, in three-inch white block letters, other Commission designations inscribed below. Looking back at the dog as we entered the compound, the only signs of the recent storm were a few puddles, our fresh wagon tracks, and the horseshoe prints in the quickly drying dirt.

Shepard was guiding the wagon toward the two largest frame buildings. About forty yards long and twenty wide, both were painted the same sulfurous yellow as the big school in Tsosie. Beyond an off-duty flagpole, the windows of the closer building displayed faded art projects that seemed to indicate three class-rooms on each side. Separating the school from the other large building was a wide space of barren hard ground. Two slightly bent steel poles there with worn plywood backboards and rusted rims faced each other from about fifty feet apart. A homemade outdoor light on a wooden pole stood at the center of the im-provised basketball court like a too-tall player forever on defense. A battered off-kilter iron merry-go-round and three dilapidated swings completed the rest of the miserable playground.

The second large building, apparently the dormitory, teed into the center of a long steel Quonset. Next to that, an old stone-and-mortar structure sent out a web of power lines to the whole complex. I saw no fences, but twenty feet or so of underbrush and piñons had been cleared to create a perimeter.

Shepard stopped the horses close to the school building, where a sign read, OFFICE. I jumped down from the wagon, shouldered my pack, and picked up the cooler.

"Is there anybody around?" I asked.

He just puckered his lips and pointed them toward the dor-mitory.

"Okay, Mr. Shepard, thanks for the lift."

Still taciturn, he turned the horses and drove off. Trying to hold back judgment of Hosteen Shepard and Raven Point, I crossed the playground to the dormitory. Behind a roof-covered boardwalk its four doors were wide open. The old structure's re-cent thick coat of dark-mustard paint poorly disguised multiple cracks in its siding and trim.

I walked through the first door onto the polished but worn linoleum floor of a rectangular room about twice the size of an ordinary classroom, its walls a lighter shade of yellow than outside. A ping-pong table, a Foosball game, three sofas, several folded-up lunch tables and stacks of wooden chairs took up most of the space. Three doors on the other side were marked OFFICE, QUARTERS and KITCHEN. Near a counter beneath that last sign, about a dozen or so identical cardboard boxes were stacked next to a tall coffee urn.

A living-room sized Navajo rug took up most of the far wall; its polygonal symmetric designs suggested a charcoal-and-grey maze with no exit. The nearest wall displayed some colorful full-sized posters. The first one depicted a tall needle-like red rock spire, the next a sandstone formation with a great portal of blue sky—WINDOW ROCK the legend said at the bottom. I set down my muddy knapsack and cooler to walk closer to the third poster, a photo of a Navajo rug featuring thin turquoise lines formed by the impossibly elongated torsos of biped creatures with square heads and blank faces.

"Are you interested in *Yei-bi-chai*?" a contralto voice asked from behind.

Dogs barked not far away as I turned to a man about five foot six with a medium build, standing in the open doorway beneath QUARTERS.

"Hi. Yay-buh-what?" In Tucson, I would've pegged him for a dark Mexican in his late twenties, all slicked up to go to a dance in his ironed light-green summer shirt, stiff new blue jeans, and a tan cowboy hat.

He came closer, favoring the toes of his polished black shoes. "*Yei-bi-chai*, a kind of Navajo god. I'm Leonard Santos—I'll be your assistant," he said with a slight lisp. Two ordinary short-haired black cats had followed him in, while a small brown dachshund-mix barked once, wiggled, then settled quietly in the open doorway.

"Sean Noland, fifth-and-sixth-grade teacher." We shook hands casually; he smelled of strong citrus cologne. "You'll be helping in my classroom?"

As the two cats made figure-eights around his legs, he looked up from noticing my muddy clothes, apparently not very surprised. "No, Mr. Noland. The agency office obviously failed to get in touch with you. I have some news."

"What do you mean?"

He glanced at the drying mud I'd tracked onto the dull but spic-and-span floor. "Well, you've been reassigned. You're now the P.E. teacher and also counselor for the dormitory."

"What?"

"Yes, Mr. Hatcher only had you and a transfer to choose from."

"Hatcher?"

"Hal Hatcher, the principal."

"First time I've heard the name. He must also teach—a school this small."

He chuckled—almost a giggle. "No, he doesn't teach. Welcome to the FIC and Raven Point."

As I let all that sink in, Leonard removed his hat, revealing thick shiny black hair in a precise bowl cut, cropped straight at mid-ear and with Dutch-boy bangs over his dark eyes and thin brows. Clean-shaven, he'd applied tan cover-stick to hide some acne on his sepia face.

"So, we call this the rec room—r-e-c, not w-r-e-c-k," he said with another smile. "By the way, you supervise everyone who works in here, including the cook—the rec room is also the school kitchen."

I rolled my eyes. "Great."

Leonard began to explain the dorm's layout. Where I went to high school, he would've been labeled a *pansy*—or worse—and subjected to abuse by some he-man types and others. My parents, who had no tolerance for such persecution, influenced me to buck high school peer pressure to live my own life and let "different" kids live theirs.

As a teacher, I'd occasionally heard staff mock a male adult or student as "light in the loafers" or something similarly judgmental. I didn't confront such comments, but I didn't give them the expected smile either, cementing my reputation as a contrarian. One day near the end of my time in Phoenix, a math teacher in the faculty lounge jeered loudly to his cronies, "These fairies deserve to get bullied!" I stated the obvious, that nobody deserved that, and then walked out, fully ready for the changes that my divorce had already set in motion.

Although I didn't know much about Navajos or the FIC, my guess was that Leonard's demeanor might be a source of gossip in Raven Point and Old Mission Agency. Up close, I noticed crow's feet at the corners of his eyes that belied his easy smile. My first impression of Leonard had been wrong—he was in his mid-thirties, only about ten years my junior.

" . . . and we have two apartments through that door," he said, finishing his explanation while pointing toward the dog with his hat. "The last counselor, Mr. Laird, got married unexpectedly to an FIC teacher in New Mexico, and they let him transfer over there."

I was shaking my head again. "Do you suppose anyone even considered whether I'm qualified to be a counselor?"

He looked regretful, almost sad. "Sometimes qualifications don't matter much out here. Hatcher told me that you played high school basketball."

"Yeah, second-string JV—why does that matter?"

"Well, the P.E. teacher is also the coach for our school team."

"Competitively, against other schools?"

"Yes, tournaments, trophies—the whole shebang." That sibilant sentence accentuated his lisp. "C'mon, I'll show you more of the place."

I pointed toward the playground. "Where's basketball practice, out there on the dirt?"

"No, we have a gym." Like a TV quiz-show model, he presented his arm with a long flourish toward a window that faced the metal Quonset next door.

"In there?" I scoffed as we passed the kitchen, where all of the stacked boxes were labeled BOTTLED WATER – 1GALX2.

The cats licked their paws as we stood by the huge rug on the wall. "When do I meet this Mr. Hatcher?"

"We were supposed to have the agency meeting next Tuesday, but it was postponed. Hatcher will be here by Wednesday for our staff meeting, probably not before."

"Who do I talk to about the counseling re-assignment?"

"You could call the agency in Old Mission if our phone is working, or you can try the radio. I'm supposed to show you the ropes and get you and the other new teacher settled in." He glanced at my filthy knapsack and cooler. "So where's your vehicle?"

"In the mud, about halfway here from Tsosie."

"Oh. No one told you about the turn-off at Old Mission?"

"From the main highway?"

"Yes, it's rocky, but no mud and a lot shorter. So how did you get in here?"

"A man named Shepard, two horsepower and a unique wagon."

"Hosteen. I bet he looked happy."

"I wouldn't go that far."

"He loves that old wagon—one of the last ones still in use around here. Hosteen's related to probably a fourth of our kids. How many dogs were with him?"

"Just one, I think."

"Good. Well, now you've met the Raven Point Chapter President and the School Council Chairman."

Not sure how to react, I told him about how I had to ditch my last two beers. "Any idea what that was about?"

Leonard raised his brows. "Hosteen's a teetotaler—not a real popular point of view."

"But he keeps getting elected?"

"Yes, he does. He's also a respected shaman, which balances it out. We can get into all that later."

I pointed to the impressive Navajo rug. "This is amazing—the design is perfect."

He nodded. "Except there's supposed to be one intentional flaw that allows evil spirits to escape," he said with another smile. "I can show you around more while it dries up outside, then we'll go out for your vehicle."

He put on his hat as I gave up searching for the rug's imperfection. "All right, thanks."

"I'll put these guys away." He turned to the felines. "C'mon, kitties." The cats walked with him to the door, where one of them in passing rubbed against the dog. I started to follow Leonard and his pets and saw a small horse in a pen outside, and then the heads of barking dogs, leaping up to look in the hall window. I turned back, opened two folding chairs, sat, and waited for him, wondering if Leonard was Navajo or if he had just learned a few words of the language.

He came back in and glanced at the two chairs. "Mr. Noland?"

"First of all, it's Sean. Can we talk a second?"

"Sure." He sat, crossing one knee over the other. "Something wrong?"

"Yeah, I'm kind of lost with this whole deal."

"Are the boonies already getting to you?"

"No, my trip was interesting. The land is incredible."

"Well, that's a good start."

"Fine, but I need a better idea of what I might be in for here."

"Some of that will depend on you." His smile became a wry grin. "I have a few more surprises, but I hoped to break them to you gradually."

"Look, Leonard, maybe you could just spill it all out. I'm not thrilled that they changed everything and didn't bother to tell me. When I get back to my truck, I'm not sure right now which direction I should drive."

"All right. Probably the next thing you need to know is that when Hatcher isn't here, you'd be in charge of everything. All part of the job."

"My God." I envisioned the chaos of every student in the school eating in that less-than-expansive room. "All right, what else?"

"Well, you should probably know that we have some kids who don't adjust well to being here. A few, usually boys, run away every year."

"You mean like over to the store or something?"

"No, they try to get home."

"How far?"

"Anywhere from a couple of miles to twenty or so."

"Twenty? What does the school do about it?"

"We go after them. Some we bring back, others we leave at home for a while, depending on the situation. A few schools on the Rez have some bad runaway stories. In my five years here, our worst was a boy who lost some toes to frostbite and got real sick."

When I waited to see if there was more, Leonard waited too.

"Do they take off in groups?" I asked.

"Usually alone—sometimes two."

"Are they homesick?"

"That can be part of it, but sometimes they just can't stand school." He sighed deeply. "For those kids, you see relief on their faces every day when they get back to the dorm."

"Why do you think they hate it so much?"

"For some, I think it boils down to failure. We should probably leave it at that for now."

6

With the icy hill glistening below us, Leonard kept the panel truck in low gear. He took his foot off the brake and let gravity take us slowly forward and down. His method seemed to work at first; I could feel the transmission provide steady resistance for seconds before there was a loud clunk and we began to roll faster. He tried to jerk the transmission back into gear, but it popped right out again. Like Campbell in the mud three months before, the rear of the long vehicle swung around on its own until we were glissading—sideways. Leonard turned into the skid, righting us, but then we were rolling again, much too fast.

"Worse than I thought—hang on!" he shouted, and the dog squealed once as we sailed down the rest of the hill. The road curved at the bottom, so to avoid the trees ahead, Leonard had to either turn or brake. He chose the former and we spun a full circle. As he yanked the wheel madly, the truck twirled again and slid off the road. A branch scraped across the roof before we came to a halt with a loud thud, the truck settling toward my side. I looked out at a cottonwood trunk a few feet from the window.

Leonard exhaled in relief and turned to me, shaking his head. "Piece a cake. You okay?"

"Yeah. Now what?"

He looked back at Marie, on her feet and eager to get out. "Let's check the situation under the truck."

Marie followed him as I pushed my door open just far enough against the tree to squeeze out, holding my parka. I put it on and came around to the rear of the long vehicle, switching on my flashlight. The dog was hobbling away from us, her snout in the snow. Leonard, coatless in a black fleece pullover, followed her with his own light.

I called to him, my hands in the coat pockets "Shouldn't we check under the truck?"

"I'm coming, but Marie found their tracks over here!"

"Good deal." He started back to me as I knelt to shine my flashlight under the truck. The couple inches of snow didn't complicate things, but the frame was jammed on a boulder, raising both left wheels off the ground. The part of the stone I could see was turret-shaped, suggesting that the mass underground was the size of an army tank.

"Geez, the rock of ages," Leonard said from behind. His flashlight beam had joined mine before he shone it on the chassis. "Not good—looks like the axle's busted."

"More fun by the moment." We stood together in the crusty snow; I put away my flashlight and quickly zipped and buttoned the parka. Hatless, Leonard had added a grey woolen scarf around his neck.

"So what do you think?" I asked.

"The winch would be a waste of time. I might catch someone on the radio, but if I can't, we just have to move on." When he aimed his light up at the road, he called Marie and she began to trot crookedly toward us, but she suddenly stopped.

Leonard shrugged. "It's so slick up there, the boys had to walk next to the road. They might not even be to Benally's yet." As he aimed his light at the truck again, I felt a chill on the back of my neck, so I pulled my hood over my cap.

Leonard shut off his light, then looked above the bare cottonwoods. "It's clouding up."

"Yeah, they said more snow is on the way."

"We'd better get moving."

"Aren't you going to try the radio?"

"Not anymore." He switched on his flashlight again to illuminate a jagged stub of aerial on the truck's roof, the rest snapped off by the tree branch.

"Perfect."

Just then, Marie, still about ten feet from us, began to growl. In Leonard's beam, she stiffened and bared her teeth toward the road above. He aimed his light in that direction to reveal a large, pointy-eared grey canine glaring down at us from about forty feet away. Marie started barking and Leonard made a loud guttural noise, but the animal held its ground, its irises reflecting the artificial light. After Leonard repeated his bluff, the stalker finally skulked away into the dark. Marie, still growling, limped back to us.

"Good girl." Leonard brushed a twig off her head and ruffled her half-floppy ears.

"What the hell was that, a wolf?"

"No, I'd say part coyote and part domestic. A big one, probably drawn to Marie's limp. Tough as she is, she'd be easy prey." Leonard started adjusting his clothes, tying the scarf around his head to cover his forehead and ears. His thatch of thick black hair seemed to serve him as well as a hat. Chuckling, he patted Marie again.

"What's so funny?"

"Not much—we're about to break one of the old taboos. If a coyote crosses your path on a journey, you're supposed to go back, or you can expect to get hurt or killed." He removed his gloves and bent over to tighten his bootlaces. "It just struck me as ironic that it is within the realm of possibility for us to have some problems out here tonight."

"Well, let's not make that a self-fulfilling prophecy."

He straightened up, pulling his gloves back on. "Right, but after an experience like that, you can see how listening to taboos your whole life could influence you to believe them."

I knelt to retie my boots as well. "Fine, but you told me you don't buy into all that, or the Christian hocus-pocus either. I think we're about eye-to-eye."

"We probably start from a similar perspective."

"What do you mean?" I looked up at him as I finished tying.

"We can talk about that on the way, too, if you want."

I nodded and stood up, jamming my frozen fingers into the coat pockets. Above us, a few stars and a bright planet glimmered through a slit in the thickening cloud cover. "How far do you think it is to the Benallys'?"

"We're about halfway—still more than two miles. Maybe we'll join the boys there."

Following his light, we crunched through the old snow back to the truck's open door. Leonard unhooked his belt, removed the pullover, and reached behind the seat to bring out a dark snowsuit with reflective lines down the sides. He stepped into it, zipped up, then found his peacoat. We walked to the rear of the truck, where I watched him put his belt and coat into the pack. He secured a small tarp over the sleeping bag and the pack frame, and then pulled out four wooden skis and sets of poles from the truck.

"What good are those on this ice?"

"If it snows hard, we'll be darn glad to have them. For now, the poles will help." He began to tie the skis together with their leather bindings. "Some teacher years ago tried to get the kids into cross-country skiing. I found them in a shed and refurbished two pairs."

"Are they supposed to be this wide?"

"They made the old ones like this. Have you used modern cross-country skis?"

"No, I've just seen them—never skied at all."

"Well, with these, you just fall in the snow a few times until you get the hang of it."

"I can hardly wait."

He strapped the four skis to his bulging drab-green pack then hefted all of it onto his back. I kept my light on his pack for a moment, noticing SANTOS stenciled in faded black letters. "We could switch off with that once in a while," I said.

"I'm used to the weight back there. You need to stay on your feet as much as you can."

The old guy's job. I pulled on the parka's hood, grabbed two of the poles and hiked up to level ground following Leonard, his snowsuit's hood hanging behind. We set off on the edge of the glazed road in calm but biting air. Leonard clipped the flashlight to his sleeve's cuff so we could follow the bouncing beam in the snow ahead.

Soon, an occasional solitary snowflake drifted through the light, and Marie headed off into the night again. "Maybe it would've been a good idea to bring Bowie," I said, referring to Leonard's Weimaraner.

"Poor Bowie couldn't sniff a roast in the next room." I heard amusement in his voice. "He'd be lost out here. Marie's the perfect dog for this, believe me." He quickened our pace a little. "The other big hassle I had with Samson was just last year—over Marie and Hawthorne."

"What?"

"Marie stays with me but she's Hawthorne's dog." He turned his head my way. "Okay, Sean, here it comes."

Flakes flicking at my cheeks, I stopped to button the hood's flap over my face. "How bad you think this'll get?" I called, my voice muffled by the material.

"No idea, but for now, the snow helps. We'll soon be able to walk on the road."

I almost had to shout to be heard. "And you once called *me* an optimist."

"Hey, if the snow gets deep, we have the skis, but if the wind picks up, then we have something to worry about—just the facts."

"Thank you, Joe Friday."

In
Two miles,
A Navajoland road
Can change from
Sand or clay
To mud
And then back—
Or simply stop
For any flowing
Summer wash.

7

At the end of our discussion in the rec room about runaways and miserable kids, two middle-aged women entered through the far door. They retrieved mops and buckets from a closet, and when they started over to meet us by the cases of bottled water, Leonard lifted the large coffee urn onto the counter. All I saw nearby was a stack of tiny paper cups, no coffee makings.

Leonard introduced them as Felicita, pronouncing it *Fuh-LISS-tuh*, and Marla. The former was thin and the latter very heavy, both of them in lightweight long full skirts and men's work shirts. Ornate silver clips held back their long black hair, Felicita's a traditional bun, Marla's a ponytail. After plenty of smiles, no handshaking involved, Leonard spoke to them in Navajo. Felicita appeared to correct one of his words good-naturedly, and then the three of them chatted and giggled a little longer before Leonard and I moved on to look at the dorms.

"Felicita speaks English," Leonard said. "She and Marla are our top dorm aides."

"And they're doing the floors?"

"They get comp time. The custodian's on sick leave. I'll be coming back later to help." He made a wry smile. "The fine print in our government contract says, 'and duties as assigned.'"

"Like chasing after runaways."

"Yeah, that's one of them."

He led me through the worn but tidy facility; it resembled a military barracks, with boys and girls separated by a wall, a door, and a small office cubicle. Both sections had rows of steel bunks and a bathroom that would have been spotless except for the orange-stained sinks and floors. We headed back toward the rec room.

"You seem to speak Navajo pretty well, Leonard."

"I'm improving with Felicita's help. I understand Navajo better than I speak it."

"Do you mind explaining how that came about?"

"Not at all. My mom was from what they call the Checkerboard Area—small separated tribal lands not far from Gallup. Over there, they call this the Big Rez. After my mom died, my grandma raised the three of us in Albuquerque."

"So you're full Navajo?"

"My mother—my father was Mexican. I guess that makes my two sisters and me more than half native." He made a self-effacing grin. "In Raven Point, I'm just another outsider."

I didn't know what to say to that. "Um, the guy at the store in Tsosie acted like he couldn't believe I was coming out here."

Leonard halted, turning serious for the second time that day. "Well, this is the oldest, smallest, most isolated school in Old Mission Agency. We're last in percentage of kids who go on with school, lowest in funding, test scores, basketball—a lot of things." His shoulders sagged as we walked on. "One thing we're first in is Special Ed kids. We have more per capita than any school in the agency. Mrs. McAdam is the teacher."

"Full-time Special Ed for this little school?"

"She and an aide work with about a third of our kids."

We came to his office. "A third of how many?"

"Almost fifty in boarding, plus a few day students who are children of staff members, including Abby's, er, Mrs. McAdam's daughter. This year we expect about the same number in kindergarten alone as in the five-six room—about a dozen students."

"Why the big drop-off?"

"A few move away, especially if they have young parents. Some kids are held back. We have two eleven-year-olds in third grade, and Billy Benally, who's fourteen, in sixth." He sighed. "And we've lost seven since I came here five years ago."

"Lost?"

"Four died from illness and three more in accidents—officially."

"And unofficially?"

"Just speculation. No sense repeating that unless you decide to stay."

"Sounds pretty grim."

"At times it is—I won't mislead you. But mostly, I don't think this is a bad place at all."

We went outside onto the covered boardwalk. Leonard checked out the clear sky and bright sunshine, pronouncing it dry enough to go rescue my pickup.

I noticed again all the power lines running from the old stone house to the compound's other buildings. "Why so many wires from that place?"

"Jon Begay, the custodian, that's his shop. Ages ago, it was the school. Jon keeps the old generators behind it in good condition because the electricity from Old Mission is irregular."

"I saw a lot of TV aerials in Tsosie."

"Yeah, they've had a signal for years—three channels. Cartoons and basketball are big hits. Some people here want to put an aerial on top of the canyon and run wires down to the compound. So far, Hosteen, the School Council, and the Chapter are against it, but it's just a matter of time. For now, movies are still the big deal in Raven Point. Ready to go?"

"Just need my knapsack and cooler."

"I'll get my pack and move the truck up here."

I walked back in, picked up my things and met him in a couple of minutes outside by a long grey four-wheel drive government panel truck, a winch on front. Leonard got out; he had swapped his regular boots for black knee-high waders, his pant legs tucked inside. I tried not to look amused as I wedged my pack and cooler behind the front seat, next to Leonard's pack.

To my surprise, he opened the driver's side door to let in the dachshund and a limping, medium-sized, long-haired, and lop-eared black mutt. The dogs scrambled over the front and second seats, then the back bench, into the open space at the rear.

"You've met Albert; that's Marie. Do you like animals, Mr. Noland?"

"It's Sean, okay? Well, I had a dog once, but my mom had allergies. My ex-wife wouldn't stand for anything larger than a goldfish. I do enjoy seeing animals in the wild."

"With a little luck, this is a good place for that."

Off we went with the front windows down, the dogs wagging their tails and scampering from one back window to another, looking out. When we passed the ancient ruin in the canyon wall, I asked Leonard about it.

"*Anaasází*," he said, "but it's so small that the archaeologists decided it was either a hunting shelter or abandoned before completion—not even any pottery shards up there. That cliff above is Raven Point, where they want to put the TV aerial."

"At orientation they said Anasazi a lot. Is it a Navajo word?"

"Yes, it means 'old enemy who lived here,' more or less. Oldest enemy is probably closer to history. The Navajo," he said, as if the term didn't include him, "pretty much didn't like anybody around—Hopis, Zunis, Apaches, Spaniards, Mexicans, and the *Bilagáana*, of course."

"Belagana is white man?"

"That's it."

"I guess that's good to know."

"I'm sometimes called *Bilazáana*—apple. You know—red on the outside and white inside." He flashed another grin. "With your blue eyes, you might get your own nickname."

"Great." We started up onto the mesa. "Do you mind if I ask why you came out here?"

"No big secret. I worked after high school for years, then went to UNM. I had to quit after my money ran out. The FIC offered to start me at GS-Five—more money than I ever made. I'm saving up now. Two more years, then I plan to go back—just need two quarters for my B.S."

"What will you study?"

"Mostly chemistry and physics."

"Really? Do you want to teach?"

"Don't know yet. Depending on *dinero*, I might go for premed."

"Good for you, Leonard."

As he picked up speed on the hard level ground, we rolled up the windows.

"Okay, your turn," he said. "Why did you come to the Rez?"

I told him a little about my reasons. " . . . my ex-wife calls it a mid-life crisis."

"Well, it'll be something different for you for sure—that is, if you stay."

"Yeah. Tell me about Hatcher. Seems strange he won't get here until the last minute."

"No secret there either. He retires in December." I was surprised by the scorn in Leonard's voice. "His wife and all their things are already in Albuquerque. Last year, he used as much accumulated leave as he could on Mondays or Fridays. We'll probably see him two or three days a week until Thanksgiving. Then that'll be it."

"The FIC doesn't care?"

He scoffed. "Sometimes Hatcher plays cards on duty with the agency boys in Old Mission. You probably met the new superintendent at Orientation—he's part Seminole. Maybe he'll have some new priorities—I don't know. Anyway, they probably won't bring in a new principal before January."

"So I might be in charge for more than a month?"

He nodded. "It's not as bad as it sounds. The place pretty much runs itself."

"Sounds like you have to run it while the teachers are gone. How does that work?"

"They have more time off in the summer than non-certificated staff. I did use two weeks of leave this summer, but I'm saving most of it." Seeing we'd come to the first of the clay, he pulled to a stop, opening his door to get out. "I need to set the hubs." The dogs yipped but stayed in back.

"I'll get this one." I got out as well and locked the mud-crusted hub on my side then climbed back in. "It isn't as slick as before, but my truck's two or three valleys away."

Leonard engaged the four-wheel drive. "If there's less viscosity here, it should be similar up there."

"Ah, spoken like a true physicist."

He chortled and started off, driving steadily around a curve, where we spotted a rabbit. The lame dog, Marie, also saw it and squealed.

"How many animals do you have, Leonard?"

"These two—Albert came here with me—and the two black cats you saw."

"I saw a lot more than that."

"The rest are strays that I try to get fixed. I leave some with my sisters in Albuquerque. They help me look for homes."

"And the horse?"

"A pony—my latest addition. The guy who runs the junkyard in Old Mission bought it for his little girl. Trigger got old and nobody wanted her. I still need to build her a shed."

"Doesn't all that cut into your college fund?"

"It does, but with animals you usually know when you make a difference. Kind of a selfish pleasure, I guess."

I waited for him to elaborate, but he just drove on. "Doesn't sound selfish to me," I said. "Have you considered veterinary medicine?"

"Yes, that's a possibility. I've also thought about pediatrics."

We'd reached the high ground and side road that Hosteen Shepard used earlier. "We're almost to the valley where I went off. How far in there to Shepard's place?"

"Maybe two hundred meters."

"If it weren't for the Olympics, I wouldn't know that's not very far."

Leonard laughed. "Someday we'll join the rest of the metric world. Anyway, it's behind a hill, a big house for out here, plus two hogans. Hosteen uses the old one for his ceremonies. He also has a garage-barn combination, and corrals for sheep, horses, and a few cattle."

"How large is his family?"

"His wife passed years ago. Maybe a dozen live there now, that I know of. An older sister, two aunts, and his four youngest kids—two sons around thirty—one's married and has two kids. He has two daughters still there, one with her husband and baby. There's another daughter who probably won't marry—long story. The Shepard women are some of the best weavers around. Three of his older kids have their own places not far away. Two more are long gone."

"Man, he doesn't look old enough for such a big family."

"He's somewhere in his sixties. Hosteen's unusual that way. Most of the men around here look older than they are."

"Why do you think he's in such good shape?"

"Clean living?" Leonard shrugged. "I don't know. He works as hard as anyone."

The road was sloping downward, the piñons fewer. "What about your family?" I asked. "If you don't mind telling me."

"Well, I guess I'm the classic floundering middle child. My older sister's a career woman, and the younger one has a good husband and two great kids."

"Man, there it is." We finally saw my truck in the valley ahead. Campbell looked forlorn, a headlight and one corner of the windshield muddied.

Leonard whistled. "My gosh, how did you get that far off?"

"I worked at it. Slicker than I thought."

When we got out, the road surface wasn't bad, but the mud in the gulley was still soft. Leonard knew his way around with the winch, so after one false start we had Campbell up on the road in about twenty minutes. I stood there, splattered with clay again from my waist down, but Leonard was still neat, just mud on the tall boots that I no longer considered comical.

Leonard raised his brows at Campbell. "In there that deep, I doubt if she'll start."

"Let's find out." I climbed in and turned the key—nothing. I got out, raised the hood, and we both peered in. Most of the engine parts that I knew by name—battery, distributor, spark plugs—were coated in grime. The air filter had come loose, and the carburetor was barely visible, choked with mud.

"Well, Sean," he said, using my given name for the first time, "I hope you're okay with coming back to Raven Point for a while, because you don't have much choice."

"Yeah, there go my big Saturday night plans in Tsosie."

He laughed. "Oh, sure." He got into the panel truck, turned it around, backed up, and brought over a tow chain to attach it. "Okay, get behind your steering wheel and don't brake unless I do." He returned to his truck and drove ahead just far enough to take up the slack and slowly pull me toward Shepard's ridge.

Approaching the summit, I was surprised to see his back lights flash, but since we were going uphill, I didn't brake. I could hear Marie start barking, then Albert chimed in. Ahead, the silhouette of a man on a horse, and then another, moved slowly through the piñons from the direction of the Shepards' place toward the crossroads.

I felt Campbell's weight strain against a stronger pull; Leonard seemed to be trying to get there first. I was about to stick my head out and shout when I heard him downshift and accelerate again. With that, my truck lurched as the first shadowy figure also tried to urge his swaybacked horse ahead.

Although neither nag was moving very fast, the situation reminded me of a B Western—a steam locomotive chugging from one direction, two cowboys racing to intercept it from the other. It became obvious that the two men were going to get there first, so Leonard gave up and stopped just short of the summit, the tow chain between us still taut.

A decrepit black horse and then another ambled out into the crossroads, paused, and then slowly moved our direction. Clad in jeans and western shirts, the men rode on blankets but no saddles. One tried to dismount, slid off, lost his cowboy hat, and fell to the ground guffawing. The horses sauntered into the brush, leaving the two men on the road. The shorter of the two gripped a bottle, but the other one picked up a softball-sized rock in each hand. About six feet tall and burly, that guy began to stagger our way while the shorter one stayed back, took a swig from his bottle, and caterwauled, " . . . an' stay offa muh blue suede shoes!"

I caught Leonard's glance in his rearview mirror. He couldn't back up, and our linked vehicles were too long to turn around on the narrow road. I was opening my door to search for my camping shovel when Leonard screamed. "Sean, stay at the wheel!"

The husky guy with the rocks swayed and wobbled ahead until he was within twenty feet or so of the panel. "Th' li'l half-breed queer an''is dogs," he called back to the other one.

The shorter guy stopped singing. "Leave 'em, Randall—the ol' man'll kill us."

"G'dam li'l fag's on our road."

"This's the main road. Yer shi'faced."

Randall stumbled to one knee, staggered to his feet and came on. "He ain't goin' by."

"Someone's behind 'im."

"He ain't goin' by either."

His dogs barking incessantly, Leonard's right shoulder dipped to engage the manual transmission. He hit the gas, mud flying behind his wheels. Campbell jerked and so did my head; we were moving straight for the guy with the rocks. Adrenalin pumped through my neck and wrists, my hands gripped tightly to the steering wheel.

Not ten feet from our foe, Leonard swerved, but the man pitched a rock at the panel truck. It grazed the roof, flew straight back and thunked dead center into my windshield. I'd raised my arm before it hit—the snowy bruise in the glass instantly spread side to side like a web.

We were moving faster on level ground, but I couldn't see ahead. Well past the first guy, I spotted the other one through my side window, plopped down next to the road with the bottle, shaking his head. Seconds later, Campbell bumped lightly into the back of the panel truck—Leonard had stopped for some reason. I poked my head out of the window and saw our attacker lurching after me from behind, rocks in both hands again. I turned forward and saw Leonard getting out.

"What the hell are you doing?" I shouted over the din of yelping dogs.

Reaching down, Leonard picked up the same thin white-and-brown mongrel that had followed Hosteen Shepard's wagon before. He shoved the dog into his front seat, jumped in after it and started off, the tow chain grabbing again. I turned back just in time to see another rock glance weakly off the back of my cab and clunk into the truck bed. I let out a long sigh as we passed the two horses, blithely chewing greens as if grazing in a meadow.

On the ridge's downhill side, Leonard hit the gas and held that speed until we started up the next bluff. He stopped at the summit, and I stuck my head out to watch him walk toward me, giving the old dog some kind of snack. The scraggly mutt knelt down to devour the food, hesitantly wagging its tail as the other two whined from the panel.

Coming to my window, Leonard smiled. "So now you've met the Shepard brothers, Randall and Carlton. Pretty exciting for your first day."

"Exciting? What if we couldn't get by him?"

"That wasn't going to happen."

"Jesus, how can you be so calm about it? I can't believe you stopped."

"I wanted to get that dog."

"Won't Hosteen be pissed?"

"No, this pooch is too old and feeble even for a watchdog. Carlton's wife probably kept him alive." The haggard canine tottered closer, its tail low but wagging. Leonard leaned over to rub its pointed ears.

I nodded to my windshield and shook my head. "What do I do about this damn mess?"

"Once Hosteen finds out, they'll really catch it—Carlton for bringing in the booze. How we handle this could get a little complicated." He hurried back to his vehicle with the rescued mutt trailing behind.

)-)

When we rolled into Raven Point, I leaned my head out the side window to see where Leonard was taking me. My cap blew back into the cab as he towed Campbell toward the four old trailers, each about the size of half a caboose. Like giant pink shoeboxes forty feet apart up a gradual hillside, the trailers had open four-foot crawlspaces below. The missing metal skirting was on the ground nearby beneath concrete blocks. The first three trailers looked vacant, but the last one had bed sheets flapping in a steady breeze on the clothesline next to a Ford pickup.

Leonard drove into the gravel driveway by the first trailer, and Campbell rolled to a stop by one of those movable three-stair porches. The trailer's front door was so short and narrow it would have suited a children's playhouse. Leonard and all three dogs got out and came toward me as I climbed out to stare at the modular hut. On closer inspection, all the trailers were more salmon-colored than pink.

"Cute, huh?" Leonard asked while Albert sniffed the white PVC pipe under the trailer.

"Why is the skirting removed?"

"Air circulation. Jon and Eddie screw them back on before winter. This is where you can camp for now."

T

TTLLLOLOYLOYD WWINWINEWINETWINETSWINETSKWINETSKY

AsAs we unhitched Campbell from the tow chain, I glanced at the trailer. "I'm afraid to ask who lives here."

Leonard gathered the chain. "Yes, that would be you, should you decide to stay."

Yeah, another perk with this job.

He pointed to my tarp in the truck bed. "Your things will be okay there until dark." I stowed my knapsack and cooler in Campbell's cab and locked up.

Leonard was waiting by his truck with all the dogs. "Jump in."

"So where are we headed?"

"To the dorm office, if you want to call the Navajo Police in Old Mission."

With all of us inside, he coasted down toward the main buildings. I turned to him. "If we call the cops, what happens to the Shepards?"

"Nothing to Carlton. Maybe jail for Randall, if you press charges. He's been in for fighting a couple times, nothing like this."

"He wasn't aiming at *me* with that first rock. What about how he spoke to you?"

"This is going to be all about your windshield. Randall would never act like that sober, or when he's involved with basketball season."

"Oh. Is he a good player?"

Leonard raised his eyebrows in admiration. "I guess he and Carlton were the best ever at Raven Point—the only time the school ever won anything. When they were in boarding school in New Mexico, they went to the state tourney together once. Carlton's a shooter and Randall's inside. It's pretty exciting to watch them play men's league."

"Did they graduate from high school?"

"Yes, but they've been back here ever since, except for Carlton's two years in the army—the only time the men's team didn't win the local tournaments." He parked in front of the dorm;

the dogs panted on the glass, ready to get out. "Oh, one other thing—Randall's the school's assistant basketball coach."

"You're kidding," I said, but he was straight-faced. "So what does that involve?"

"He nods to the kids when the coach tells them something he agrees with."

"Quite a system." I exhaled audibly. "Is there an alternative to pressing charges?"

"Well, Randall could take responsibility for the window repair and work it off." Leonard checked his dogs in the rear; they'd settled again. "Carlton's a mechanic, army training and all. He helps the family with his part-time work at the Old Mission junkyard. And he barters his skills around here. Sometimes Randall helps him."

"So they fix my truck or it doesn't get fixed?"

"If you handle it, you'd have to tow it to Window Rock, maybe even Gallup. The Shepards could fix and clean your engine here in return for the cost of the glass, and Carlton could install the windshield if you have it shipped C.O.D. to Old Mission. The junkyard should have the tools." He called the three dogs; we all got out and made our way up to the boardwalk.

I turned to him. "All right, what do we have to do to get this deal going?"

"You're willing to hang around for all that?"

"I'm in no hurry, and I can check out the whole situation here."

This
Coal-tar Raven
Rocking Lightly
On an updraft
From Canyon De Chelly
Thinks she's
A fancy bird of prey.

8

As we walked along the boardwalk in front of the dorm, the three dogs perked up at the sound of a loud vehicle beyond the school. Leonard had been telling me that we shouldn't go out to Shepard's place until Monday morning to negotiate over the windshield. " . . . Hosteen sometimes holds ceremonies on Sundays to defy the missionaries. The windshield thing won't come together without him." Just then, a brown Cadillac about ten years old with a bad muffler belched up to the school office. "There's Miss Dot and Miss Mona."

"Who are they?"

"Dot Stringfellow has kindergarten, and Mona Johnson, first and second. They share the other quarters in the school, across from Hatcher. Want to meet them now?" A tallish heavy woman got out wearing a scarf against the fresh breeze and hurried toward the school with a box in her hands.

"No, she seems to be on a mission."

"They're not due until Wednesday—probably on the way to their cabin near Flagstaff. I expected Mrs. McAdam, the Special Ed teacher, and her daughter to be here by now. The new five-six teacher, Mr. Beale, should show before Wednesday." Leonard held up a hand, fingers crossed. "Hatcher said Mr. Beale will be a big change for us. The last teacher in that class was, um, pretty mean to the kids. He finally got his high school transfer."

"Great, I'm sure that'll solve it. So I'm the only teacher here so far?"

"No, Miss Wilson—the last trailer up the hill. She teaches third and fourth."

"Maybe I'll have a little chat with her."

Over at the school, the hefty teacher was already leaving with a smaller box. She handed it through the passenger-side window, then walked around to get behind the wheel. After backing up fast, she floored the sedan in a jackrabbit start, leaving behind a swirl of dust before the Caddy rumbled by the store on the road to Old Mission.

"So, ready to see the school?" Leonard asked.

"I think that can wait. Maybe we'll start with the gym."

"All right." As he smiled, his eyebrows rose again.

"Okay, Leonard, is this another 'Oh, by the way?'"

"Well, you can see for yourself. Just give me a couple minutes to take care of the pups and change my clothes."

I walked around back with him past a worn and dented blue VW Bus, which he identified as his "wheels." He settled the new dog in the pen with a half-dozen other mutts and one large, sleek shorthaired grey dog that looked to be a purebred. The wiggly hound cowered away from lame Marie, who was apparently top dog in the yard. Leonard's scruffy brown pony contentedly flicked its long tail and chewed some hay right among the dogs. Two tough-looking long-haired adult cats, one a grey tabby and one black, wandered inside the fence while three smaller ones, two of them black as well, roamed warily outside.

After we entered the back door, I headed down the hall and stopped to use the staff bathroom, where I was momentarily repulsed by the brown toilet bowl before concluding that the water was just very hard. After that, I waited in the rec room, stooping to pet the sleek black cat that had followed me from the apartments.

Leonard soon joined me in a fresh short-sleeve yellow dress shirt and his regular polished boots. "Isn't *Łizhinii* a sweetheart?"

I stood slowly from a squat. "Yeah, what does, uh, Zhinny mean?"

"'The black one.' My other cat is *Chiidi*—'ghost.' She doesn't warm up to strangers like *Łizhinii* does."

"I've never been around cats much."

"We can certainly fix that if you'd like."

"No thanks."

He started ahead of me for the door to the boys' dorm, his smile fading. "We get more stray dogs here than cats. The kitties I do get are often black, which is a revered color in the Navajo creation story—it represents the north."

"You don't sound like much of a believer."

"I also don't believe in Noah's Ark, manna from heaven, or magic cures for lepers."

"Amen," I said as we moved by the girls' bunks.

"Some Navajos have borrowed that black taboo from the white man. The city pounds are full of black cats—the last to be adopted, if they're lucky."

"What about that fancy grey dog out there? Was that a stray?"

"No, Bowie's a Weimaraner. Hatcher's wife bought him last year as a pup, but Hal didn't take to Bowie, so I board him—he may as well be mine."

We went out through the far door of the girls' dorm and onto a short connection that joined the main boardwalk to the nearby gym. Leonard unlocked the right side of the double door near the center of the windowless Quonset; we entered, and he flicked some light switches. We rounded a long ceiling-high cinder-block barrier, possibly a wind block for the winter.

I looked up at rows of wire-protected lights, maybe a hundred watts each, that poorly illuminated the warm gymnasium. I scanned the oblong room. Each end of the Quonset had a dark stage, the one to the left much smaller. From an apex of about twenty feet, the ceiling formed a downslope on each side all the way to the floor, leaving just enough space for a single row of chairs or benches, but anyone over five feet trying to stand there would have to duck.

"Man, this is something." I faced Leonard. "Why is it so hot in here?"

"It's an oven or a freezer until October, when Jon turns on the steam heat."

After one step over a long, low bench we were on the basketball floor, its seams visible between sections of old yellowed linoleum. The court was nowhere near regulation length, its center circle not ten feet from the key in either free-throw lane. Although patched and uneven in spots, the playing surface did have clearly painted black lines, and the nets, rims, and metal backboards looked practically new.

There was even a small electric scoreboard, apparently made of scrap metal, above the right stage, where P.E. equipment was scattered—poles, mats, nets and large cartons overflowing with random crap like bent badminton rackets, Hula Hoops, and jump ropes.

The smaller stage held a few tables and stacks of wooden folding chairs under a large carefully drawn mascot half-encircled by HOME OF THE RAVENS. Unfortunately, the artist must have used a scrawny dark-grey blackbird for a model.

Both stages were only about three feet above the floor and not ten feet beyond the baskets. I could almost see players hurling themselves onto a stage after errant passes. "What happens when the ball hits a light or the ceiling?"

"Out of bounds. The men's team fixed it up last year. Carlton made that scoreboard himself. Randall did the lettering and drew the, um, raven a few years ago. The men's team call themselves the Old Ravens, so it all works out."

I noticed a drinking fountain, its porcelain basin almost as dark as the staff toilet in the dorm. "Um, that crappy fountain—hard water?"

"Yeah, that's as clean as it gets—iron deposits. I'll tell you about that after our tour. So what are you thinking, something about a silk purse and a sow's ear?"

"Actually, it seems sort of comfortable. Teaching in here might be better than force-feeding English."

"So you're still considering the job?"

I was taken aback by how hopeful he sounded. "Maybe you can tell me a little more about the counseling."

"Sure, let's go out and talk." He shut off the lights, and we went outside into what had become a clear day with a tranquil breeze. Leonard inhaled the refreshing post-rain atmosphere, looking up at the azure sky. "Man, what a day."

"Does that mean this isn't very typical?"

"It is for this time of year. The rest can be . . . more challenging."

"I'll bet. So, the counseling?"

"Right, let's sit for a minute." Still genial but more serious, he pointed to the edge of the boardwalk. We sat there, facing the desolate but sunny playground.

"First," Leonard said, "this is rarely the kind of counseling where you talk with a kid one on one and try to sort out serious problems. There are lots of cultural barriers; what we try to do in the dorm is provide as close to a family environment as possible. Once in a while, one of the girls will open up to Felicita or Marla. In five years, I've had three boys bring a real problem to me—not even once that I know of with the last two counselors.

"Most of us end up doing things with the kids on our own time—birthdays, holidays, tutoring, movies, library night, school and community events. Miss Wilson and Mrs. McAdam help out when they can." The way he singled out those two teachers suggested that the other returning teachers and principal didn't bother.

"How many on the dorm staff?"

"Not counting the cook, who helps out sometimes, it's Felicita, myself, Marla and three more female aides—one's half-time and also subs. And the counselor, of course. We try to have at least two people on duty after school and in the evening, but on graveyard, it's only one person with another on call." He stood up, ready to move on.

I got to my feet to walk along with him. "You sound a little discouraged."

He couldn't hold back a sigh. "Well, six adults in loco parentis for fifty kids just doesn't cut it, although we do have a hardworking staff."

We passed the dorm and waved casually at the two women I'd met. They were dragging a floor polisher from one door to another. "So the big lady is Marla, and the one in the Navajo bun is, um—"

"Mrs. Etcitty. Felicita is a GS-Four—monitors the girls like I do the boys. She also has a lot of first aid training, so she acts as our nurse. Felicita does most of the day shifts and stays in the other apartment during the school week. Marla has more graveyard than anybody."

When we came to the panel truck, Leonard reached into his pocket to hand me a full key ring. "These are for your elegant trailer, the dorm, and the gym—most of your domain."

I took them reluctantly. "Not quite yet."

"Yeah, I'll know you're actually with us when you take the school keys from Hatcher." Serious again, he added, "I have at least two reasons to hope you'll do that."

"Oh? What are they?"

"For starters, I think you'd work out here just fine."

"Thanks, I guess. The other reason?"

"If you stay, I'd ask you to help me with something I'm concerned about. It would be completely up to you, and I'd understand if you decide not to do it."

"Uh-oh, here it comes."

For once, Leonard didn't smile back. "Remember that stained fountain in the gym?"

I nodded. "And the dormitory sinks."

"Wait until you see the toilets."

"Yeah, I saw the staff bathroom."

"So we all share the washing machines in the dorm, but some staff try to do their wash in town so they don't end up with orange underwear."

"From the iron?"

"Yes, it's a nuisance, but innocuous unless the levels are extreme. It's bad enough, though, that the water has a metallic taste. The spring before last, the agency tested the water and they told Hatcher last fall to tell us to run it a full minute after six hours of non-use. When I asked Hal about the report, he just gave me generalities, said the water was hard but within standards."

"Then why did they tell you to flush it out?"

"Exactly. When I asked to read the report, Hal said I'd have to go to the agency. So I did, and they refused, saying they treated the water and are just being careful by having us flush it out. When I tried to go higher up, some guy suggested in Commission-speak that I might want to butt out if I liked my job. They took more samples this spring, so by now there's a second report that they won't let me see."

"What is it you're so worried about?"

"I just want to be sure there's nothing harmful in the water."

"Do you think that's really possible?"

"Yes, there are a few possibilities. In the meantime, we stay low-key about it and use the big coffee pot in the kitchen for water, plus a cooler between the dorms. Because of the taste, most of the teachers use coolers in class and buy water for their quarters."

"So what could I do about it?"

"If you stay, your school keys might open the bottom drawers of Hatcher's file cabinet—they're padlocked. You'd be in charge when he's gone; you could take a peek."

"I see. Did you try to get the last counselor to look for the report?"

"He would've gone right to Hatcher."

"How do you know I won't?"

He arched one eyebrow confidently. "I think I'm a pretty good judge of character."

"All right. If I'm here, I can at least give it a try."

"Thanks. Just between us, okay?"

"Right," I said, wondering if the issue was worth all the intrigue.

"Believe me, I'd be glad if it turns out not to be serious. By the way, the water in the trailers isn't as bad as the school, but you still might want—"

"To drink something else. Got it." I started to leave. "See you in a while."

"If you need anything, I'll be over there with Felicita and Marla."

ן-ן

Still thinking about my conversation with Leonard, I passed the school and crossed the main road to reach the trailer. On second look it seemed even smaller, its paint job almost matching my maimed and comatose truck nearby.

I retrieved my cooler from Campbell and carried it up the shaky steps, then fumbled with the keys to unlock the door. Like Alice through the looking glass, I had to duck and turn sideways with the cooler to make it through the runty doorway.

A pair of two-by-three windows in the living room, their shades up, let in wedges of sunlight to expose a scarred tan linoleum floor, a worn brown Naugahyde armchair, and a two-cushion olive-green couch. The fake knotty-pine wall panels continued into a kitchen the size of an ordinary bathroom. It had a cheap two-chair dinette, a few pine cupboards, a porcelain sink, and a white refrigerator and stove, both half-sized. Near the sink, a round shaving mirror hung from another small window, this one louvered, its glass splattered with grease from the nearby stove. The sink was orange, but not so darkly stained as those in the dorm.

After setting the cooler on the dusty table, two strides down the narrow hallway took me to another mini-door. I opened it to find what was literally a water closet—a toilet just inside the door and a shower stall with a cloth curtain hung from the warped ceiling panels. I peeked at the toilet bowl expecting a turd-brown color, but it was the same orange as the kitchen sink. Then I laughed out loud, realizing I'd be able to sit on the pot and reach through the doorway to move a pan on the stove.

A few feet down the hall, I bumped my head peering into a puny windowless bedroom with a double bed and dresser that took up most of the space. A small window barely brightened a second even smaller bedroom, furnished only with a fold-up cot. A door in the hall opened out to a drop-off, five feet to the ground.

Home sweet home crossed my mind, followed by *What the hell? The crappy little place is big enough for me—if I stay.* I definitely wanted to talk to that other teacher up the hill. Maybe her perspective would reassure me I wasn't crazy to consider staying in Raven Point.

I went out to Campbell to retrieve my knapsack, left it on the bed, then unpacked the cooler into the refrigerator, chiding myself for not insisting on more milk at the store in Tsosie. *Man, all this in one day.*

Starting up the hill past the next identical trailer, I spotted a raven, perched atop a power pole not twenty feet away. The husky corvid, lustrous as obsidian, bore little resemblance to the mascot painted in the gym.

"Hey, mama," I said quietly, assuming its gender. She seemed to turn her long black beak my way, but instead of cawing she made a deep and confident *clock-clock.* The raven stayed right there and repeated *clock-clock* as I moved slowly by. Then, hopping a few inches straight up, she unfolded her impressive wingspan and flapped just once to let the breeze carry her aloft. Her mate appeared in the sky and circled upward with her in the thermals, soaring as delicately as any pair of eagles.

I watched the ravens become black specks before I moved on. The third trailer's only distinction was a homemade plaque— McADAM burned into the wood. Beyond it, on a clothesline by the last trailer, bedsheets had been replaced by towels and washrags, waving in the breeze along with two velveteen shirts, one black and the other dark green.

Wondering if the teacher was Navajo, I made my way up her wobbly steps and knocked on a door like mine, except for a red-and-white bumper sticker with Navajo words and diacritical markings. The only one I recognized was *Dine'é.* A plastic nameplate above the door read, MISS ELIZABETH WILSON.

I knocked and heard, "Just a sec," then stepped back down to wait. A pallid woman in glasses, maybe in her late thirties, opened the door. She was so short and thin that the small doorway seemed custom-made for her. With her long, dark-brown hair gathered behind in a knot, she was in Navajo dress—a carmine velveteen blouse with a long sack-like tan skirt.

"Well, hello," she said from four or five feet above me, her narrow face mildly surprised. As we stood there, she was holding a silver and turquoise squash-blossom necklace that she put over her gawky neck.

"Hi, I'm Sean Noland."

"Elizabeth Wilson. So you're the other new staff member?" She sounded formal and stayed in the doorway, not offering her hand, and I didn't feel compelled to offer mine either.

"Well, they re-assigned me—"

"I know—counselor and basketball coach."

"And P.E.," I added, but she stared at me doubtfully for a long moment. Noticing stress lines around her green eyes, I judged she could be reasonably good-looking if she gained enough weight to fill out her bony features.

"Oh, excuse me," she finally said. "Please come in. I was just making tea before going over to the school."

"Thanks. I do have a couple questions if you don't mind."

She nodded and backed up. I climbed the steps, lowered my head and walked in, almost stumbling over one of three fish-tank terrariums. Each held a plastic pond and a solitary animal, basking under artificial light—a salamander, an ordinary painted turtle, and a three-inch frog.

"No snake?"

"No, too many taboos." Lifting a half-gallon bottle of store-bought water, she added some to her steaming teakettle. "Some of the children will not even look at snakes, let alone study them. Water creatures don't have many taboos, except not to harm them, so amphibians are perfect for science as well as my Navajo classes. Would you care for tea or instant coffee?"

"Coffee, please—a shot of milk if you have it."

Puttering at the small stove, Miss Wilson fit perfectly in her snug kitchen. As for the living room, the blinds were drawn in order to shade what seemed to be her shrine to indigenous cultures. A large colorful rug tacked to one wall had a design like the poster in the rec room—thin, elongated, square-headed Navajo gods. I had forgotten Leonard's word for them. A black saddle blanket with white fringe covered the back of her small sofa. The other main piece of furniture was a ceiling-high bookcase with a small stereo, pottery, baskets, jewelry, and carved figurines; some of the artifacts looked ancient.

Between the windows she'd hung what I guessed was a time-worn baby carrier, its wooden back frame made in halves with a curved piece jutting at the top, a footrest at the bottom, all of it held together with weathered leather strips. I gazed down the hall as she fixed the drinks and saw that her extra bedroom was an office with full bookcases around a small desk, several colorful *ojos de Diós* suspended from the ceiling.

I took a seat in one of her dinette chairs as she brought a cup over to me along with a plate of vanilla sugar wafers. While she went back for her tea, I sipped some of the coffee. "Just what I needed. Thanks."

"You're welcome." She sat in the other chair, dipping a tea bag in her cup. "So, has anyone mentioned to you that our P.E. classes have basically been supervised afternoon recess?"

"No, that's news to me."

She made a dubious half-smile. "Are you completely new to the Navajo?"

"I'm from Tucson. Grand Canyon is the closest I've been before." I read her slight cringe as *God, another tourist.* "And where are you from?"

"Chicago." She left the tea bag on her saucer. "When did you get in, Mr. Noland?"

"It's Sean—today. Leonard's been showing me around. He told me about the job change."

She sipped her tea, unsmiling, and said, "Welcome to the FIC."

Not yet, lady. I nodded at the apparently standard Commission joke then bit into a crunchy wafer before swallowing some coffee. "So what's the deal with this principal, Hatcher?"

"He usually works out fine because we hardly ever see him. You will be in charge much of the time, but it's nothing to worry about. We all cover our own responsibilities. Jeannie handles the mail and official papers; all you do is sign them." *And stay out of our way*, her imperious tone implied. "Do you have other questions?"

"Um, what did you mean by Navajo classes?"

She brightened, seeming pleased by my inquiry. "We have some extra funds expressly for indigenous language and culture. I have two Navajo classes—third to sixth, and then K through two—rotating with your times on Tuesday, Wednesday, and Thursday afternoons."

"I see. So those will be large classes."

"For here, yes. Around twenty-five in each."

"I assume you also teach ESL in your regular class?"

"Yes, but with my own materials. I expect our students to be bilingual."

"Makes sense to me."

That brought another hesitant smile. "Good."

I sipped more coffee. "So you must have studied native cultures in college."

"Yes, especially the *Dine'é.* I am working for my doctorate in Multicultural Ed."

I nodded to the wooden object between the windows. "Beautiful piece. What's it called?"

"*Awééts̓áál*, a Navajo cradleboard. Each part has a practical use and also represents an aspect of nature. Mother Earth, Father Sky, the sun, rainbow, lightning, and so on."

"Interesting." I glanced at the other artifacts. "That's quite a collection for someone—"

"My age? Actually, most of it is in storage. Some pieces I acquired; the others were handed down from my mother. She was a museum curator and also had her own collection." Her face turned more serious. "What have you taught before, Mr. Noland?"

I gave up insisting on my first name and quickly filled her in on my teaching background.

"I can see why they hired you for the five-six class," she said, "but may I assume that your only preparation for being on the Navajo was orientation in Gallup?"

After I nodded, she took some tea, and then jeered. "The Navajo Way in two hours with Mrs. Joe, of all people, and then they expect you to be a counselor for these children."

"Yeah, that's sort of what I thought—"

"Nothing against you, but a counselor here should have thorough training on the basics of Navajo mythology. Without an understanding of the *Diné'é* concept of right thinking, evil, and the achievement of harmony, how can they expect you to understand a culturally conflicted child?"

"I see your point, but I think Leonard would be helpful." She covered a scoff with her fist, which really annoyed me. To calm down, I gazed at the rug on the wall to look for its flaw. I faced her and spoke again. "Leonard also told me that a lot of the kids are in Special Ed."

"He and Mrs. McAdam are quite the worrywarts on that subject. Most of those children end up qualifying because of their English."

"But he said the number of kids is disproportionate with the other schools."

"That's his misinterpretation. Leonard and I came to Raven Point the same year. He is very good at what he does, and I appreciate his support for my classes, but he is not an educator."

He is half Navajo, I felt like saying. I wanted to hear the Special Ed teacher's take on all of this. "Um, I noticed before that you said 'Navajo mythology.'"

"Yes, that is the correct term."

"Do you mind if I ask if you are a Christian?"

Her thin face stiffened. "Yes, Catholic, as a matter of fact, and I believe you are implying some sort of analogy—yet you have no knowledge of the Navajo Way."

I waited to be sure the lecture was over. "You're right on both counts, but I'd bet that what you call mythology is a religion just as much as Christianity or any of the rest."

"Many Navajos practice both, but you have a right to your opinion."

"Yes, but I apologize—your religion is none of my business." I took a last drink, got up, and stepped to the sink to rinse my cup. "Well, thanks for the info and the coffee." I turned to her.

She nodded and stood, teacup in hand. "No misunderstandings, Mr. Noland. I am glad you are here and that the five-six position opened up again."

Wondering why she cared about the latter, I attempted a smile. "Good to meet you." I walked to her door, thinking that she was probably glaring at my back.

9

Leonard was right again. The light snowfall soon gave us enough traction to leave the edge and walk on the road toward the Benallys' place, our poles clicking on the ice beneath the new accumulation. Marie showed up in Leonard's flashlight beam, snow clinging to her matted fur. She limped along with us for a while, then took off tracking again into mostly stunted piñons.

"Did Hawthorne name her Marie?" My voice was loud but stifled, my lips damp against the coat's lining.

"No. He probably just called her *łééchąą'í*—animal obsessed with poop."

"What?"

"Or poopy pet—rough translations for dog. After I saw how smart she was, I named her after Marie Curie. Hawthorne calls her that now when he visits the yard."

I pulled open the top buttons so I could speak more clearly. "And the wiener dog, Albert, is for *Einstein*?"

"Original, huh?"

I chuckled, noticing that the snowfall had thickened. "How did you end up with Marie?"

"After she hurt her leg last year, Hawthorne hid her out in the tules from Samson so he wouldn't shoot her. The leg healed like that by the time she came home, so the next time Samson was drunk, Hawthorne hid her again. When school started he told me about it, so I went out there with him to get the dog. We had to pass the house, and when Samson heard us, he fired off a couple of shots. One came pretty close. I didn't call the cops, but he still carries a grudge."

"Jesus. Besides Peter and Hawthorne, how many others live out there?" We'd started out side by side but I was having to work to keep up with him.

He turned back to me. "Let me know if you need to stop."

"I'm doing okay."

"Anyway, Peter and Hawthorne are the youngest. Their mom died when Peter was four. Most of the older kids got out after that. Besides the two boys, there's still a teenage daughter, Ruth; and a son about twenty, David—and their elderly aunt."

"The girl's not in school?"

"She was in boarding at Fort Defiance until this year. Honor student, played basketball, and she wanted to return for her junior year, but Samson said Ruth was boy-crazy, that he'd only let her go to some school up in Utah. She refused and has been trying to find a way out ever since."

"Is she the one Hawthorne's worried about?"

"Her and David, I'd guess. They all get along better when Samson's sober, of course, but even then he's no prize—mostly obstinate and quiet." Marie, with a thin layer of snow yet to be shaken from her black fur, emerged from the trees to take her place next to Leonard.

"So Samson probably lost that eye when he was drinking?"

"No, supposedly an accident with some firewood when he and Hosteen were kids. He still blames Hosteen for it."

The snowflakes had turned fluffy but dry. We stopped talking for a while as the traction improved even more, the tips of the poles now silent as they struck only snow. Several minutes later, a breeze came up. I buttoned the hood over my face again, and Leonard used his scarf like a bank robber to cover his ears, nose and mouth, but he still didn't use his hood. Although we were on an uphill grade and I'd fallen back a little, we were making steady progress. His light flashed off to the side to reveal bushier piñons, some of them over ten feet tall.

The snow pattered hard against my hood, and my rubber soles squeaked with each step. Soon the breeze turned to a light wind, slanting the heavy curtain of falling flakes. It wasn't long before our boots made less noise as we began to push through the deeper snow.

Leonard stopped and shouted back. "Not letting up. Starting to drift a little." I saw him check his watch, then put away the flashlight, useless in the near-whiteout. "It's almost five."

"How far to the Benallys'?" I called back to him.

"Maybe a mile. Close enough there's no sense to mess with the skis."

"Good." I could make out his ghost-like form just well enough to see that he finally put up his hood. After he waited for me to catch up, we moved on, using the trees and bushes to keep us on track. Marie walked between us, no longer searching for the boys' trail. The opaque snowfall and ambient silence felt more serene than spooky, which I attributed to Leonard's confidence in dealing with our situation.

After another half hour or so, the wind abated some, but the thick snow was still falling at a slight angle. Although we were slogging uphill through small drifts, I still felt okay—probably due to running with the kids and the men's basketball team. All the same, I was looking forward to some rest.

A few minutes later, we smelled smoke and Leonard said, "Piñon wood. Getting close."

I followed him and Marie onto what was apparently a narrow side track beneath the snow. Relieved, I noticed the dim shape of a cabin in the pines, traces of first morning light above, with smoke and steam that billowed from a chimney pipe. We hiked on level ground past a boarded-up hogan the shape of a giant cupcake, then an empty corral, a derelict pickup truck, and an outhouse before we came to the rectangular log cabin. It didn't look old or weathered, its gently slanted roof covered with more than a foot of ice and snow.

Dogs started barking inside, prompting a whine from Marie. Leonard stopped to look at the place, pulling down his scarf. "Good, May's awake. That old hogan back there is where she and Walter raised Billy from when he was two. Come on."

I unbuttoned my hood as we moved on. "How did that come about?"

"Short version—Hosteen watches out for the Benallys and comes to Billy's meetings. Billy's mother, May's niece, died in a crash with her husband, but the boy survived; the Benallys took him in. Hosteen told the school that May lost her only baby and couldn't have more."

Leonard sounded dubious at times during his account, but I didn't ask why. He waved at a brightly lit window on the right side of the cabin, where someone peeked out through a fogged-up pane. "If we're real lucky," he said, "they're both in there getting fed."

Most of the snow had been scraped off the flat roof and stairs of an enclosed wooden porch. So he could take off his pack, I removed all the ski equipment from Leonard's back and stuck the poles and skis into the deep snow by the cabin.

The door to the porch was cracked open a foot or so by a tiny woman with a wizened face, a colorful Pendleton blanket over her head like a shawl. She motioned for us to enter, and then Leonard greeted her in Navajo. Holding the frame pack at his side, he pointed his lips away, asking something about Walter.

She answered in a few words. I understood "Walter" along with the abrupt Navajo negation I'd heard many times by then. Leonard and I climbed the three steps, kicking snow off of our boots. We followed her in with Marie through the door and onto the porch. Leonard's flashlight revealed an interior of unstained lumber, a small bench on one wall, and two shovels in a corner. While the temperature wasn't much better than outside, it felt good just to be out of the breeze.

As we stomped more snow off of our boots, Leonard spoke to May; I heard "Hawthorne" in his question. She answered quickly, and I picked up "Noland," "Hawthorne," and that Navajo word for dog in his reply. When he finished, she looked at me with just a trace of a grin.

"Walter's gone," Leonard told me, "and Hawthorne left after he dropped off Billy. She'll tell us more after we go inside."

As we sat on the bench to unlace our boots, the dog rushed through the inner door with the old woman. "Marie knows this place," Leonard said. "Aunt May sometimes takes in strays or tells me about them."

We removed our boots and walked into the cabin, where Billy, in jeans and a flannel shirt, was already horsing around on a throw rug with Marie and two other dogs, one about Marie's size, the other a small mutt. I took off the parka and carried it with me as I started across the cold wood floor to Billy. Leonard nodded to me with approval while he unzipped the top half of his snowsuit and pulled out his arms.

Not surprisingly, the boy kept wrestling although I was standing right by him. "Billy, we're really glad you're okay."

Much taller than his great-aunt, Billy let Marie go but stayed on the rug, looking up at me with a full smile I had not seen before. He brushed back his dark bangs, grown long since school started. "Play good?" he asked, his D sounding like a T as he touched his chest.

"You sure did, Billy."

He glanced to where May and Leonard were talking, and then back at me. "I stay?"

"Yeah, for a while."

Billy went right back to Marie, so I looked around the cabin's large room. A gas lantern at each end cast shadows over well-used beds, sofas, chairs, and dressers along the plastered walls. They had tacked up a trading post calendar, a few small pictures, and one framed poster that was near me: the iconic shot of American servicemen raising the flag on Iwo Jima. I saw two cats, one black and the other orange, sleeping in a faded-blue stuffed chair. Pinned up by its sleeves to a clothesline above them was Billy's black and green mackinaw.

Leaving my parka near the cats, I realized I was sweating, but then a chill shuddered through my body. I stepped toward the home's source of heat, something like a boiler I once saw in a museum steam locomotive, but this one had an oven beside its hearth, plus an iron slab on top. I sat on a wooden chair near the stove and heard sizzling oil in a heavy iron caldron as steam billowed from a speckled-blue coffee pot. Firewood and chunks of snag filled a crate nearby.

After Leonard left May to greet Billy and the dogs, she shed her blanket, revealing grey hair in a traditional bun, a store-bought brown wool sweater, and a long, heavy cotton skirt. At a slow but steady pace, she walked to a sturdy table on the other side of the big stove. Next to a bag of flour, a blue cylinder of salt, and a Crisco can, she kneaded a batch of dough, her elbows pumping like pistons. Beyond the table, May even had a sink, its spigot likely engineered to draw water from a gravity tank that I didn't see out in the storm. If that system was functioning so late in the year, I wondered how they kept it from freezing. Her kitchen also had four varnished pine cabinets, plus a door to a cold box, likely with a closable vent to the outside.

While Leonard played with the dogs and Billy, I got up and walked away from the intense heat to the center of the room. Like a square harp made of wood, a Navajo loom stood there near a yellow dinette table with varied plastic-covered and wooden chairs. May's weaving project was about a third finished—another rug with precise geometric designs, this time in black, brown and white. Not far from the loom, a worktable held steel tools and punches, waiting for the leather artisan to emboss some belts that lay there.

Leonard left Billy to get something from his pack by the door. On his way back to May, he unwrapped some produce and a few long candles, giving them to her before he walked over to me at the loom.

"What else did you find out?" I asked as we watched Billy, still tussling with the dogs.

"Hawthorne ate here, then left more than an hour ago with food, blankets and matches. Samson's on a binge, all right. May and Walter tried to pick up David, Ruth, and Aunt Gerry for Thanksgiving, but Samson ran them off. May's mainly worried about David."

"What about the girl?"

"May says Ruth and Geraldine know how to stay away from Samson when he's drinking, but David—"

"What?"

"David is, um, slow like Billy. He was still in school when I first came to Raven Point. Aunt May tries to keep tabs on him and Geraldine, who's her cousin. Gerry takes care of David like May does Billy. Walter sometimes picks them up at Samson's to get the kids away from him and give the ladies some time together."

"Pretty confusing."

"Yeah. Anyway, before the snow started, Walter went to get Hosteen, and now he's probably stuck over there. I guess it was Walter's old Buick we saw on the Tsosie road. He's not supposed to drive anymore, but he still uses the back roads."

"What's wrong with him?"

"Gradual dementia." He glanced at Billy. "May thinks Hawthorne will be okay outside, but she said we should try to get to his house before he does."

"And do what?"

"I guess try to talk Samson down."

"But he won't even speak to you."

"Yeah, that's about the size of it."

"And how are we supposed to catch up with Hawthorne?"

"He's breaking through deep snow by now, and we'll be on skis."

A house trailer here
Tugs at its anchor
Like a chained mad dog
While gusting sand
Draws delicate designs
On the inside
Of airtight compartments.

10

Since I had yet to make my decision whether to stay or go, it seemed possible that my visit with Miss Wilson might have been my last with a Raven Point teacher. An intermittent windstorm shook and rattled the trailer as I slept into Sunday afternoon, something I hadn't done in years. Wondering if such adolescent habits revived for guys pushing fifty, I went out and walked around the deserted compound in a funk, annoyed by the dirt blowing in the warm air. Deciding not to pester Leonard, I returned to the dinky trailer and ate fruit from a can, watching dust drift under the door to form tiny dunes on the linoleum.

I unpacked a few books and avoided a day of self-pity with some distracting reading—Saroyan's *The Human Comedy*. I lost myself in the daily trials of Homer, Ulysses, and the Armenians of World War II Central California, stopping now and then when an anchor caught and thumped from under the floor, straining to keep a gust from carrying off the trailer.

Hosteen and his two sons came into Raven Point early on Monday, well before Leonard and I had planned to go out to their place. After the buzzer from the dorm woke me, I waited outside by Campbell, about two hours after dawn on that cool, still morning. With Hosteen driving, the Shepards and Leonard rolled up in a grey-primered, muddy and battered dual-cab four-wheel-drive Ford pickup. In spite of the truck's appearance, its motor sounded tight and well-tuned.

After they all got out, the hassle over the windshield was resolved just as Leonard had suggested. The Shepard brothers just glared away from the conversation while Leonard and Hosteen did most of the talking. We'd have to wait for the glass to be shipped C.O.D. to Old Mission to complete the arrangement, but Carlton inspected Campbell's motor as Randall handed him wrenches from a toolbox they brought. Before they left, Carlton released the brake and for some reason rolled my truck into some short brush about thirty feet down the slope from the trailer.

The principal, as predicted, had not arrived, but Leonard told me that Mrs. McAdam, the Special Ed teacher, had left a message relayed by radio from Old Mission—the Raven Point phone line was out again—that she and her daughter would be arriving very late on Monday night.

)-(

Managing to rouse myself by mid-morning on Tuesday, I was in limbo with nothing much to do but have a can of fruit and take a shower. After I got dressed in jeans and an old work shirt, I looked out one of the small windows at a passing dented dark-blue Dodge pickup. Its bed was partly covered with a canvas tarp that fluttered in the light breeze, held down only by slack ropes. The truck had so much cargo in back that I couldn't see the driver. It crossed the road, swung around, and parked parallel to the school's front door.

I stepped outside onto the top stair and watched a woman—Mrs. McAdam, I assumed—climb down from the driver's side. Still dubious at best about my situation in Raven Point, I nevertheless wanted to hear the Special Ed teacher's take on the issues Miss Wilson had raised. I closed the door, walked down the stairs and started for the school.

No more than five-five, the fair woman was in blue jeans, rolling up the sleeves of a green plaid flannel shirt. Her thick dark-blonde pigtail swung behind her as she came back to remove the loose ropes from the tarp.

The passenger door opened, and a tall girl walked to the back of the truck, stretching her long arms. Dressed like her mother, except in a red flannel hanging loosely from her slight frame, she also wore a single long pigtail, but hers was black. They worked together to fold up the tarp that had been covering stacks of boxes, plastic storage tubs, a stuffed armchair, and several wooden painting easels.

Inches shorter than her daughter, I couldn't pinpoint the woman's age. From where I stopped at the edge of the main road, they could pass for two young women moving into a college dorm. They propped open the school's front entrance as they began to carry items from the truck bed to set down near the door. Crossing the road, I saw the daughter making more trips because her mother kept stopping to sort and organize. If they saw me coming, they gave no sign, going on about their business.

As I came closer, the lanky girl turned and looked at me askance, wisps of wiry black hair escaping her braid. She had fawn-colored skin and long black lashes that set off her thin young face. I was surprised that regardless of her height, at least five-nine, she was no more than eleven or twelve years old. Her mother pushed away a large white plastic storage tub, faced me for a moment, nodded, and then turned back to open a box. Now I had some idea of her age—maybe five years younger than me, in her late thirties or early forties.

Like her daughter, she didn't use makeup, and they shared the same alert hazel eyes. Having endured the war of dental braces with my ex-wife and Rebecca, I noticed that this mother and daughter had not stooped to such vanity for their slightly uneven but healthy-looking white teeth.

As if Mrs. McAdam had just left a sunny hiking trail, freckles formed a pert mask across her ruddy oval face. Her nose, mouth and chin were rounded and pleasantly symmetrical, and she carried some extra weight that seemed to fit her solid frame and firm curves. She was physically attractive in a sturdy way I had sometimes wondered about during my two marital relationships with intentionally thin women.

"Hi, you must be Mrs. McAdam." I hoped it wasn't obvious that I had checked her out.

"Yup, that's right." Her brows, also dark-blonde, arched dubiously. "It's Abby." She pulled off a work glove and thrust out her hand.

"Sean Noland. New hire." I met Mrs. McAdam's earnest grip, her hand softer than her backwoods appearance implied.

"Another record crop at orientation?" she asked rhetorically as the girl returned. "Mr. Noland, my daughter, Elizabeth."

Occupied with a poster tube, the girl made a cursory nod, probably glad that she didn't have to shake hands with another white person pretending not to notice her biracial background.

"Hi, Elizabeth. So you have the same first name as Miss Wilson?" I asked stupidly.

"Bingo." She walked away again.

"Sorry—sore subject," Abby said. "I forgot to say 'Beth.' She had Miss Wilson for two years. Now she'll be with you in fifth grade." She rummaged through one of her boxes as she spoke. "So you're in the first trailer. Thought you'd get the second."

I had pegged Abby for a lifelong southwesterner, using "git" for "get," lots of casual contractions, and an occasional *yup*. "I guess that's for the other guy," I said, and then explained how Leonard tried to break the news tactfully that my assignment had changed. "…I'll save you the trouble—no need to say 'Welcome to the FIC.'"

Abby maintained eye contact for a moment, breaking her serious demeanor with a brief smile. "Good, sounds like you and Leonard are getting along. We haven't seen him yet." She gathered some loose art paper as Beth came back and climbed into the truck bed.

"Can I give you two a hand?"

"Sure," Abby said, "just help us unload."

I gave Abby the last of the paper. "Leonard's already saved my hide a couple of times." Closing a storage tub, she glanced at me inquisitively.

Beth scowled at her mother and jumped down, hauling out an easel with congealed dried paint all over it. "I'm taking this into the room."

"Okay," Abby said, bringing down the next easel as Beth left.

I reached up and lifted out another one, surprised by its weight. Abby stopped working and turned to me. "So how did Leonard save your hide?"

I gave her a brief rundown of the incidents on the road. "... and Carlton's starting to work on the motor while we wait for the glass." I pointed over at the truck.

"I saw the windshield. That sort of thing doesn't happen much in Raven Point. Randall I get—surprised Carlton was involved."

"I thought it was strange that he left my truck down there before they took off."

We set two more easels down and stood near them. "Carlton's quiet, but he's proud," she said softly. "He's probably contrite. Saves face for him to work on it down there."

Abby's use of "contrite" didn't seem pretentious, just part of her eclectic style of speaking. I grunted at her statement, doubting that the Shepard brothers felt much remorse.

Her brows rose with uncertainty. "I get the feeling you don't know if you're here to stay."

"Yeah, it's kind of wait and see." I nodded toward the school. "Listen, I don't have much to do for now. Maybe I could help you take all of this in and get a look at the school."

"I'd definitely appreciate that." She hauled out a case of water like those I'd seen in the kitchen and set it by the rear wheel. "Planned to be here a week ago, but my Chevy died. Took days to find this ol' lizzie, but at least I didn't have to tow a trailer."

After we finished unloading more cases of water, she pointed to some larger boxes in the middle of the truck bed. "You mind bringing down those books while I go in for the dolly?"

"Sure. So where did you drive in from?"

"Durango, Colorado—where I grew up. Took a class this summer; we spent the rest of the time there with my dad."

Beth was back, looking pouty. "You're gabbing about Grandpa?" She glared at me as I reached for a book box. "I'm in charge of those."

"Yes, dear, soon as they're inside," Abby said. After Beth left with another easel, Abby turned to me, shaking her head. "Sorry about that. So where you from?"

"Tucson."

"Oh, I like that country down there."

"Yeah. Unfortunately, I've been living near Phoenix for a long time."

She laughed, sincere and unforced. "Not my favorite place."

Maybe our mutual antipathy for Arizona's capital city was a small sign that we'd get along. She carried off an easel, and I began lifting the heavy boxes one by one from the truck to the ground. As I finished, Abby returned with a furniture dolly and manhandled a book carton onto it. I added two boxes on top, and she was right behind with another, ignoring my attempt to help her. I put the fifth and last box on the pile.

"Good, all in one trip," she said. "I'll lead the way so you know where we're heading."

"Right. Where'd you get all the books?"

"Bought some, the others were donated."

I stepped onto the bar to tilt the dolly, and pushed it after her to the front door, where Beth was moving things onto an A-V cart she'd brought out from the school.

"Hold the door, please," Abby told her. "We'll put these in your library."

Beth shrugged as we passed her and went in. The hall to the left looked like an elementary-school museum—scuffed brown linoleum floors, white volleyball-sized light fixtures, wooden doors with glass on the top half, and then long shelves over rows of coat hooks on walls layered with goldenrod paint. To the right, the shorter end of the hall had two doors on one side, the first with STAFF stenciled on its glass; the second had a nameplate, likely an apartment. Across from it was a third door to a small office; through its glass top I could see an interior entrance marked PRIVATE.

I rolled the cart to a stop in front of a large wooden trophy case, the kind typical for a high school gym. Its bottom shelf held just two small trophies, some ribbons, and two black-and-white team pictures of boys. The upper shelves displayed color photos of men's teams plus numerous plaques and tall trophies with golden male figurines in every possible basketball pose. On the wall above the trophy case, someone had painted a small version of the blackbird-like mascot I'd seen in the gym.

Abby came back to the trophy case. "Mr. Noland?"

"Sorry. So this must have something to do with the Shepard brothers."

"Yup, Carlton built it with community money." She pointed ahead. "Mine's the last room on the right." I swung the dolly to the left, rolling it past a dark-orange drinking fountain toward the classrooms. Through one door, I could see long shelves, a movie projector, a rack of colored butcher paper, and a hand-crank ditto machine.

Abby turned to me, chuckling. "By the way, seen our gym yet?"

"Yes, quaint. The whole basketball thing seems pretty bizarre to me."

"Yeah, but it's important to the community." She looked up at me as if I were six-foot-five. "Did you play?"

"A little, but I've never coached."

We passed another classroom. "Shouldn't be much pressure with basketball," she said. "The school hasn't won a game in years, but everyone loves to watch 'em try. There's one boy who can shoot the ball well, Hawthorne Shepard—first cousin to Randall and Carlton. I'm afraid only six or seven might play, if you include Billy Benally."

I halted the dolly at the last door. "I think Leonard mentioned Billy."

"Turns fifteen in April. Billy's the manager, but he practices with the team." She grasped the doorknob, then faced me without turning it. "He's the slowest kid we have, but very sweet. He has Navajo Studies and gym time with the upper grades, the rest with me." She sighed deeply. "We can't keep Billy again; I have a year to find a school that might be useful for him." Abby opened the door.

"Can I get a couple more questions off my chest?" I asked, still in the hall.

"Shoot."

"If I decide to do this, how would it go over if I actually teach P.E., not recess?"

"I think most of the kids would like it. Hal and the staff won't care as long as the kids are over there for the whole period. Come on, we can talk for a minute in my mess."

She moved boxes and tables, clearing a path so I could roll the cart into her surprisingly large and bright room. She or Beth had left the lights on, and the shades were at the top of four tall windows that looked out on the dirt playground. Her classroom had a jumble of ordinary school furniture plus an assortment of haphazardly placed materials: terrariums, magnifying glasses, a microscope, a telescope, manipulatives, plants, a water table, an abacus, hand-drawn charts and maps, a Navajo saddle blanket, and at least a dozen vivid posters depicting sandstone formations, animals, minerals, and Anasazi ruins.

Below a gallery of student artwork on one wall, milk crates were stacked four-high to serve as cubbies. The long counter near the door had a sink surrounded by jars, tempera cans, brushes, crayons, colored chalk, glue, scissors, and more craft materials. When we passed by, I saw the familiar dark-orange porcelain, a small blue plastic water cooler, and a pillowcase tied over something in the sink.

"What's under there?"

"The drinking fountain."

"Right, I heard a little about the water." I walked up to an ice cream tub atop a lazy Susan. I spun the device, peering through its slits on the side to see a hand-drawn stick figure perform a jumping jack. "This thing is great," I said.

"A zoetrope." She sighed. "I left my room mostly as it was. We do learning centers."

"Whaddaya know, John Dewey's alive and well." I wanted to take back my name-dropping, smart-aleck comment as soon as I said it, but Abby nodded.

"Yup, I think he'd approve. Anyway, now I barely have time to reorganize. Thank God the agency called off Tuesday and my aide starts on Wednesday."

"How many aides in the school?"

"Dot's and mine plus one floater, Jeannie, who's also in the office." She looked around. "There's room now to get into the library." She pointed to an alcove of full bookcases positioned around throw rugs, lounging pillows, beanbag chairs, an overstuffed settee and a reference table with an old typewriter. I pushed the dolly over to park it behind the bookcases, where she had taped up pages of student writing.

I put my hand on the boxes. "Do you have room for all these?"

"Yes, they go on some new shelves above the primary books. Most of these books are for kids who can read. Beth chose a lot of them. This collection is for the whole school."

I left the books to follow Abby to a corner where an overflowing desk occupied a cubicle formed by tall metal file cabinets. Scores of black-and-white photos covered the back of the first grey cabinet. "Photographer?" I asked, reluctant to point out the rough, haphazard photos of the reservation that included very few people, and one of those was a grainy close-up of Beth.

Abby was looking at her desk. "I dabble in it, but the kids took those. I have five old Brownies they can check out, and they write about whatever they shoot."

"Not much written about people then."

"For some kids it's a taboo to take pictures of people." She dragged over two of the larger student chairs, and we sat near the photos. "Sorry, my desk is another disaster area." She was polite but obviously ready to work. "So, Sean Noland sounds Irish."

"Yeah, both parents. I'm third generation. You?"

"Same, more or less, but Scottish and English."

My gaze drifted to Beth's image on the cabinet. "Um—"

"Her father was Jamaican."

"Sorry, none of my business."

"It's okay. You have family with you?"

"No, divorced."

"Well, that's none of *my* business."

"No problem. We both have smart daughters. Mine is studying music in college."

She nodded. "So what other questions about the school?"

I glanced back at her sink. "Um, the water deal must be pretty annoying."

"That's one word for—" She stopped herself as if she'd said more than she wanted to.

"Does Leonard pay for all that bottled water in the kitchen?"

"Most of us chip in. He orders what the FIC allows and brings in more."

"And those cases by your truck?"

"For in here. Beth and I have more at the trailer. I bring some in on every trip."

"I see. Leonard is sure an interesting guy."

"What do you mean?" Her tone sounded just a touch defensive.

"Well, he seems so even-keeled, and he's pulled in so many directions—with the FIC, and all the cultural things, I guess. Not to mention some other interests he told me about."

She appeared to relax a little. "Most people don't get that there's a lot more to Leonard than meets the eye."

I decided to change the subject. "I also chatted with Miss Wilson. She seems dedicated."

"Dear Elizabeth." She glanced at her messy desk. "Don't get me wrong, we've all learned a lot from Miss Wilson. Her knowledge of Navajo culture is one of this school's assets."

After already hitting a nerve with Leonard, I held my impulse to bicker about Wilson.

"Something wrong?" she asked after I didn't answer.

What the hell. "I'm sure she does know a lot, but it bothered me that she calls native religion 'mythology,' as if Christian miracles are based on reality."

"Oh my." Her eyes opened wide. "You said that to her?"

"Pretty close. I don't think she was very happy with me."

"You touched on her dilemma," Abby said, her tone suddenly academic. "It relates to the one problem I have with her. Elizabeth is so effusive about Navajo culture that it affects her judgment about learning deficits, except for obvious kids like Billy. And I'm not talking behind her back; she hears this directly from me."

"She mentioned your difference of opinion. So why are so many kids in Special Ed?"

"It's not just their English, believe me. I've been doing this for sixteen years, ten on the Navajo, and I've never heard of a cluster like this. At least half of the kids here are well below average in learning ability, and more than half of those are in Special Ed."

Her assertions grew more heated with each sentence. "I've tried every kind of reputable test—language, developmental, cognitive, learning styles, manipulative, motor skills. I even had a Navajo grad student from UNM try two tests in Navajo. We have the highest percentage in our agency for sure, maybe the whole reservation for all I know. Even worse, nobody wants to talk about it, especially the FIC."

"Why not?"

"Because the longer the kids are here, the worse it gets, which nobody admits except for Mona in first and second grade. It's the only time we agree on anything. She blurts it out to anyone, but for the wrong reasons."

I'd warmed up to her enthusiasm. "You just put it right out there, don't you?"

"Well, you went right to the heart of it."

"I meant that as a compliment."

"Oh." She shrugged. "I'm not accustomed to a lot of support for my, um, zeal." Her face softened. "Shot my mouth off too much already. It's better you make up your own mind about what goes on around here."

"Okay, just tell me if Hatcher is really gone as much as I've heard."

"Yes, thank God."

"You and Miss Wilson agree on that one."

"Yup, Hal's an FIC classic. Taught band a few years, then in charge of these little schools for twenty-five. If you stay, you'll get the general drift in the morning."

"You sure he'll show up?"

"Has to. Hal does the minimum." She grimaced. "He plays clarinet, especially with a shot or two under his belt. We tried to get him to teach some music to the kids—" She stopped herself again, shook her head, and got up. "Look, for what it's worth, I think you'd get along here okay if you can learn to handle the FIC games."

I stood up as well. "That's about what Leonard told me. Thanks, I think."

"Sure. I'd better get busy."

We headed back to the library as Beth was wheeling in the A-V cart and simultaneously reading a paperback. She closed the book and put it down. "Great, you two just keep blabbing while I do all the work. Mom, guess who's here already?"

"Not Hatcher."

"Still doesn't know my name. He said, 'Hey, Miss McAdam,' and then went into his apartment. I saw Leonard showing the second trailer to some funny-looking little old man."

"That'd be the other new teacher." She turned to her daughter as I removed the first box from the dolly. "Your teacher, Beth. Mr. Noland here is the counselor."

"That guy out there?"

"Yes, any family with him?"

"Not that I saw." She opened one of the boxes of books.

"Probably another FIC lifer. Any sign of Dot and Mona?"

Beth shook her head and left; Abby turned to me. "So our southern belles didn't even beat Hatcher here. Tomorrow should be pretty lively in this place."

"Why's that?"

"New teachers sometimes bring out old battles."

"Which you'll let me figure out for myself," I said, amused. "Hatcher still owes me an explanation. I think I'll go see him for a minute when I leave."

"Probably won't answer his door. He'll come out later to be sure the school's locked, then hole up with his Benny Goodman records."

"I see. So, are you an FIC 'lifer'?"

"No, neither a tourist or a lifer. The tourists give it a try and are gone in a year, or sooner. That's why there's always such a big group at orientation every year."

When Beth came back, she was more interested in her books than scowling at me. I opened two long cartons and groaned like an unhandy father on Christmas morning at the hieroglyphic instructions, piles of planks, plus bags of braces, bolts, nuts, and screws.

Beth was sorting books and said, "Don't bother. I can do those shelves blindfolded."

I believed her, especially since Abby had explained that Beth essentially ran the library, cataloguing it and setting up a check-out system. "Sounds good to me," I said, setting the instructions on a carton. I took the dolly out to retrieve the armchair and Ab-by's water, well aware that Beth also wanted me to move along because she sensed and resented that I had "noticed" her mother. Although I did find Abby both interesting and attractive, the child had no idea, of course, that I was increasingly comfortable with my loner status.

When I brought in the last load of water Abby was preoccu-pied with organizing her materials. She looked up and thanked me for my help, so I took the hint and left, telling her that I'd be around if she needed a hand. Following Abby's advice about Hatcher, I went out and headed to the trailer, feeling better about Raven Point but still not sure whether I would stay.

11

Aunt May knew Leonard's preferences, serving us beans and rice plus coffee and fry bread. Before I finished, Leonard went outside, so I watched May toss snacks to her dogs and feed Marie something more substantial. When Leonard came back in, he said it was snowing so hard that he could barely see the daylight.

"What time is it?"

"Just before seven. This is your last chance to use the facility." He loaded his pack with provisions May had set out: home-dried jerky, raisins, oranges, two bottles of water wrapped in socks, and fry bread that wouldn't stay hot for long. He also accepted two blankets and a small tarp to wrap into an extra bedroll he strapped under the frame pack, making the whole thing almost as tall as May.

Leonard told her something in Navajo, then relayed it to me. "I said if anyone came by to tell them I expect to arrive out at Samson's by eleven, depending on the weather."

He carried his pack out to the porch—he called it a mudroom—and then came back in. We thanked May, and I called goodbye to Billy, who just watched Marie hurry over to us. I retrieved my coat from the two comfortable cats nestled into it and followed Marie and Leonard out to the porch. He left a tin can just inside the cabin door, shut it, and turned on his flashlight.

"May is amazing," I said.

He was searching in his pack for something. "One of the best—here or anywhere."

"They have a good set-up compared to some places I've seen out here."

"A regular estate in the country." Leonard frowned at something inside the pack. "Excuse the sarcasm." He glanced at me. "At their age, self-reliance doesn't come easily, especially with Walter getting worse." He took out his windbreaker, checked the space it had occupied, then stuffed it back in.

"What's in that tin can you left inside?"

"Wax. I asked May to melt it for our skis."

"So they slide better?"

"That's the concept. Would you bring them in, and the poles?"

"Sure." He dug into his pack again while I put on my boots, parka, and gloves. I went out with Marie, but she hobbled away, her muzzle down in the snow as before. The breeze had stopped, but the snow was falling very hard and straight down, like sugar cascading from a scoop. Leonard had swept the stairs, so I stepped down easily into some deep accumulation. I brushed off the skis and poles with my gloves, banged their ends on the stairs, and hurried back into the mudroom with them.

"Still coming down hard," I said. Already in boots, Leonard handed me his flashlight, and I inspected the poles. "They're made of bamboo."

He took the two longer skis and put them on the floor. "Yeah, that's what they used back then. Those two longer poles go with these skis." He reached back and opened the cabin's door just a crack.

"Why does it matter?"

"Longer skis for the longer person." He retrieved the melted paraffin and then took a small stiff paintbrush from a pocket of his snowsuit. Marie scratched at the door, and I let her in. As I held the light for Leonard, he slathered the bottom of one ski, furrowing his brow.

"Is something wrong?" I asked.

"No. It's cold enough that this should be about right. Otherwise we're just breaking trail. We'll see." He quickly waxed the other three skis and left the can under the bench. I helped him lash all four skis, waxed sides out, to the back of his pack.

"Well," he said, "here goes something, I hope. Bring the poles, okay?"

I bundled up completely, then took two poles in each hand. Leonard cinched his army belt around his zipped-up snowsuit, lifted the pack by the frame, turned it sideways, and pushed the outer door open with the skis.

I went out behind Leonard and Marie. There was still no let-up to the storm, but at least we could see each other as he hefted the pack onto his back. When I handed him his poles, he pointed one of them toward the outhouse. "You want to go now, or in the snow later?"

"You convinced me."

"Okay, we need to start off on the level ground between here and the loo."

"The loo? Where did you pick that up?"

"British movie—little words with big meaning. Follow me."

"Jolly good." I stomped behind him with my poles into the storm for a short while until we stopped and he had me detach the skis from his pack. I handed him the shorter ones and speared mine into the snow.

"Have your torch?" he asked, enjoying the wordplay.

"Yeah, limey, and a match to light it."

He laughed as I started with my poles for the outhouse in his earlier tracks, almost filled with fresh powder. I had to remove the parka to take care of my business in there, grateful that I had a "torch." After securing my coat and hood again, I tramped through the snow back to him.

Leonard's gloves were on again, his scarf around his neck, and he'd already strapped on his skis. I pulled the front of the hood off of my face to talk. "Just like the Ritz," I said, glancing at the outhouse. "Why a two-seater?"

"Beats me." He pointed down at his skis. "All right, Sean, you can see that all I did was slip a boot into each brace and strap the leather bindings around the toes. I don't suppose you've ever used snowshoes."

"No."

"A lot of this will be more like snowshoeing than skiing, especially with this old equipment." His poles hanging by leather loops from his wrists, he leaned forward. "See, my heel is free— makes it almost like walking."

"I'll bet, and how many more hills are out there?" I took my skis and was about to put them down.

"Hang on a sec." He strode off several feet, then almost out of sight. I took a step toward him, holding the skis.

He turned and skied back. "The wax seems okay. All right, back to your question. I remember two places that qualify as hills. The first one is long but not steep. We probably won't even slide very fast."

I laid my skis down in the snow, one at each side. "And the other hill?"

"You'll have the hang of it by then. Let's get moving." He watched me strap on my skis. "That looks good."

I stood, realizing I had left the poles just out of reach. Leaning for them, my skis crossed and I fell into the powder. "Crap." Skis still attached, I uncrossed them, sat up and grabbed the end of one pole, using it to slowly prop myself upright. I brushed snow off of my clothes.

Leonard waited there, not able to keep a straight face. "Well, that's lessons one and two. You're off to a good start."

"Yeah, don't cross your skis. What's the other one?"

"The poles always stay with you."

"Right." Following his example, I put a gloved hand through the loop at the top of one pole and grabbed the grip, repeating the process on the other side.

"All right, you're ready. I'll break trail—just follow in my tracks as best you can. We'll take it really easy for a few minutes." He vanished into the whiteout with Marie.

That's my lesson? Skis straight, I stepped sideways and got into his tracks, then lifted the left ski ahead, and set it down straight. I did the same on the right, then repeated my baby steps. "Where are you, Leonard?" I shouted, my voice muted by the hood again.

"Not far," he called back. "Did you get started?"

"I guess that's what you could call it."

"What did you say?" Seconds later, he and the dog materialized from the curtain of snow. Marie eyed me and sat back on her haunches as if disgusted. "Sean, you're walking, not skiing. Picture someone on skates, and stride a little so the skis can slide."

"Fine." Starting with my left leg, I slid ahead without stepping, but as I felt the ski glide, the tip of the other ski caught behind me in the snow, and I fell down off to the side. "Shit." Right ski forward, I got up awkwardly using both poles, and then brushed myself off again.

"We're lucky that back ski didn't snap. You started out okay, but you need to get the other leg sliding before you finish the first stride."

As patient as he was, I felt really dumb, but followed his instructions and carefully made two strides. Amazingly, both skis glided a little until I came to a stop.

"Good, Sean. Now repeat the movements and push with the poles while you're sliding."

Obviously crossed my mind, but I just nodded. I got into his tracks again and started off slowly until I was actually gliding about as much as I was striding. Marie made a crooked leap and came down on all fours, then watched me as if to say, *Finally! Let's go!*

Leonard had stayed close. "Don't go passing me now." He pulled his scarf over his nose and mouth again, and then took off.

"Fat chance." He probably didn't hear me grumble. All I could see of him was the dim outline of his pack. Worried about the two hills ahead, I wasn't ready to consider skiing as fun, but at least now we had a chance to catch up with Hawthorne.

A
Century of
One-year reforms
On Navajo children
Make them equal…
In confusion
With everyone else.

12

After I left Abby, I decided to drop by the next trailer up the hill to meet the new five-six teacher. It was midafternoon when we both ducked our heads slightly so we could see each other from opposite sides of his doorway.

Beth's description of the man was fairly accurate. A few years my senior, maybe in his early fifties, Jimmy Beale was skinny and pale, but not all that little, about five-ten with a combed but unruly brown mane with hints of grey. Black and white hairs spiked from his nostrils, and a slight excess of flab on one jowl made the right side of his pocked face seem lopsided, as if it lacked muscle tone. He wore a faded green polo over stiff new blue jeans, cuffs rolled up to clear his white sneakers, which would have earned him "Where's the flood?" at my junior high. A half-smoked cigarette drooped from the lazy side of his mouth in that casual way that suggests a new one would soon replace it.

We greeted, stating our assignments, although it wasn't really news to either of us. Beale's green eyes and thick dark brows seemed almost inanimate when he asked me timidly to come in for a drink, apologizing moments later for only having the two cans of root beer he took out of the small fridge.

"This is fine," I said, sitting at one of his dinette chairs. I opened the can and took a sip of the perfume-sweet soda. "Do I detect a slight southern accent, Jimmy?"

"Maybe. I'm from northern Virginia, west of D.C." His dull mien unchanged, Jimmy walked to the sink and started scouring. "Almost done, be right with you."

He seemed to be settled in already, traveling light with no unpacked boxes or amenities in sight. Humming contentedly between occasional coughs, he glanced my way and impassively praised the weather as he rinsed the sink. He was so much at home in his kitchen that I resisted making a wisecrack about our identically austere and compact quarters.

Jimmy lit a new cigarette on his way over to sit with me. "Care for one?"

"Thanks, I don't smoke." I was relieved that all the doors and windows were open.

"The sink's still a little orange, but not like what Leonard showed me in the dorm."

"I assume he mentioned to run the drinking water, especially at school."

"Uh-huh." He seemed unconcerned, coughing into his fist. "He told me the job change was a big surprise for you. Welcome to the FIC." His use of that phrase sounded habitual, not sarcastic as the others had said it. "You did me a favor, ya know." He drank some soda.

"How's that?"

"I had fifth grade at a big school in Chinle Agency. This suits me better, except I have to add sixth-grade curriculum." He flicked the end of his cigarette on the rim of a small glass ashtray, already brimming with butts.

"How did you find out about the opening?"

"Elizabeth Wilson—she's a teacher here. She heard about it and told me."

"Yes, we've met."

"Oh. Elizabeth and I used to be in the same school; she knew I was trying to transfer." He stopped for a short fit of deep rattling coughs. "Excuse me. Anyway, she called when it opened up again. Thanks to her, I was Jimmy-on-the-spot."

I forced a smile. "I doubt there's a big line of teachers waiting to get into Raven Point."

"Yes, but I'll like it here. I didn't get along quite as well with the Navajos after Elizabeth left. She helped me understand things better." He coughed again. "She just knows so much; I'll be going with my class to her Navajo lessons." His understated tone suggested a sincere but platonic appreciation for Miss Wilson.

After I didn't respond, he spoke softly. "How do you like it here so far?"

He had unwittingly put me on the spot. "It's quite a place. I'm, um, going to give it a shot." If Jimmy detected my lack of enthusiasm, he didn't show it, or maybe he didn't care. As he blew some smoke away from the table, I kept the conversation going by telling him about some geographic contrasts between Southern and Northern Arizona.

He stated the obvious, that his hometown in Virginia was, "Way different from the Rez."

Our discussion petered out quickly, and we soon said our goodbyes. Judging that it wouldn't be hard to get along with Jimmy, I walked by his old Pontiac sedan and decided to cut across to the road and check out the store. It turned out to be like half a mini-mart in somebody's living room, mostly basic dry goods, candy, soda, packaged and canned food, nothing fresh or refrigerated.

"Hi," I said to the chubby teenage girl in a faded Disney T-shirt who came out from the back with a metal cash box. Not answering, she just waited with the money. I spent nearly all of my remaining cash on two gallons of bottled water, powdered milk, a quart of apple juice, and four cans of ginger ale.

For most of the rest of that Tuesday, I occupied myself with unpacking and trying to make things more livable in my new hearth and hovel—minus the hearth. I went over to visit Leonard that evening, but he was out, then when I came back to my trailer, I met him walking down the hill. "Evening," I said. "I just went over to see you."

"Been visiting; you were next. Jimmy told me he thought you were staying."

"Yeah. We'll see how it goes."

"I'm glad to hear it."

I felt trust and sincerity from his comment. "Thanks, Leonard."

We walked off for the dorm, and he began to go over how I fit into the schedule. Tuesday to Thursday, I'd be off in the mornings, teach in the afternoons, then take up dorm duties at dinnertime. I had full shifts on Fridays and Saturdays with Sundays and Mondays off. Before I left, Leonard gave me a thick pamphlet with FIC guidelines for counselors. I fell asleep that night before I'd covered half of the dry material.

ᕮ-ᕭ

I hoped the situation at school would begin to make more sense the next day—all of us together, including the principal and the two primary teachers. Leonard told me that our meeting was for GS-Five and above, so he would be there as well. Afterwards the teachers would have the option of using leave for the rest of the week. With Campbell on the blink, I wasn't going anywhere, and the three teachers I'd met needed all that time to prepare, plus the two extra days—Labor Day, then student check-in on the following Tuesday.

Breakfast was coffee and a stale doughnut on Wednesday morning. I stood at my small window, watching the compound and another cloudless cornflower-blue sky. I knew there'd be some cleaning ahead, so I'd put on patched jeans, tennis shoes, and an old summer shirt.

Two guys in their late teens were walking by outside in dark slacks, business shoes, white dress shirts, and black ties, each carrying a thin valise. One was tall and tow-headed, the other short with black hair and darker skin. They had similar boot-camp haircuts, a combed tuft between wide swaths of closely-shaved scalp.

Salesmen, out here? I picked up the counselors' guide and my spiral-bound notebook. Outside, Old Glory was atop the flagpole, limp on that calm day. I heard a door slam uphill and looked back to see Abby starting down, again in a flannel shirt and jeans. I waited by my stairs and saw that she carried a closed apple carton, holes in its sides.

"Morning," she said, finishing a yawn. "I heard you're staying."

"Morning. Yeah, I'll give it a shot."

"Let me know if I can be of any help." She sounded more alert and also seemed pleased.

"Thanks." I pointed to her box. "Something crawling around in there?"

"Toad and a salamander Beth found this summer. Elizabeth convinced me that amphibians are more useful critters than the reptiles and rodents I had."

"I heard that speech too."

"I met Mr. Beale; he seems low key. The kids'll like that after the last guy, but I'm afraid he'll have a whole new experience with Beth."

Probably so. The two formal young men were back in view, talking to a Navajo man in a pickup parked at the store. "What are those two guys selling?"

"Book of Mormon—one of several thumpers who visit us."

I liked her habit of dropping the first word from old slang like *Bible-thumper* or *tin lizzie.* "So what are the others?"

"Old Mission is all-flavors Protestant, with a clinic and small hospital." She nodded to the Mormons. "Those two jelly-pants LDS boys are second year, when they tend to get pushy."

"Jelly pants?"

"That's what our kids call slacks," she said, smiling. "Because they wiggle like jelly."

I didn't quite get it but laughed anyway. "Does Hatcher let the missionaries in?"

"He follows policy. They're allowed for school activities, and they rent space for fellowship, as they call it, but Hosteen keeps a close eye on them. His brother Samson is also on the Council and always backs the missionaries. Samson is LDS but drives his pickup to whoever has the best handout, although the old pirate is legally blind."

I wasn't sure how to react to Abby's scorn for Hosteen's brother, whom I hadn't met. I glanced at the missionaries as we crossed the road. "Is one of them Navajo, or maybe from another tribe?"

"Navajo, adopted—grew up in Salt Lake. Knows less of the lingo than blondie does."

We walked past three vehicles parked in front of the school, the dusty brown Cadillac I'd seen before, and two four-wheel drive government pickups, the same dull grey as Leonard's panel truck. "What does Hatcher drive?"

"One of the trucks—leaves his car at the office in Old Mission."

We walked into the hallway where a short elderly Navajo man in khakis and a blue mesh baseball cap deftly manipulated a droning floor buffer that probably weighed more than he did. He was polishing to the middle of the floor; the other half looked clean but not waxed. Down the hall by the storage room, a thin young man was preparing to mop the linoleum in a cowboy outfit—spangled shirt, Tom Mix hat, tall patterned boots, and blue jeans. The old man beamed at Abby, showing black gaps in his crooked yellow teeth.

"Hi, Jon," she called over the noise, and then started off on the non-waxed side of the floor toward her room. "That's Mr. Noland, the new counselor and P.E. teacher."

Jon Begay turned off the machine. I was about to offer my hand, but he kept hold of the bar. "Hi, Jon. I hear you're the one who keeps this place going."

"Mis-ter No-lan," he said, pointing his lips in the direction of the gym. "Good," he added, his final D like a T. He nodded to his busy helper down the hall. "Muh' gran'son Eddie. Janitor." Close in age to the Mormon missionaries outside, Eddie was about five-nine, sleek black hair over his nape. When I raised my hand in greeting, he looked at me long enough to stiffen his shoulders—proudly or defiantly, I couldn't tell. Jon flicked the switch and guided his machine again while I skimmed my manual and waited for Abby by the office.

She walked back from her room and said, "You didn't need to wait, Sean."

"If I have questions, I think I'll probably want to be near you or Leonard."

We passed another of the stained drinking fountains and walked into the staff room past the faculty toilets. A man and two women, the three largest people I had seen in Raven Point, except for the one dorm aide, chatted at the far end of a long table that filled half the small windowless room. Beale and Wilson were at the near end, Jimmy listening to her speak quietly. On a card table in the corner behind them were a coffee pot, hot-cups, condiments, several cans of cola, napkins, and two plates of store-bought cookies. The off-white walls were sparse, just a small blank chalkboard, a black clock, and a framed yellowing likeness of Abe Lincoln.

Several minutes early, Abby and I got coffee and sat down, leaving a chair between Jimmy and us. He and Elizabeth smiled our way, drank their coffee, and then she continued talking in a whisper. Abby and I merited only dour passing glances from the two obese primary teachers, who had sodas and a stack of sandwich cookies between them. Standing with one hand propped on the table, Hatcher nodded and raised a chubby forefinger to us so we'd know he'd be over soon. The large man went on listening to the muted story from the nearby primary teacher.

Abby started working on some Special Ed forms, so I pretended to read my dorm manual, furtively watching Hatcher. Either his portly face hid his age well, or else he'd be retiring before age sixty-five. Coffee in hand, he was about six-two, carrying most of his three hundred-plus pounds from the waist up. In tan slacks cinched by maybe a size-fifty belt, he wore a light-blue, short-sleeve dress shirt and a bolo tie with a red stone. He had a large oval head, thin but curly auburn hair, and a few freckles around an unwavering toothy half-smile. If his eyes weren't so droopy, he could've been a double for Jingles, Wild Bill Hickok's sidekick in the old TV series.

Not knowing Dot from Mona, I guessed that both were around five-seven and somewhere in their forties. The one talking to Hatcher weighed maybe 250 pounds; the other teacher was even heavier and held a walking cane. Both women had similar dishwater-blonde pageboys and wore pastel flowered smocks. Tweedle Dum and Tweedle Dee came to mind, but that didn't work because of their very different faces. The larger woman had squinty small eyes and pasty rolls of skin that hid her features and expressions.

Her roommate, still holding court for Hatcher, did not have much extra weight above the neck; she had tan skin and lined thin brows, her hair likely dyed over a darker color. She used light makeup that accentuated an even mouth and dark-brown eyes. She finally finished telling her joke, and Hatcher obliged with a brief chuckle.

"Okay, get this one," he said, and lowered his bulk into a chair to begin a story of his own. An occasional word or phrase slipped out, especially *okay* at the beginning of every other sentence, as the teacher listened attentively, occasionally making a short drawled comment like "Aw, c'mon now," a forced smile replacing her scowl. The other teacher leafed through a magazine and ate cookies. When Hatcher finished his apparently risqué joke, he blushed and his admirer hooted with laughter as the principal gave a brief, self-satisfied smile.

Leonard walked into the room right on time and again in slick style—an ironed, yellow summer shirt, creased jeans, and polished boots. He poured himself some coffee and sat across from Abby and me with his cup and a cookie. Smiling as usual, he reached out to lightly touch hands with both of us.

When Hatcher got up to haul his mass in our direction, his face was torpid but with that same false but steady smile. The primary teachers sneered toward Jimmy and me, and I got their unspoken message loud and clear: *So, new factions, the one who counts is on our side.*

The principal shuffled up to Jimmy and me with a limp handshake. "Hal Hatcher," he said, and then correctly guessed our names. He nodded to Abby and Miss Wilson before turning to Leonard. "Thanks for showing our new folks around, Mr. Santos." His accent was similar to Abby's, with a bit more cowboy drawl. Hatcher turned to Jimmy and me. "Okay, after we finish this morning you two let me know if you have any questions. Oh, and Mr. Noland, I'll need to show you around the office before noon today."

I nodded; he lumbered away to sit beside the two heavy teachers. He extracted a pile of papers from his briefcase and lay them on the table. Still sitting, he faced us. "Okay," he said yet again, clearly a habit. "Besides my retirement, the big change is our two new teachers here…." He repeated what everyone already knew about our assignments. "I'm sure you two have met everyone by now, so tell us a little something about yourselves."

Although I had not met everyone, I briefly complied, and then Jimmy did the same. His light Virginia accent had the two primary teachers whispering to each other.

"Okay, that's fine," Hatcher said, "and welcome to our little staff. Maybe you're bridge players?" He glanced at the nearest of the two women, the thin-faced one. "Miss Mona and I need two more to make a game."

At that, Mona's frown changed to a weak smile. The larger one, Dot, ignored Hatcher—so I finally had their names figured out.

Jimmy turned to me. "I've played some bridge."

"Sorry, not me." I intended to sound unenthused but not abrupt.

"Well," Hatcher said to no one in particular, "an old dog can learn to take a few tricks." His quip didn't bother me, and only Mona reacted, looking my way with a scowl.

And an old bi—I let that thought go when I saw Dot pouting, apparently not pleased with the camaraderie between Mona and the principal.

Hatcher finally started on the business at hand, yapping in a dreary monotone for twenty minutes about standards and regulations, which gave me some time to jot a stitch or two about my contrasting earlier impressions of Eddie Begay and the Navajo missionary.

"Okay," Hatcher was saying as he handed out forms, "we have a lot of paperwork to fill out by noon, more than usual because they postponed the agency meeting."

Once we started working on them, I thought that the meeting was going to be short and uneventful, but Hatcher resumed speaking. "Okay, before you folks get too involved with those, we have something to discuss about our schedule."

Elizabeth spoke up right away, putting down her pen. "We already approved it."

"Yes, Miss Wilson, I looked it over again and found a problem. I'm concerned that Miss Dot's and Miss Mona's students have lost reading time over the last few years. They're just not as prepared as they should be to read in the higher grades."

Elizabeth glared at Mona, then faced Hatcher. "*I'm* the one who gets them in third grade, and there has been no significant difference in their readiness."

"Now, darlin'," Mona drawled with a condescending grin, "you know your reading scores went down again. The K-two kids need more time for letters and sounds. Forty minutes three times a week is just too much for Navajo class. A half hour on Monday and Friday's more'n enough."

Wilson's lips tightened, her narrow gaze darting at Hatcher. "That's half of their time. You can't just do that. Those funds have minimal instructional requirements."

"Okay, Miss Wilson, now please take it easy." Hatcher spoke with lengthened vowels and cloying composure. "I found out this summer that the policy says Navajo class is voluntary, like a high school elective. Parents can sign a letter for their children not to take the class."

"Why would any of them do that?" Elizabeth asked, even more livid.

Mona smirked, brows raised. "I have two letters here, one from a Council member, requesting less time in Navajo class for his second-grade boy, and the other's from the parent of a first-grader." She extracted papers from an envelope.

Elizabeth cut her off. "Don't bother to read them. What did you promise Samson to get him and his neighbor to sign those?"

"Excuse me?" Mona severely arched her brows. "And what are you implying by that?"

"I am not *implying* anything. You probably—"

"Okay, ladies," Hatcher looked at Wilson as he got himself up. "Please, let's not be unpleasant and get everyone all upset."

"How can you let her pull this?" Elizabeth turned away, fuming.

Abby cleared her throat. "Hal, Mona only has two letters, but she wants all of K-two cut back."

"Yes, I tend to be in favor of that for the reasons we mentioned, and the schedule would only need a minor adjustment."

Abby glanced at me, saying to Hatcher, "It would also affect P.E."

Mona jumped in before Hatcher could answer. "No need to change recess if Navajo class is on Monday and Friday."

I faced her. "Excuse me, but I believe I'm teaching Physical Education, not recess."

Hatcher, still standing, seemed surprised by my comment before he looked down at me. "And what about basketball, Mr. Noland?"

"After school, like everywhere else."

Mona turned to Elizabeth. "See now? The only schedule change would be yours—giving you more time to improve your reading scores."

Elizabeth glared back. "I certainly do not need any teaching advice from you."

Mona scoffed. "Sticks an' stones, honey."

"Okay, ladies," Hatcher said, still not very perturbed. He sat again.

Elizabeth faced him. "If you do this, they will take back our Indian Ed funds."

"I don't believe so, Miss Wilson. For the other hour of Indian Ed for K-two, I can get you comp time to organize an after-school program, maybe with one of our weavers."

Elizabeth threw up her hands. "Wonderful. Show me one boy who wants to do that."

"Okay, Miss Wilson, I'm sure you could suggest a suitable class." Hatcher's pretense of neutrality concluded with a quiet decree that he wanted to hear final comments on the subject.

"My position's clear." Mona's expression was triumphant.

"The whole point," Elizabeth said, "is to make Navajo Studies part of the academic…." She went on, finishing with an impassioned plea for supporting the language and culture the children bring with them to school.

"As an enrolled one-quarter Cherokee," Mona said to Elizabeth, "I resent the implication that I don't support their culture." Her angry jowls shook. "You can't tell me—"

"You've both made your point," Hatcher stated. "We need to go on."

Mona clenched her teeth and Elizabeth turned away, sputtering through her thin lips. Abby cleared her throat, facing the principal. "I have something else to say."

"Of course, Mrs. McAdam."

"I support Miss Wilson's position." She zeroed in on Hatcher. "And I'll remind you that most parents aren't behind this. It's a staff-proposed schedule change, and we have an established process for that."

Hatcher made a frustrated *tsk*, as close as he had come to showing an emotion. "Okay, Mrs. McAdam is right, we do need to vote. Any other opinions before we do that?" Jimmy's face was blank; Leonard remained silent, although he had been nodding in favor of Elizabeth.

"Okay," Hatcher said, "we also agreed that I have an extra vote if we have a tie. The question is, do we change the Navajo Studies schedule for kinder through second to a half hour on Monday and Friday? I vote yes." He turned to Mona.

"Yes." She smugly eyed Jimmy and me, as if daring us to differ with our new supervisor.

Hatcher looked past Mona. "Miss Dot?"

"Yes," she uttered quietly, the only time she spoke during the meeting.

"Leonard," the principal said.

Mona broke in. "Not being a teacher, he shouldn't be voting on this—and he's biased."

"Aren't we all," Abby replied, but Mona coolly ignored her.

"He does have a vote," Hatcher ruled. "Okay, Leonard."

"No," he answered, and Mona just shrugged.

After Abby and Elizabeth both voted no, tying the tally at three for each side, Mona still seemed unfazed.

Hatcher didn't even look up. "Mr. Noland?"

I saw Mona's eyes dagger in my direction. "I vote no."

Mona's hostile face changed to a grin for Jimmy before Hatcher said, "And Mr. Beale?"

"No," he said, as softly as Dot did in the affirmative.

Mona's jaw dropped before she gathered herself. "Fine. Then we'll just have to get a majority of the K-two parents to sign off." She pointed at me. "You, Leonard, and what's-her-name over there can give out our letters at check-in and show 'em where to sign."

"I believe you're referring to Felicita Etcitty," I said, "and I don't think it would be right for us to promote your agenda."

Her nostrils flared. "And how would you be promoting my *agenda*?"

"That's exactly what it would be," Leonard interjected. "They can't just sign; we'd have to interpret the letter for some and explain it to others, including the ramifications."

"Oh, I know what you'd do." Mona turned to Dot. "Ramifications," she said with a snarl, just loud enough for all to hear.

Unruffled, Hatcher got to his feet slowly, getting everyone's attention. "Okay, folks, I need everyone to calm down," he said, his face placid. "I have a compromise. I agree the letter is not the dorm's responsibility, but I see no reason why the K-two parents can't be informed at check-in that Miss Mona and Miss Dot need to speak with them before they leave. Now, any more questions?" He looked around. "Your papers by noon, please." His listless smile still in place, he gathered his things and left, apparently content that the issue was resolved.

Sullen, Mona got up behind Dot, who was wrapping the remaining cookies. Mona picked up their papers, and then with her other hand helped Dot to her feet, guiding her toward the door. I realized Dot was practically disabled, using the cane and Mona for support in order to walk.

Jimmy and Abby were listening to a rant from Elizabeth, so they didn't hear what Mona said to Leonard as she passed behind him. "Gonna get you, boy," she muttered.

After they left, Elizabeth said, "Well, that's that. Thanks for your votes." She began to clean up what had been her "turn" for refreshments.

Abby and Jimmy helped her, so I leaned over to Leonard. "Why is Mona so pissed? They still get to talk to the parents."

"That's just it. Mona won't talk to them unless they speak English, and she won't use an interpreter. It's mutual; most parents avoid her, except for Samson and a couple of his cronies."

We pushed back our chairs and got up. "Why him?"

"Just another way that Samson tries to antagonize Hosteen."

"They have a Cain-and-Abel thing going on?"

He lowered his voice. "I may as well fill you in before you hear about it somewhere else. They were raised by the same parents; Hosteen's a few years older, adopted back when there weren't many records. Outside the family, that's about all anybody knows, and most people around here don't bring it up, except for Samson when he's drinking."

"I see. None of my business, but at least I'll know not to mention it."

"You'll understand it all better in a few days."

"Not sure I want to. So how does Mona think she'll get back at you?"

"I don't know, but she'll try something."

13

However long we'd been skiing, it felt like an hour to me by the time Leonard finally stopped and waited with Marie. The snowfall was still intense, but we had enough daylight to give us about ten feet of visibility. The road was nothing more than a wide white lane marked here and there by bushes and short piñons.

I strode up to Leonard in his tracks and pulled the hood's flap off my mouth. "Man, I'm sweating under here."

Marie disappeared into the storm and Leonard took off his pack and pulled down his scarf. "You're still working too hard. Thirsty?"

"No."

He unzipped the top of his snowsuit to remove his fleece layer before zipping up again and stuffing the pullover in his pack. He handed me a bottle covered with a sock. "Take a drink anyway, and it might help to warm the water in your mouth before you swallow. Then you've got to get regulated. You don't want sweats and chills out here."

"I had the chills hiking once. The parka isn't right for what we're doing, is it?"

"No, it isn't."

I swished and drank a couple gulps of water, handing back the bottle.

"Okay, now take off your hat, then open the parka and flap it for a few seconds to let out some body heat, and then put it all on again. Don't zip the coat, just button it."

He watched me while I followed his instructions, finishing with my cap.

"You're shaking a little, Sean."

"Just a shudder. It stopped—the parka feels good again."

"You could be on the edge of hypothermia." Marie was back, waiting under a solitary pine by the road. "All right, the skis are working okay, and we're not far from the first hill. Once we get there and are ready to go down I'll have a couple of pointers for you. While it's level and we're still working hard, you should undo the coat again but leave it on. After the hill, we'll have to adjust your clothes. All right, start off in a slow walk-slide again, just a slight push with the poles. Try to find a middle ground between hot and cold."

"Okay." I undid the front buttons. "Your outdoor knowledge is pretty impres—"

"Yeah, if I'd used my head, we would've driven around."

We started off at a slow pace. "You couldn't have known the hill was that icy. Where'd you get your experience, Leonard?"

"In the Guard. Mostly we cleaned fire lines and breaks. Got me started hiking and backpacking, mostly on the Rez and around Grand Canyon."

"Maybe you could show me a couple of good hiking spots this summer, if you don't mind having an old fart along."

"Sure, we'll do it."

My face started to get cold, so I stood still for a moment, buttoned the hood and started off behind him again. "The Guard didn't help you with college?"

"Not for weekend warriors, unless you activate."

After we'd skied on a few more minutes in the steady snowfall, I felt another chill. "I need to go a little faster, Leonard, or button the damn coat."

"Right, it has to be your pace."

"Should I go ahead of you?"

"No, you'd be breaking trail and sweating for sure. Tell me when it feels okay."

He moved a bit faster, and I skied to within a few feet of him and settled into a rhythm. "I think this is pretty good for now." After ten minutes or so of moderate exercise, my temperature balance seemed better.

Not far ahead of us, the dog hobbled out of sight. "Marie," Leonard called not very loud, and she came back to us as we stopped. "All right, Sean, this is the first hill." I looked ahead into the snowfall but couldn't make out a slope. I jammed my gloved but freezing hands into my pockets.

"How do you feel?" he asked.

"I can barely feel my hands, but I'm okay—starting to get cold now that we stopped."

"Go ahead and button your coat and hood now. Like I said, it's a long and gradual downslope. You should be skiing with minimal effort over the next several hundred yards."

"This must be the fun part." I exposed my hands, buttoned the parka and hood, and quickly put my gloves on again.

"Okay, I'll push off pretty hard," he said, "but you just start in my tracks with a regular push. If you do get moving pretty good, keep the skis straight and bend your knees a little for stability. Falling isn't the problem—it's the work it takes to get up again."

"Got it." Watching him start off with a hands-high thrust to glide away, I took a deep breath and got into his tracks again. Responding to my easy push, the skis seemed to slide ahead with a mind of their own, though not much faster than before. Then the speed picked up but didn't feel all that precarious. In fact, the slight pull of gravity gave me a thrill until I hit a mogul and barely kept my balance. *Geez, take it easy*. I bent my knees and skied on.

Leonard had slowed down and turned to me. "Good, keep it up!" he called, and took off again. Still in the crouch, I mimicked how he gripped his poles, pointing them straight back.

In a few minutes, I skied to a stop where he waited on level ground, skis turned sideways, his scarf down, and snow dusting his hair—it was good to see his smile. "See, you're an old pro, Sean."

Pleased just to be on my feet, I freed my face to exhale, then stuffed my hands into the parka's pockets. "Yeah, no sweat," I said, then laughed at my unintentional pun.

"Good, that's the whole idea."

"I saw you make that fancy turn when you stopped. How do you do that?"

"Now's not the time. You'd probably fall a couple times just getting the idea. If you're still interested later, I'll teach you."

"Okay. Where's Marie?"

"Not far. She found a scent—could be anything. We need to adjust your layers now so you can stay regulated. How're you feeling?"

"Fine, I guess—just my hands." I watched him put his pack down, then noticed that our drop in elevation had taken us out of the piñons.

He pulled a black windbreaker from his pack. "It'll be hard going again in this valley.

The snow will probably be more irregular with drifts and hummocks. I'll pack your coat; you can use this."

"You won't need it?"

"I have a couple more layers in here."

I swapped my parka for the windbreaker, then he reached into the pack to take out a long red wool scarf like his grey one. "That jacket's lined but there's not much to the hood, so take this. Tie it over your ears, nose, and mouth like I do. Loosen it if you get too warm."

I put his jacket on over my sweater and shed my gloves long enough to tie on the scarf, my hands already numb before I pulled the gloves on again.

He handed over a pair of socks. "Slip these over your gloves." While I did that, Leonard tied my parka to his pack. "Not snowing quite as hard," he said. "It's about four miles to that next hill. Maybe half of the going is flat before we start to climb again. At the bottom of that hill, there's an old hogan where we can get out of this for a while." Just then, Marie showed up with something orange in her mouth.

"Good girl!" He took the peel to inspect it. "Fresh—show me, girl!" He held it out to her; she snatched the orange peel with her teeth and took off away from the road.

Leonard turned and followed the dog's tracks. "Keep going, Sean. Take it slow but steady."

"Okay." The snowfall didn't seem less intense to me, and Leonard was nearly out of sight.

"I'll catch up to you in a few minutes," he called back, his voice already faint.

Though uneasy with my sudden isolation, I bundled up and slid forward a few feet, and then had to begin forcing my skis through some drifts and mounds. Breaking trail was going to be as difficult as he had warned, so I made myself go slower so as not to work up a sweat. I soon felt cold and had to pick up the pace again.

After repeating my hot-cold balance regimen at least a dozen times, I stopped to listen. The only sound was the snow ticking on my flimsy hood. I saw the skeletal silhouettes of some nearby bushes, but the cold air began to filter through to my T-shirt; I had to get moving. After skiing on, I tried to find that rhythm again.

During the next minutes, the snowfall did lessen until there were only ice sparkles in the air. I stopped, looked up and spotted a raven soaring below the grey clouds. My mind transported to the bird's point of view, peering down at a skier, a dark midge moving erratically over a white matte. I shuddered, breaking my reverie, and quickened my pace. Soon, in a similar shift of consciousness, I imagined the perspective of a sinewy coyote-dog, stalking me in the bush. The salivating canine spotted me, alone and more vulnerable with each stop and start. *For God's sake, Sean, knock it off.*

Telling myself there was no reason not to expect Leonard to catch up with me soon, I looked up. The grey overcast had descended again and it was snowing more steadily. I plodded ahead, stumbling once but not falling. There was still no sign of anyone, so I went on, beginning to conjure up calamities like a blizzard, or Leonard with a broken leg, either of which could fulfill the Navajo taboo about a coyote crossing your path.

"Bullshit," I said, then remembered the real half-coyote's eerie appearance out of the night. I shuddered again. "Crap, now you're just scaring yourself." I stopped and tried to scan all around, but with some ground fog and the increasing snowfall I couldn't see beyond ten feet. I pulled the scarf down, watched my breath turn to steam, and then listened. For the first time, that ambiguous phrase, "deafening silence," made sense to me.

Call out for him. I didn't do it, not wanting to sound as anxious as I felt. *Idiot. He doesn't play macho games.* "Hey!" I shouted, but I wasn't sure my voice carried, as if yelling into a closet. I listened again to the absence of sound until a chill got me moving.

After I pulled the scarf up, my breath made a snorting sound in the material—at least there was no more abject silence. The skiing turned even more laborious on a rising grade, making me breathe much harder.

A few minutes later, I heard a loud crack, maybe a stick breaking somewhere behind me. I stopped, turned that way, and pulled down the scarf to hear a dull galloping in the snow; the specter of the coyote-dog came to me again. I took a defensive posture, pointing my poles toward the approaching noise, trembling, until the beast suddenly appeared from the fog.

"Don't skewer my dog!" Leonard called as Marie frolicked crookedly past me.

I let the pole tips fall. "Man, I'm glad to see you."

"We got disoriented until Marie found the road." He slid to a stop a few feet away. "I was about to yell before I heard you. Did you hear me call back?"

"No. Any s-sign of Hawthorne?" I tried to be casual, as if accustomed to easily switching from panic to the business at hand.

"Marie found where he stopped. There wasn't much snow covering the orange peels and his tracks. I'd say it was less than an hour since he came by."

"That's g-good."

He moved closer. "You're white as a sheet, Sean."

"G-getting cold again."

"Then we'd better get moving." He skied ahead to where Marie waited, and then turned back as I started off. "You made good progress, especially breaking trail."

I caught up to him. "J-just call me D-daniel B-boone."

"Daniel Baboon—good one."

Mr. Optimism is pretending. "Yeah."

He started skiing again. "Okay, back to your pace—let me know."

I was staying with him, but my teeth still chattered. "Almost s-seems easy, following tracks again."

"Good. It will be hard going up to the summit but easier not to fall."

"How s-steep after the summit?"

"Steeper than that last hill but not a drop-off like before. At least it won't be icy."

My body shuddered again. "Hot d-dog."

A

Retired

Rawboned Sheepdog

On three legs

Will follow

A wagon or pickup

Five miles

To the trading post

And back.

14

Hatcher was ready to leave the school after he lackadaisically explained the basic paperwork. Holding personnel forms to deliver to the agency, he handed over the extra set of school keys, saying he didn't expect to return until Tuesday night. Leonard told me later that if anything came up, he knew how to locate Hatcher in Albuquerque and also Old Mission, where he would likely be hanging out with his buddies the day before school started.

After the principal was gone, Dot rolled by the office in a wheelchair that I hadn't seen before. Without stopping, she glanced at me and called back a single blunt phrase, her drawl not as obvious as Mona's. "We're on leave—be back Monday night."

She was gone, so I examined my new keys and approached the tall cabinets. I ignored the first one, which I knew was brimming with the myriad forms, regulations, and manuals required for even the smallest of government facilities. I inserted a key into the second cabinet, the lock opened, giving me access to the two top drawers that contained cumulative files, testing, and the Student Council cashbox. The bottom two drawers were secured with a padlock, jury-rigged with a chain that passed through both handles as well as holes drilled into the cabinet's frame. When I asked Hatcher about the bottom drawers, he just said,

"The bank account, personnel, and old records. We'll go over those later."

Hoping to find the water report for Leonard, I tried the other keys with the padlock, but none of them worked. "Shit," I said, then looked through Hatcher's desk for hidden keys. Failing that, I opened the top drawer to see if the cumulative files might tell me something else about the kids. I found the usual musty registration forms and cardstock archives, the latter covered with tiny old student photos, forgotten grades, and vapid teacher comments. In the fifth and sixth-grade section, six of the thirteen students had an extra file stuffed with testing, arcane forms, and obscure data for Special Ed.

After locking the cabinets, I thought about my immediate responsibilities, most of which had little to do with the school office. I needed some sort of itinerant workspace in all three locations, so I put my page of "administrative" notes in an empty drawer of Hatcher's desk. Figuring I'd need some materials and supplies for the gym, I went down the hall and through the door marked STORAGE. I saw it was once a classroom, now divided into two smaller rooms.

I walked past surplus student desks of all sizes, discarded equipment, shelves of old books and scanty classroom supplies before I came to the interior door. One of my keys worked; I went in and found the shades down, presumably to hide the room from prying eyes. Stacked almost to the ceiling in places was a trove of boxes and cartons of all sizes. Black stenciling indicated contents: BATH FIXTURE, OFF. SUPPLIES, RDG. WORKBOOKS, JUMP ROPES, KINDER FURNITURE, and yes, KITCHEN SINK—and so on—perhaps enough stuff to get a couple of classrooms and at least one apartment off to a good start.

"Our taxes at work," I said, spotting some piles that seemed to belong to the kitchen. I peeked inside some open boxes to find them partially full of canned government juice, fruit, peanuts, and evaporated milk. A few feet away, store-bought cases of candy and soda sat unopened save one, half-full of chocolate bars. *Somebody's stash?*

Returning to the main stacks, I moved aside three heavy boxes containing new electric typewriters to find four large cartons marked TWO DRW FILE CAB. I found a dolly in the outer room, and then trundled one file cabinet and a typewriter all the way over to the gym, where I unpacked them onto a long table on the larger stage.

I stopped by the dorm on my way back, left the dolly on the porch, and found Leonard in the rec room unfolding one of the long collapsible utility tables. He was dressed more informally than I'd ever seen him—old jeans, sneakers, and a T-shirt stained orange by the iron. "Hey," I said, and then helped him unfold the last two grey Formica tables.

We stood by one of the dusty attached benches; I noticed some rags and a spray bottle of liquid cleaner on the floor. "'Duties as assigned' again?"

He nodded. "Janet—she's the cook—doesn't start until Tuesday, so I'm just setting up the tables for registration; give 'em a good cleaning first."

"I'll help. I like your nice shirt."

He looked down at himself. "Yeah, good for doing this anyway."

"Right. Sorry, but no news on the water—he left me keys for everything but the padlock." I told him what Hatcher said about the two drawers.

"Damn," Leonard said, quiet but intense, the first time I'd heard him swear. "I don't think we'll see what's in there until he's gone for good. Thanks for trying."

"Sure. I didn't know you were this upset about it."

"Sean, I haven't been completely straightforward with you."

"So? I'm sure you had a good reason."

"Let's talk for a minute." We sat on one the benches. "I took some water samples into Albuquerque this summer."

"You did? So you have your own information now?"

T. LLOYD WINETSKY

"Such as it is. I took samples from three fountains—one in the gym, the dorm, and the school hallway. Unfortunately, my suspicion was right. All three had high levels of lead."

"What? Lead? Jesus, no wonder you've tried to stop everybody from drinking the water. How serious do you think this is?"

"Don't know for sure. What I was looking for was a clear indication, so I didn't flush the pipes before I took samples. To prove anything, I'd need pre- and post-flushing levels from the entire facility, like the FIC supposedly did. Even if I had my own pre- and post-levels, they'd treat me like a disgruntled Indian crank with unofficial data that I could've doctored."

"My God." I thought about his discovery for a moment. "Doesn't lead poisoning usually happen when little kids ingest old paint?"

"Yes, it has a sweet taste, believe it or not. In the bad old days, they used lead in toys and even food containers. Britain banned lead paint decades ago, but we still haven't done it. There isn't a lot of cause-and-effect data yet on human lead consumption from water, but the current science says it can cause mental disability and some physical symptoms."

"Damn, Abby's Special Ed cluster. She said the longer kids are here the worse it gets."

"Yeah, she's convinced of the correlation. You and Abby are the only ones who know what I found out."

"There must be something we can do."

"In my wilder moments, I've considered taking a bolt cutter to those drawers—a felony, of course, even if I found negligence by the FIC. I guess we'll have to wing it until Hatcher's gone—keep preventing access to the drinking water as much as we can."

"What if I brought up the problem with the agency?"

"A new employee? They'd ignore it and peg you for a trouble-maker."

"Wouldn't be the first time." We cleaned the tables, brainstorming a while about the water situation, then Leonard explained some other FIC folly he'd encountered.

~130~

When all the tables were clean and in place, he told me how the rec room would be set up for registration the following Tuesday. We arranged a time for the next morning to go over the dorm procedures. Before student check-in, I also had to tap my creativity and figure out what to do for my two large P.E. classes, plus basketball. Lesson plans would have to wait until I triaged the battered P.E. equipment, mostly stuffed into cupboards or left in random piles and boxes in the gym. I was going to need every daylight hour, if not more, to get ready for the start of school in Raven Point.

)-)

Jimmy, Elizabeth, and Abby were equally busy in their classrooms, so I didn't see much of them until Saturday night, when all of us crammed into Abby's trailer for a potluck. Having socialized very little with teachers over the years, I balked when Abby invited me, but she smiled and said, "Oh, come on, Sean, don't be a pooper." That chopped-off expression made me laugh again; perhaps I was more taken with Abby than I'd thought.

Jimmy and I were the last to arrive, having combined resources to contribute "spaghetti a la Canadian hot dog" along with garlic-powdered Wonder Bread. Abby, Jimmy, and I had not changed out of work clothes, but Leonard, in a crisp summer shirt and ironed jeans, was stirring some pinto beans. Abby prepared Spanish rice and also served as bartender near an impressive lineup of beer, wine, and hard liquor technically prohibited by the Navajo Tribe. Beth chopped vegetables in a blouse and skirt that made her look like a teen. Elizabeth, who brought a foil-wrapped stack of Navajo fry bread, wore her turquoise necklace and a crimson velveteen top.

I was impressed by how comfortably Abby and Beth had appointed their quarters, in stark contrast to my already messy trailer. They had moved their dinette table to the living room and partitioned off the kitchen with a small knotty-pine sofa covered by a bright Pendleton blanket. The western motif continued with a matching wooden armchair, framed prints of wild horses, quaking aspen, a wolf, and some Monument Valley promontories called Three Sisters, named for a nun and two pupils, according to Abby. She said the formation was a favorite backdrop for film director John Ford, whose movie cavalrymen fought off hordes of painted Apaches played by local Navajos.

Elizabeth, greatly amused, informed us in a professorial tone that Apaches and Navajos, ancestrally and linguistically related, had a long history as enemies. She, Jimmy, and I sat around the table and sampled chips, nuts, and carrot sticks, chatting mostly about what had to be accomplished before the first day of school. Beth took orders for a second round of drinks; I asked for another whiskey chaser with a bottle of the ale her mother brought from Colorado.

"Hey, one rule," Abby declared from the stove. "Only five more minutes of shop talk. Frankfurter spaghetti and Navajo tacos comin' right up!"

"A toast to that all-American menu!" Elizabeth's high spirits surprised me as she held up her highball. Not far from her on the sofa, I clinked her glass with my empty bottle. Meanwhile in the armchair, Jimmy, reeking of a cigarette he'd smoked on the way, lifted his beer an inch or two. Beth brought my drinks, then shrugged when I thanked her before she headed for the kitchen.

As Leonard sat with us in a dinette chair, I took a gulp of ale, tossed down the chaser, and then remarked, "You two probably won't be surprised that Hatcher told me Mona backed off on her K-two letters."

Elizabeth raised her drink again. "Yes, and cheers to all of you for supporting Navajo Studies!"

Leonard lifted his glass of red wine. "And a toast to absent colleagues."

"And thank God they're absent." Elizabeth took a drink.

"Now, none of that," Abby said with mock seriousness as she brought over a can of diet cola and sat on the other dinette chair.

"I would've invited them all, and Hal probably would've come. Besides, your toast was sincere." She winked at Leonard. "Right?"

Leonard answered in an exaggerated southern dialect. "Ah mus' confess t' havin' a smidgen a' hostility fo' one of ah suth'n belles. How's mah ack-sent, Jimmy?"

"Probably work down in Richmond." He smiled on the non-droopy side of his face.

Abby shook her head. "Pretty bad if Leonard gives up on you. Time's up—no more school talk."

Already feeling the alcohol, I polished off most of my ale, and then cleared my throat. "Okayyyy, folks." My best Hatcher impression won some chortles. "As temporary big cheese of little Raven Point School, I hereby declare that the proclamation made by our colleague from the State of Colorado is okayyyy."

The adults all laughed except Jimmy, who looked dumbfounded as I raised my bottle toward Abby. "And now a toast to our lovely hostess!" I blurted, but quickly amended my toast. "I mean, to our lovely hostes*ses*." But I knew the damage was done when Beth retreated from the kitchen to her room.

Still exhilarated, Elizabeth clapped. "Such gallantry from our P.E. department. Hail to our lovely hostesses!"

No amount of alcohol in my system could make me forget my gaffe. After Abby went to Beth's room, I shut up and tried to pay attention to Elizabeth and Leonard's discussion of Navajo vocabulary.

I was relieved when Abby returned to the kitchen. "All's well. Come and get it!"

During the meal, Jimmy and I took some gentle ribbing for our "unusual" spaghetti. "Don't feel bad about the leftovers," Elizabeth confided to me. "We have two non-carnivores here, Leonard and Beth." Abby's daughter had come back as quietly as she left, fixed a plate and carried it back to her room.

As the meal wound down, Jimmy began to clear away drinks, and Beth came in to help Abby with the dishes. I took plates and garbage over there, avoiding eye contact with either of the McAdams.

By the time I returned to Leonard and Elizabeth, they were critiquing movies based on great books. I listened for a while and made one comment before Beth joined the group, purposely not facing me. She was quiet at first, but then spoke eagerly to the topic.

Dishes dried, Jimmy came over, but he began to nod off, and the gathering began to break up. Before leaving, I self-consciously thanked Abby for having us over.

}-{

I planned to spend Sunday and Labor Day in the gym. It wasn't likely that the three veteran teachers who'd stayed around would need anything from me, and Leonard went to Albuquerque to visit family and take a dog to his sister. Sunday was quiet and cool, and I spent most of the day in the gym, sorting, discarding, and setting up a work space on the larger stage.

By ten on Labor Day morning, it was hot and stifling in the gym, and I began to think about having P.E. outside on Wednesday. After propping the doors open I discovered a wire jury-rigged to the drinking fountain, obviously Leonard's work. Even though I had brought cold water in a thermos, I attached the wire to the handle to let the fountain run and went on sorting equipment, my T-shirt and Bermudas soaked with sweat. I cooled off by splashing some water from the fountain on my head and face, then unhooked the wire.

At midday the doors blew shut. I hurried over, opened them and saw a thunderstorm firing up on the ridge to the south. When I propped the doors more securely, a welcome rush of advancing cool air brought with it the sweet smell of wet earth. I walked around the cinderblock partition and back to the stage.

As the storm crackled and rumbled closer, the gym lights flickered, so I returned to the door to savor the deluge as it swept over the compound, falling so hard it sounded like hail ricocheting off the Quonset's metal roof. I dragged a gym mat over to the doors and stretched out on it, watching the storm and breathing the fresh air all the way in.

After my relaxing break, I finished sorting and began the dreaded task of cleaning and dusting. In the afternoon Abby showed up in jeans and an old denim shirt, carrying a blue cooler like the one in her room. She walked over, her hair wrapped in a coppery bandana that set off her pretty hazel eyes as she looked up and set the cooler down on the stage.

"Well, hi," I said, letting go of a wrestling mat I had just sprayed and wiped down.

"Afternoon." She sounded businesslike but pleasant. "Now that you've heard more about our water, I brought this extra cooler. You know where the supply is in the kitchen. The last counselor always got annoyed with Leonard for using the coffee pot for water in the dorm, then Laird started drinking it himself." She nodded to the fountain. "He wouldn't even attach the wire in here; Leonard came over every day at noon to do it."

"Man." I squatted near the edge of the stage. "We'll use the cooler for sure. Thanks."

She nodded. "Looks like you had a lot of work."

"Yeah, but I found a few useful things." I put my hand on two new floor hockey goals I discovered in the school storage room. "Never used."

"Good for you." She eyed the orange traffic cones I'd set up on the floor. "Beth told me the fourth-grade boys used to help with basketball scrimmage while the rest of the kids played or sat around. I'm sure your P.E. classes will be a definite improvement."

"Yeah, I hope so."

"Actually, basketball's what I came to talk to you about. Beth wants to play."

"She does?"

"Fifth and sixth graders are expected to get involved, but Beth won't deal with Mona and Student Council, and cheerleaders are out; she's never been much for that sort of thing."

I grinned. "Gee, I wonder how that happened?"

"Yeah, I'm glad she's so into books and animals. My dad had a lot to do with that."

"Leonard told me she's taking care of his little zoo while he's gone."

Abby nodded. "I promised her a dog after school starts. She already has one of Leonard's cats and loves the pony, of course. Anyway, Beth usually gets along with our boys, but her playing on the team could complicate things a little for you."

"Well, she doesn't seem too thrilled to be around me."

"She'll get used to you; it's not that. The larger schools have separate girls' teams, otherwise they don't play. I don't think there's a rule against it, though."

"I don't see how there could be anymore. Do you think Hatcher would see it as a problem?"

"Not if it doesn't involve him. If you're okay with all this, we'll see if Beth stays with it."

"Sounds good to me. What if she gets laughed or yelled at?"

"Maybe at another school, but she'd handle it. If Beth's on the team, she'd need someplace to dress at away games."

"I think we could work that out with the other schools."

"Thanks." She took some steps as if to leave, then stopped. "Sean, don't fret about her surliness with you. This too shall pass."

I shook my head. "I did manage to embarrass all three of us the other night."

"She was a little embarrassed, but you're probably the first male other than family to say she's 'lovely.' She wasn't all that bothered."

"Sorry—not a big drinker, but I get pretty happy when I do."

"No apology needed." She started for the door. "Beth was embarrassed," she said with a laugh, "not me." With a wave she was gone.

As I got back to my cleaning I obsessed a little over Abby's parting comment and the tone of her laugh. Did she mean *Forget about your drunken toast*, or *Call me lovely whenever you want*, or something else?

That evening I went out on my steps and gazed down at the school. Through Jimmy's dark room I saw Abby's lights on across the hall and thought about dropping by. I let it go, telling myself I wouldn't pester her during preparation anyway. Leonard's VW rolled into the compound; I had a couple of questions for him but decided they could wait until morning.

)-(

After getting up early on Tuesday, I hurried across the road past Mona's Cadillac and Jon's truck, the only vehicles parked at the school. I entered the dorm and saw more stacks of little paper cups by the coffee urn on the kitchen counter, a flowery cloth bag now cinched over and around the nearby drinking fountain.

I found Leonard in the office, sporting one of his neat semi-cowboy outfits as he placed files on a side table. I was surprised to find him blank-faced, even dour. I decided to rib him a little. "Morning, Mr. Santos."

He kept working. "You're early. I'm moving some of my things over here."

"Why?"

"It's your desk."

"It's *our* desk—I already took a drawer." I pulled open the second one, showing my manual and a few supplies inside. "I have a drawer in Hatcher's desk, too, but most of my things are in the gym."

"If you're sure."

"I am. When you need to type up a form, where do you do it?"

"In the school office." He put some files back into the larger bottom drawer.

"I'm bringing us a typewriter and a small file cabinet. They can go on that table."

"Where'd you get them?"

"They were in storage. I already have one of each on the stage."

Leonard's usual smile made its appearance. "I forgot you have a key to Fort Knox."

"I don't get why all that stuff is just gathering dust in there. We'll go later and see if the dorm needs any of it. I also found cases of food, some of it open, and a lot of candy and pop."

"All that is supposedly for Student Council." He sat on the edge of the table.

I'd apparently touched on a serious subject. "So Mona has a key to that room?"

"Yes, it's not much of a secret that she borrows"—he made air quotes—"whatever she wants for Dot and herself, anything from food to furniture. Not even Jon dares to enter their apartment. Hal inherited the arrangement when he came here—just looks the other way."

"Man. So, what makes you seem a little down today?"

He absentmindedly straightened some registration cards on the desk. "It's that obvious?"

"For you it is."

"I'll get over it before we get busy."

"Do you want to tell me what's wrong?"

Leonard stared at the dorm windows and let out a deep breath. "We have a special Council meeting next week. Hosteen came by this morning and said that Samson's called for a personnel hearing." He faced me. "That means there's a complaint, apparently against me."

"From Samson or somebody else? And about what?"

"Samson, I'm sure, but I don't know what he's up to; neither does Hosteen. Mona probably stopped to see him on their way out."

"They're back now; I saw the car. Why is Mona only on *your* case when five of us voted the other way?"

"Just the way she is, I'll leave it at that. But she'll have her eye on you now like she does Abby and Elizabeth."

"Fine—happy to be on that team."

"Yeah, we're great examples, like kids squaring off for a playground fight." He shook his head. "I don't have anything to hide, so I'll just deal with her little game at the meeting."

"Still, it's crappy to have that hanging over you. What can I do?"

"Just be there. Thanks, Sean."

"Sure." I looked out at the quiet rec room. "I saw that colorful cover on the fountain."

"Yeah, Felicita made the bags last year for all the dorm fountains. We remove them when Hal brings in FIC visitors, but otherwise, he ignores the bags and coolers. His wife always ordered drinking water for their apartment—playing the FIC games like all of us.

"Right, I'm getting the picture. So how soon will the kids start coming?"

"There's a sixth-grader, Martin, already here and making his bed. They'll trickle in all day, some after we close for the night, a few more tomorrow. It works out best this way, especially for the new little ones in Dot's class."

"That's a frightening thought."

"She's not so bad when she's away from Mona. Dot plants herself at a big round table in her classroom, then her aide and the kids do all the legwork. Once they get to know her, the kids scurry around Dot like baby chicks. Mona knows better than to bother her during class, especially after Dot told Mona to move down the hall. After school, they're buddies again."

"I don't quite get it."

"Out of school, Mona fusses over Dot like the kids do, always making sure she has whatever she needs. Even when they're in public, which isn't often."

"Almost like a caretaker."

"I guess, but that's all I know and *want* to know about their deal."

The outside door opened; a big boy entered in jeans, red T-shirt and sneakers. Leonard's smile rekindled as he picked up one of the five-by-eight registration cards. We left the office and walked toward the boy, who'd set down his battered suitcase just inside the door. In his early teens, thin at about five-eight, he had a "bowl" haircut like Leonard's, except the boy's black bangs hung down to his brow.

"Hi, Billy, good to see you." Leonard grasped him firmly by both shoulders.

The boy didn't resist, nor did he hug back. "Lennert," he said, his eyes down, "Walter jus' wanna talk." Like Hosteen did before, Billy directed his lips outside.

"Sure, you can leave your suitcase there for now. I'll go see him." Leonard turned to me. "Billy, this is Mr. Noland. He's new here." The boy was still looking down. "Say hi, Billy; he's a good man."

I recalled Abby telling me that Billy was her oldest and slowest student, but Leonard's reassurance that I was a "good man" still seemed strange.

"Hi," the boy said, taking a peek at me from under his bangs. His dark face was glum, but he had even features, filled out like an adult's.

"Hi, Billy," I said, feeling foolish because I hadn't expected him to look so normal.

He turned to Leonard. "My teacher?"

"He's the counselor and coach. Mr. Beale's your new teacher; you'll like him too."

"Walter jus' wanna talk." Billy walked over to the windows.

Leonard spoke to me under his breath. "Walter's his great-uncle—old and, uh, reticent—doesn't speak English. Probably not a good time—"

"Just go ahead. I'll stay with Billy." I walked to the windows and stood several feet from the boy. Leonard went out but came right back for a leash he kept by the door. We watched him approach an old barge of a Buick, where a scrawny mutt sat in its shade. He reached into his pocket for morsels he always carried. Leonard gave the dog its treat, then led it around on the leash to the passenger-side door, where the old man got out—apparently Billy had been driving.

Walter was badly stooped, making him shorter than Leonard. Wearing a straw cowboy hat and faded denims, he accepted the registration card Leonard brought for him to sign.

As they started their conversation, I turned to the boy. "Your dog, Billy?" After a barely perceptible shake of his head, he still didn't look my way. Out at the Buick, they had finished their business. Bracing himself with a hand against the car, Walter slouched around to the driver's side, got in with difficulty, and then drove off with insufficient speed to raise any dust.

After Leonard beckoned us with the registration card, we went out and followed him around the dorm to the animal pen, where Billy put his hands on the wire fence to watch the pony. As some of the dogs barked and most of the cats went into hiding, I wondered about Billy's situation but didn't want to ask Leonard with the boy standing right there.

Leonard turned to me, petting the quiet but nervous mutt outside the gate. "Another stray—followed their car all the way here."

I patted the dog. "Can I ask you something about your, um, enthusiasm for animals?" He nodded. "Does it relate to your not eating meat? Elizabeth mentioned it at the potluck."

"Well, that hot-dog spaghetti was mighty tempting." Leonard petted the stray again before putting him in the pen; the dogs inside sniffed out the new arrival without incident. "Good pups," he said, then turned to me. "Back to your question: I shot game for my family when I was young but stopped hunting after it was no longer needed."

"And eating meat?"

"Well, as a man of letters, you probably know Sinclair Lewis."

"What? Sure, *Elmer Gantry* is a favorite of mine. Why?"

"There's a line in *Arrowsmith*, a doctor's observation. I can only paraphrase it. The doctor doubts the superiority of man to the cheerful dogs, graceful cats, unagitated horses, and adventuring seagulls. That sort of sums it up for me. I sometimes have a little bit of meat to be polite, just enough to remind me that I don't like to eat it."

The menagerie remained peaceful, so Leonard led Billy and me through the back door into the hallway, then the rec room. "Lots of introductions for you today," he said. The dorm staff had arrived to move out the sofas and set up games, reading material, snacks, and registration papers on the tables. Felicita had a private station in her apartment to check vaccination records, inspect the kids for medical issues and lice, and trim some of the boys' long hair. Leonard told me they had recently modified the long-time practice of giving all the boys a short butch.

"There's Jeannie," he said, explaining that the part-secretary and part-teacher's aide was there to handle the school's paperwork. Leonard led me toward where she was chatting with Marla, the very heavy night aide I'd already met. Like Marla, the secretary was about five-five with a round pretty face, flawless mocha skin, and long black hair held by silver clasps. She was probably ten years younger than Marla and fifty pounds lighter, though also stocky. In a tan business suit too small for her, the outfit seemed formal for Raven Point.

Before Leonard could introduce us, she offered her hand and blurted, "I'm Jeannie Whitney, and you must be Mr. Noland. I'll be working with you in the office sometimes," she said in perfect English.

We shook hands. "Hi, Jeannie. I'm Sean. Are you two sisters?"

She laughed. "No, Marla is my *mom's* little sister." Shy Marla, in loose work clothes, just nodded. I found out later that Jeannie was just two summers away from earning her degree in education.

The morning turned out to be busier than expected with more than half of the boarding students registering by noon, but Leonard and Felicita were prepared for the check-in to run efficiently. As we processed the kids I saw a few who had light skin, hair, or eyes—apparently not full-blooded Navajos. I wondered how they were treated by the others.

A third or fourth-grade girl came up to me, pointing her lips at a boy who was walking away. "Jus' wanna be mischief," she said with a pout.

"What?" I replied, but she glared at me as if I was a dunce, then turned to Leonard, who was standing nearby. He solved their little spat and came back to me.

"So that's how she says *mischievous?*" I asked him.

He smiled. "You'll get used to it."

Many of the children arrived in iron-stained socks and T-shirts, scuffed shoes, worn-out pants or cotton skirts. Old play clothes, I thought, before Leonard told me that most spend the summers on chores like herding livestock, processing meat, cleaning wool, gathering wood, hauling water, and harvesting natural plants or garden vegetables.

Following Leonard's example, I tried not to be pushy when greeting the kids, but most of the girls and maybe half of the boys were as shy with me as Billy. I noticed that Leonard rarely touched the younger children, but some of the older ones were noticeably pleased to see him; a few returned a brief hug after Leonard's avuncular embrace to their shoulders. Most parents left after their children's health check-up, and many of the older kids went straight from Felicita to the dorm to shower and change into their school clothes.

By midday, Felicita was relieved not to find one case of lice, but she did have to send four kids to the clinic in Old Mission. There was also the expected complication of settling the kindergarten children, a few of whom cried for their mothers. Instead of placing the little ones together, Leonard, Marla, and Felicita paired each of the kindergarteners with an older child. Although he didn't actually smile, Billy seemed pleased to be the temporary "pal" for his small male cousin. All in all, we seemed to be off to a good start in the dorm. I wondered if the first day of school would turn out so well.

15

With the snowfall intense again, we trudged up the second hill. I kept trying to regulate my temperature by adjusting the skiing pace, but I was alternating between chills and sweats. In a few minutes we ascended into some piñons and stopped. Leonard saw me shiver and said, "We're within a mile of the summit." He set his pack down, untied my parka, and brushed it free of snow. "Put this thing on for a while, then we'll get going."

I pulled my scarf down. "Thanks," I said, enveloping myself in the down coat.

"Take some water, slowly again." After handing over the sock-covered bottle, he took the flask from his belt. I sipped, swished, and swallowed water three or four times. This time I felt like I wanted more.

He finished taking his own drink. "That's probably about enough. Any dizziness?"

"Just s-sort of a weak feeling." I took a last sip and handed him the bottle.

"We *have* been up all night. Going down this hill might energize you some."

"If you say so," I said, not trembling as much.

"Once we start down it's the same deal as last time, except it's longer and we'll be going faster. The main thing is to stay on your skis if you can. Feeling a little better?"

"Good enough." He took back the parka, tied it down, and I pulled up the scarf and thin hood. He hunched on his pack again, and we started off as Marie came back to check on the delay.

Within minutes, the snowfall thickened to near-whiteout conditions. I caught up, and Leonard pointed ahead into the storm. "As long as the wind holds off, the snow's so deep that it should be fairly smooth when we start down. You'll do fine; it starts just ahead."

I felt like asking how he could know that. "Just the facts, right?"

"Hey, I'm as ready as you are to find that old hogan. After we start, if you feel like you're going too fast, drag your poles to slow down. There are a couple of curves; you'll have to go slower there to stay in my tracks. If you do fall, yell out right away so I don't get too far ahead."

I nodded, pulled up the scarf again, then watched Leonard and Marie vanish in the snowfall. I breathed deeply, trying to ignore my isolation as I skied into his tracks. I'd expected gravity to take me at any time, but I just slid to a stop on level ground. With my next effort, two long strides got me moving right away. Then my body sensed the downward angle and I was suddenly moving faster than on the quickest part of the last hill. "Good God," I said, squatting into a crouch, the ski poles back for balance.

As Leonard predicted, I met only slight dips in the deep snow, but my downhill speed seemed to increase exponentially. Definitely alert, even excited, I began to worry about how I would handle the first curve.

I didn't have to wait long until g-forces urged me to keep going straight instead of veering to the left in Leonard's tracks. I leaned that way and dragged my poles, staying more or less on course through the curve. I felt more confident skiing straight down again, and I heard Leonard call, "You okay?"

"Yeah!" I yelled, as loud as I could into the wool.

I managed the next curve the same way, but then the downhill grade was even steeper. Snow pelting my eyes, I wondered if "a couple curves" could mean three, but I made myself concentrate on balance, trying for more drag with the poles. Barreling down the hill, the snow began to clot in my lashes, but I didn't dare lift an arm to clear it away.

When the grade leveled slightly, I slowed enough to wipe my face once, thinking the worst must be over. Then I saw Leonard's tracks turn hard to the left. Before I could compensate, I skied across the curve and shot over the edge.

Skiing almost straight down through deep powder, I tried to dig in the poles to avoid piñons and large bushes. I skied right over a thick clump of brush that scraped my legs and crotch, slowing me enough to consider a quick Hobson's choice between falling sideways or grasping the top of a piñon. I tried the tree, but the branches slithered through my hands and I shouted, "Going down!" Tumbling heels over head, I made two-thirds of another revolution until the deep snow kept me from rolling farther down the slope.

I didn't move for seconds, listening to the quiet. It came to me that if the proverbial bear in the woods had watched me roll into the snow, it had to look cartoonish, especially after being goosed by the bush. I turned onto my back, only the right ski flailing above me in light snowfall. I sat up, keeping my leg with the ski to one side so I wouldn't sink deeper into what seemed to be a profound drift. I brushed snow off my face and opened my mouth wide. "Leonard!"

Looking around in the silence, I saw that the tallest of the piñons was six or seven feet below me, its top only a few feet above the snow. The second ski, intact and just within sight, was caught in some brush thirty feet or so downhill. I raised my arms to check the poles—the right one was okay, but less than four feet of bamboo dangled from my left wrist.

"Leonard!" I shouted again, trying to get to my feet with the one pole, but the ski slid, and I flopped back deeper in the drift. I listened to the stillness again, reminding me of when I spooked myself about the coyote.

I sat up and pulled the sock and glove from my right hand. Reaching for my right boot, I managed to untie the binding, and then sat up and jammed the ski into the snow, but it didn't hit anything solid. Hands and face freezing, I put on the glove, called out again, and then wrapped the scarf around my head.

I debated between waiting for Leonard and trying again to get back on my feet, which would probably work up a sweat. After calling for him again and waiting, I extracted my hand from the loop of the good pole and leaned forward as far as I could to push the end of it against the piñon's trunk with the idea of using gravity to help me stand. As I intended, the round doo-hickey on the end of the pole caught against the narrow trunk, so I put both hands on the grip to shift more of my weight ahead. At first, the lower half of my body started to come free, but the pole broke through the tree, so I fell back on purpose rather than rolling down the hill.

"Shit!" I sat up and freed my torso, but my ass and legs were completely buried. While I brushed off, I saw that both the ski and good pole were now well out of reach.

I took the pole fragment and jammed it straight down into the snow, thinking it would somehow help me find ground or some other purchase. Calling Leonard every minute or so while repeatedly plunging the four feet of bamboo into the drift, I started to shiver and feel dizzy.

"Sean, keep calling!" came faintly from above.

"I'm here!" I blared before Marie showed up and licked my face. "Hey, g-girl—good dog." Feeling a surge of energy, I stabbed the pole fragment into the snow again and again, vaguely aware of a swooshing sound of skis behind.

"What're you doing, Sean?" Leonard made a sideways stop next to me.

"Trying to get up."

"Stop. You're doing all that for nothing."

"What?" I held up my wrist and looked at the dangling piece of bamboo as if I hadn't seen it before. "Well, I'm s-stuck in here pretty good."

"I see that. Quite a drift you found. Let's get you out of there."
I was trembling. "How?"

"Sideways. It's steep but not that far; I had to leave my pack up top." He unsnapped the flask from his belt. "Same as before, don't gulp it cold." After swishing and swallowing I saw that he'd sidestepped several feet below.

"Okay, toss me the water," he said.

After I did that, he clipped it on next to his sheath. "Ready?" Leonard thrust the grip end of his poles toward me. I grabbed them, and he made more sidesteps downhill, pulling me at least a foot closer to the surface. "Okay, let go of my poles; don't try to stand yet. I'm going after your other ski." He skied down there in seconds before clomping a stride or two back uphill. "I'll try to toss this just over your head," he called. "If you miss, don't lunge for it."

When he launched the ski, I fumbled it in the air but held on, then stuck it in the snow. I watched him gradually sidestep back up, stopping for a couple of minutes at a sturdy bush to cut branches with his knife. With brush and a ski pole under one arm, he approached using the other pole for traction.

"You look like crap, Sean, but we're getting out. Hold these." He dropped the branches and a long stick into my arms, and then stamped his skis until he'd flattened an indentation in the snow all around me. After he put down the brush to form a mat on the compacted snow, Leonard retrieved my good pole, came back, and took the stick from me. "All right, use my poles, keep your feet on the branches, then stand up. I'll help you."

I took his poles and dug them in; he grabbed my arm and I slowly got up. "All right, what n-next?"

"How're you doing?"

"Not great." I shuddered again. "Just t-tell me what to do."

"Did you see my sideways stride on the way back up here?"

"Sort of."

"Well, that's what we both have to do now."

"You only have one p-pole."

"And this stick. It's good enough to get me up there."

After helping me strap on my skis, he demonstrated the side-stepping method. We started off with me in the lead, one parallel step up at a time. My skis sometimes slid, but I just leaned into the vertical bank to keep from falling. Repeating the monotonous sideways and upward movement time after time with Leonard's encouragement from behind, I couldn't tell if I was making much progress. My head down, I kept going until I thought I was spent.

"Don't stop, you're almost here." Somehow his voice was coming from just above me. I made several more straddles and finally reached Leonard's hand. He pulled me up to where I could sit and rest with my skis over the edge. "Be right back, Sean."

Marie waited with me, her long tongue all the way out. "Yeah, g-girl, me too." Dizzy, hot, and completely soaked, I shed the scarf, windbreaker, and my hat to wait. "Where *arrre* you, Leonard?" I sang foolishly into the light snowfall.

He soon skied up to me and put down his big pack. "What's going on?" he asked, putting down the pole and stick he was using.

I laughed. "I d-don't know. I was thinking about t-taking off my sweater."

"We have to change your wet clothes."

I watched him untie my parka from the pack and flap it a few times as you would a dusty throw rug. "Who's gonna s-see that?" I laughed again. "How about smoke s-signals?"

"In this overcast, Kemo Sabe?" Straight-faced, he draped the parka over me, buttoning it part way. "Leave that on for now." He began to stamp the snow around me again.

"Y'know, the masked b-bastard called him s-stupid all those years?"

"Yeah, now pay attention." He laid down a small tarp. "I want to see you try to stand on your own. It's almost level here."

"What about all my b-bracelets?" I giggled, holding up three straps—two attached to the good poles, the other to the fragment.

"Just move over and try to get up. I'll guide the tips into the grommets."

I couldn't stop laughing. "What's a grommet?"

"The metal holes in the tarp. Go on, Sean."

"Yes, s-sir." I swiveled the skis and moved my ass over there, then tried to squat. When I couldn't shift my weight onto the poles, Leonard pulled me up by the armpits.

"Pretty shaky," he said.

I leaned on his shoulder, then steadied myself between the ski poles. "B-but I'm up," I said, still silly. "Let's go."

"Yeah—stay right there." He pulled some clothes out of his pack, shielding them with his body from the light snowfall. "Now take off the parka and everything else above your waist."

"What?" I giggled again. "G-gladly." I dropped the poles, removed the parka and gave it to him. I stripped off my sweater and T-shirt, snowflakes tickling my skin. "Feels good."

"It's not supposed to." He handed me a dishtowel. "Now dry off as fast as you can."

"Okay, don't get p-pissed." Grinning, I dried off my chest, shoulders, and head before the shivers got worse. Leonard took the towel to wipe my back, and handed me a rust-stained T-shirt. "Too s-small," I said, pulling it down. "I'm getting c-cold now; is that good?" He ignored my idiocy, handing over his fleece sweater, the parka, and my hat. I put them on with his help.

"Zip and button the coat and hood, with the flap over your face. We're almost ready."

I managed to do as he said, and then put dry socks over my gloves. While Leonard secured his pack, I was still trembling but the parka felt good. It finally dawned on me how ridiculous I'd been to want to remove my clothes. Instead of wondering what to do next, I stared at Marie, running around with a stick like an excited puppy at a lake on a summer day.

"Sean!"

His shout broke my daydreaming. "Yeah."

"Well, how do you feel?" He hefted his pack and secured the straps in front.

"Uh, I'm okay. B-been acting pretty weird, haven't I?"

"It'll be funny later on." He reached out for his pole and stick, embedded nearby in the snow. "Just a few hundred yards to the bottom of the hill, and it isn't very steep now. Should be easy going, so keep your coat buttoned and your face covered. Let's go."

He skied off slowly, his good pole and the makeshift one dragging behind. I followed in his tracks and seemed to glide casually, as if I knew what I was doing. After five minutes or so of effortless skiing I was shivering again.

We came to level ground, where the tips of a few squat piñons stuck out from the snow. Leonard left the main road onto a side trail, where it was hard going again, breaking through drifts and over mounds. He pointed ahead with his stick. "C'mon, we're almost there."

After a few hundred more feet, I was warm and dizzy again, starting to fall behind. Leonard raised an arm toward the outline of a tall white mound just ahead. The prospect of shelter must have kicked in some adrenaline. I skied up to him and the old hogan. It had about two feet of ice and snow layered on top, much less on its rounded sides.

"Look up there," he said. Wisps of smoke escaped through the top of a crooked stovepipe at the roof's center.

"Good. The door?"

"Other side." Leonard and I skied around and caught up to Marie, sniffing tracks that led to a wooden door. Someone had scraped away enough accumulation to allow the door to open a couple of feet. Drowsy and shaking, I watched Leonard set down his pack and stab his skis into the snow by the door before he used a nearby board to scrape back more of the powder.

He untied my skis for me. I stepped off, then he speared them into the snow with the others before lifting the door latch. "Wait one sec," he said, and then walked inside with his flashlight. Leonard came right back out and grabbed his pack. "Come on." Marie and I followed him in; he closed the door. As my eyes adjusted to the near-darkness, I saw a flicker of flame at the end of a long barrel.

Leonard aimed his flashlight toward an unmoving lump under a blanket near the stove. One arm hung out, covered by the unmistakable black-and-green sleeve of Hawthorne's mackinaw coat, an open sketchpad and pencil on the ground nearby.

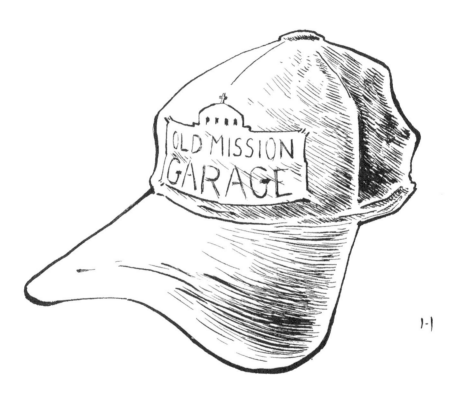

This
Navajo on a mission,
Adorned
In jelly-pants,
Black tie,
Crew cut, and
The Book of Mormon
Has plenty to say—

While this young
Navajo cowboy
Silently boasts of
His Levis, Lamas,
Stetson and Skoal.

16

On check-in day, a few fathers asked me about kids' basketball as well as the men's practice times in the gym. Samson Shepard's boys, Hawthorne and Peter, came in with their much older first cousins, Carlton and Randall, who brought in registration cards signed by Samson. Like Billy and two other big boys, Hawthorne carried a well-worn mackinaw, patterned with black-and-green squares; the smaller boys had similar jackets, but with black-and-red or gold. Leonard explained that a Phoenix department store had donated the mackinaws years before along with pink, red, and purple nylon coats for the girls; most of them had been passed down as the kids grew.

Carlton and Randall were in working garb: T-shirts, old jeans, and oily boots. They wore bandanas under the brims of smudged green baseball caps with OLD MISSION GARAGE on the front. Although I'd seen them tinkering with Campbell from a distance, I hadn't spoken to the Shepard brothers since our meeting with Hosteen the week before. I did discover one morning that they'd cleaned my motor, but I decided not to go back to the trailer for my spare key to see if the truck was already running.

Neither of Hosteen's sons looked at me until after the wiry, muscular Carlton registered his own two boys, a kindergartener and a third-grader. Standing with his small sons, Carlton seemed older and shorter than before. His taller, heavier, and slightly younger brother stayed back while Carlton came over to me, wearing a red headscarf with blue and white patriotic streaks. In one short hushed sentence, he told me that my truck was running, but not good yet, and the windshield hadn't come to Old Mission. Before they walked away, I told Randall that basketball practice was after school the next day.

"Not two-fifteen?" He started for the door.

"No, right after school," I said, and he walked out behind Carlton.

By the time the cook served cold sandwiches, canned fruit, and juice for dinner, I was already an hour into my first evening shift. Leonard, an aide, and I played games with the kids and had some registrations that kept us busy until after lights out, when the aide left. Leonard took the first hour at the between-dorms desk, while I updated some office files and took care of a registration.

After we switched for the second hour I read a paperback under a small lamp, hearing only an occasional cough or moan from the children. When Leonard came in later with two newly registered brothers, we swapped places again. I walked back to the rec room, worrying that Hatcher wouldn't show and I'd have to spend time over at the school the next day.

Near the end of my first night, Marla came in for graveyard shift, and I was relieved to see Hatcher's truck pull in over by the flagpole.

}-{

Technically off duty on Wednesday morning, I put on tennis shoes, sweat pants, and then a light jacket over my blue Arizona T-shirt. I walked over to the dorm before ten to find out how everything was going. Felicita was registering a family with Leonard, who had stayed on well past his graveyard shift but was about to leave. He said eight boarding students were missing, mostly little ones, and that he would start home visits after he had some sleep.

Leonard also told me that Jeannie always escorted the first class to P.E., but it was up to me to swap them afterwards with the older group. As if reading my mind, he then said that nearly all of them had sneakers except the kindergartners. He'd given instructions to the aide to have the kids change their shoes at noon. "That's it, Mr. Noland. Good luck with your classes."

After he left, I took two gallons of water over to the gym, poured it all into the cooler, and went back for cups before reviewing my plans.

Just before one-thirty Jeannie brought in twenty K-two kids and said there were five missing, including a day student. About an equal number of boys and girls, they'd be by far the youngest children I had ever taught. Jeannie, in her snug suit again, told me nearly half of them spoke little or no English; she asked if I would like her to stay for the first two days.

"Is that okay with Mr. Hatcher?"

"Yes, I'm in the office two hours in the mornings, but I haven't finished arranging the rest of my schedule, so I'm free this time today and tomorrow."

"Great, I'll claim you for both days." I turned to my students, who waited quietly together. "Good afternoon," I said with a smile that I hoped wasn't too ingratiating.

A few mumbled, "Afternoon." Many of them had met me before, and I knew a few names, so they didn't look all that anxious, especially with Jeannie there.

The forty minutes went by surprisingly fast. It took a while to get the kindergartners and a couple of others into their socks, Jeannie setting the example by taking off her business shoes while speaking to them in Navajo. It took even more time to form three lines and space them apart between the traffic cones, but we accomplished it with military overtones, marching here and there, which the kids seemed to enjoy.

I'd planned for a game next to learn more of their names but decided that could wait a day. I started with simple stretches and basic calisthenics, all of the children complying after some help from us. Jeannie taught the words "stretch" and "exercise" to some; a few kids started to giggle, which spread to the whole class while they mimicked my movements.

When I stopped and said we were going to run two laps, some second-graders quickly interpreted for the others, so I realized it was not essential to have an adult interpreter there. I started off with the children filing in behind me, some with big smiles. Jeannie stayed in the middle of the gym, encouraging them in Navajo and calling out, "running laps," which many of the kids repeated back to her.

We finished running, and a few of the youngest started for the drinking fountain. "Whoa, let's not drink that water, okay?" I called. "Those who really need a drink, line up at the stage; the rest come on over to start a game." Surprisingly, only four of them got a drink.

Instead of starting my planned game, I asked first about their favorite one. After some second-graders interpreted again, a tall boy called out, "Nordit!" Most of the kids repeated that word and scattered until only two tiny girls remained with an older one who was still explaining the game. I'd figured out that "Nordit" was "Not it" when one of the little girls chased after the girl who interpreted. The other one walked right up to Jeannie, touched her, and fled. Jeannie poked my shoulder, so I ran off after the biggest boy.

After our rambunctious game of tag with two players "it," the older children helped some of the little ones with their shoes. Most of the kids lined up at the stage for a drink and tossed their cups in the trashcan.

"Whew," Jeannie said with her genial smile, "tomorrow I'll dress more appropriately."

We walked the class back to school and found Elizabeth and Jimmy in the hall with their students, including Billy, Beth, and some others I knew by name. As Jeannie led the K-two children to the door for Navajo class, Elizabeth turned to me. "Mr. Noland, I have three absent; Mr. Beale just one, and we do have scheduled transition times."

I'd been staring at another wired fountain and its bubbling ochreous water, not a single kid near it. "Oh, sorry. I'll be more prompt tomorrow." I glanced at my new group, another twenty or so again, more girls than boys this time. "So is the procedure that I need to get the non-basketball players to the dorm after P.E.?"

"I imagine so; this is all new." She turned to my new group of students. "I see that some of you have books to read—good. Starting tomorrow, all of you need to take your homework with you to P.E. so that you don't have to come back here for it." She started for her door.

"That's right," Jimmy said quietly to the kids before he entered his room.

As the third- through sixth-grade students followed me to the gym, I noticed that nearly all had on sneakers in various condition. Four boys were in P.E. trunks, the rest of the class wore long pants, including the girls. As we walked, a few kids muttered in Navajo, except one boy clearly said "recess" when we approached the gym.

"Not recess," I told them. "This is P.E." I took out a whistle that I didn't even use with the first group and put it over my neck. As soon as we walked around the barrier inside, a few kids with books plopped down on the floor. Two small boys ran over, vaulted up onto the larger stage and raced for a huge box that once contained the recess balls. Puzzled, they came back to the front of the stage as I approached.

One of them, a thin fourth-grader who showed up at check-in with a butch haircut, glared at me. About five-one, he had buckteeth and fairer skin than most of the others. "Basketballs?" he asked me.

"Benny, right?"

He just nodded. The boy was so active that his health problems had slipped my mind. Felicita told me Benny Yazzie had juvenile diabetes, and she gave me a bag of small chocolates to keep in the gym in case he weakened noticeably when his blood sugar dropped. In case of shock, she had insulin and other medicine for him in the dorm. Benny also didn't know much English and usually just said single words.

"No balls in P.E. today, Benny. You two can come back down." I turned to the others. "The rest of you over here too."

After they all complied, I asked two girls to remove their street shoes. The class followed my directions to line up for calisthenics, then one boy, Hawthorne Shepard, raised his hand. He not only had the reputation as the school's best basketball player, he was also the best "drawer," as a dorm aide told me. Hawthorne often carried his supplies around in a loom-knitted grey woolen shoulder bag in case he found time to practice his art. Muscular for his age and already as tall as his cousin Carlton, I guessed that Hawthorne would eventually be at least as big as Randall. Like most of the boys, he had dark brows, eyes, and trimmed black bangs. He also had a long scar on one cheek but did not seem self-conscious about it.

"Yes, Hawthorne?"

"What about basketball practice?"

"After this class. Anyone who's interested can stay on after P.E."

"Even fourth grade?" Hawthorne directed his lips at Benny and another small boy.

"Yes, anybody in here," I said, then those three boys exchanged grins.

Most of the class did the calisthenics and jogged energetically without complaint, except Beth, who griped a little and exercised lackadaisically. Afterwards, I told them I was going to show them a game of tag for big kids. They quickly picked up on the rules for "Capture the Flag," using two Frisbees for flags.

At the end of P.E. many of the kids got a drink from the cooler before I blew the whistle and gathered the class near the stage. "All right, anyone who wants to play basketball, please sit on the stage. The rest of you wait here."

Hawthorne and two others in shorts hopped up there with ease. The fourth boy in shorts, very chubby, just stood near them in front of the stage. Hawthorne waved to Billy, who ran over and vaulted up backwards, followed by the two small fourth-graders—Benny and his friend. Hawthorne, taller than all the boys but Billy, welcomed the others with friendly soft slugs to their arms. "Billy plays?" Hawthorne asked me.

"Sure, if he wants to." Everyone turned to Billy, who nodded. I asked the seven boys to say their names. As they finished, Beth walked sullenly over to stand in front of the stage, away from the other players, not saying her name.

"Good, Beth," I said, "that makes eight."

A couple of boys laughed until Hawthorne spoke in Navajo to them before turning to me again. "Girls can play?"

"Yes, as far I'm concerned."

A third-grader was already halfway to the stage; I recognized him as Carlton's son. The very small boy stood with the over-weight sixth-grader, turned, and proudly said, "Raymond."

"Okay, Raymond." I faced the rest of the class. "We need one more for a full team. Last chance, or line up at the wall by the door, please." They walked off except for two girls, one large and one small, who giggled together until Beth motioned for them to join her. Hands covering their faces from the nose down, they hurried over to stand with Beth. They said their names quietly after I asked.

"Great, that's eleven. You guys hang on." I quickly jogged over to the kids who'd lined up at the barrier and escorted them over to the dorm, making sure an aide saw them. On my way back Randall walked up in work clothes, except for some snazzy black court shoes.

"Hi," I said. "Ready to run them?" He nodded, and we went into the gym. Randall stood by the boys, now in front of the stage, while the three girls waited several feet away.

"Okay," I said to the team, "first day, we're going to learn some basketball vocabulary and do some drills. Then we'll see who can make a layup." I pointed to the black line under my foot. "What's this called?"

"Line," Benny said with a wide smile, a few boys snickering.

"Benny's right, but every line has its own name. You need to learn all the basketball words right away because Mr. Shepard and I will say them to you when we're coaching." The boys turned to Randall; I was relieved when he nodded. "All right, who knows the name of *this* line?" I pointed down.

"End line," Hawthorne said, and Benny echoed his words.

"Good. How many end lines are there?"

"Two," Hawthorne answered.

I jumped up onto the low stage and motioned for Randall to join me. "Okay, Hawthorne, go ahead and run to the other end line, step on it, and yell out its name."

He jogged to the far end of the court, stomped his foot and said, "End line."

"Now," I shouted, "everybody run off and step on one of the two end lines." The girls went to the closest one and stood silently, while all the boys ran down to Hawthorne and said, "End line," Benny's voice the only loud one, which made the boys grin. By the time we repeated that process with sidelines, free throw lines, the mid-court ten-second line, explaining each one, we had our eleven players standing all over the court.

I blew the whistle from the stage, Randall a few feet away from me. "All right, learn those words for homework; you older kids help the others. Tomorrow, you'll learn more words like 'key,' 'lane,' 'backcourt,' and 'frontcourt,' but now it's time to run. When Mr. Shepard calls out the name of a line, sprint to it from where you're standing." I heard a couple of kids translating "sprint."

As if we'd prepared together, Randall pulled out a whistle of his own, blew it, and called, "End line," just loud enough for them to hear. The group divided, running to opposite ends of the gym. Randall smiled slyly, and then called out louder, "Other end line!" They all ran across, mostly laughing, as if it was hard not to collide with the kids running in the other direction. They laughed less and less as Randall repeated "End line" or "Side line" several more times before bringing them all together with "Ten-second line!" They ran to mid-court, most of them bent over, gasping as if they'd run for miles.

Randall gave them a short break, then called out lines again. While they ran, I saw that Hawthorne was the only boy who could outrun a thin sixth-grade girl not five feet tall whose name was Mary. Beth ran effortlessly just behind her, so she was also fast. Four other boys ran well—Benny, his small friend Simon, tiny Raymond, and George, a short fifth-grader. They all looked pleased just to be on the team.

The third girl, Winifred, a chunky pre-adolescent about five-four, followed directions well but could barely keep up with the last three boys—Billy, Calvin, and Martin, a sixth-grader about five-two with what looked to be a congenital limp. I couldn't tell how fast Billy could run because he wasn't sure when or where to go, so he just stayed with chubby Calvin—the alert, coordinated sixth-grader whose stomach and thighs spilled from his undersized shorts. I found out later that Winifred and Calvin were twins, day students related to Jeannie and Marla.

"Thank you, Mr. Shepard," I called out. "Everyone, last sprint—to this end line." They complied, and I jumped down from the stage, landing awkwardly with all my weight.

"The whole world shake," Hawthorne said with just a crease of a smile.

I straightened myself. "What? Oh, yeah—earthquake."

Hawthorne chuckled, then so did most of the boys. Next, we had the kids do a standing jump against a wall. The highest vertical leaps came from Hawthorne, Beth, and Billy, aided by their height and long arms. Then Randall demonstrated and super-vised simple layups. The only boys who made more than half were Hawthorne, Benny, Calvin, and Martin, regardless of his inability to push off on the bad leg. I seemed to be the only one surprised when swift but diminutive Mary made almost every layup.

Finally, we asked them to split up evenly and shoot around. The girls, Calvin, and Billy went to the far basket; the other six boys stayed to shoot at the goal near the larger stage. When Martin said something in Navajo to another boy, I picked up "good basket" in his sentence.

I moved nearer to Randall in front of the stage. "What's 'good basket' all about?"

"This one's better," he said, and went on watching them shoot.

I saw that Hawthorne was indeed accurate within twelve feet or so with his unique left-handed jump shot, and he was nearly ambidextrous under the basket. Beth launched the ball awk-wardly like the beginner she was, but still did not seem to try very hard. Little Benny kept flinging up two-handed set shots from twenty feet, and half of them went in. Three kids didn't know how to dribble very well, and two of the smaller ones couldn't get the ball up to the rim.

Nevertheless, I felt generally pleased with their effort as I fol-lowed them back to the dorm. While the team changed for din-ner, Leonard and I spoke in the rec room. I told him that Randall was helpful in practice, though he'd left before I locked up the gym.

Leonard answered with one of his big smiles. "If Randall already backed you up, he's with you. The kids seemed pleased when they came in. That's an improvement right there."

"If you say so. What's the deal with the 'good basket'?"

"I guess you could call it tradition. The Ravens, old and young, always have that basket in the second and fourth quarters. Ev-eryone thinks they do better there, even when they lose. By the way, your three girls are pals. Sometimes they quibble with the two cheerleaders, but it's nothing real serious."

"Good to know. Mary and Winifred tried hard, but Beth's just going through the motions."

"Don't worry, she'll come around."

Wondering why he was so sure of that, I lowered my voice. "How did Hawthorne get that scar on his face?"

Leonard turned more somber, watching Janet cart some condiments out to the tables. "Nobody knows for sure. It happened two years before I came. The school records say it was an accident at home. Some say Samson hit him, which is one rumor around here that I believe."

"Jesus."

"Yeah, speak of the—um, remember we have the special Council meeting at six-thirty. I have a movie all set up, and two aides are on for us."

"Right. Have you heard what Samson's problem is?"

"I have a guess, but we'll just wait and see."

)-)

On our way over to the school after dinner, two second-grade sons of staff members were heading for the dorm and laughing. "Hey, guys, the movie's starting," I said to them.

They didn't answer and kept chortling from behind us. Then we heard the boys chanting, *Bilagáana-Bilasáana, Bilagáana-Bilasáana, Bila . . . ."*

"Does that bother you?" Leonard asked me.

We walked on. "No, it's pretty funny. I like the rhyming."

"Yeah, just the plain truth."

"Right. Most of the kids are reserved, I guess, but they do let you know what's going on—a choice word or two, gestures, body language. I think I'll probably get them better than their parents. Won't be the first time."

Leonard briefly grasped my shoulder. "I think you're already hooked."

I scoffed a little as we approached the school. "So you aren't that worried about this deal tonight?"

"Not about any accusations," he said, and then told me the meeting was in Jimmy's classroom because it had the largest furniture.

When we entered, about two dozen people were settling in, seven of them up front at two tables facing the audience, many of whom waited in wooden folding chairs behind three rows of five student desks. We joined Jimmy, Elizabeth, Abby, and an older couple in the desks by the door.

In a blue muumuu, Mona sat by the windows, indifferent to a blazing red-and-orange sunset while she leafed casually through a magazine. Ahead of her in that row, the two jelly-pants Mormon missionaries whispered incessantly to a local young couple who looked trapped, smiling without comment.

Hatcher, Jeannie, Hosteen, and Felicita spoke quietly at one long table. The principal and secretary were in suits while both Felicita and Hosteen wore satin shirts and traditional hair knots, hers tied with white yarn. The other three council members waited at the other table. Jon Begay, in his usual khakis, sat by two men in dark trousers and plain summer shirts, their hair short, combed, and parted like the LDS boys. The younger of those two councilmen could pass for another missionary, and the second one was Samson, whom I had only seen once from a distance, but he was unmistakable with his black eye patch.

Regardless of his neat attire, Samson looked more aged and worn than his older brother, Hosteen. Taller than most Navajo men I'd seen, I guessed he was about my height but scrawny, with loose skin on his arms and neck suggesting that he'd been muscular at one time. Samson's wizened, liver-spotted face and single bloodshot eye accentuated his frail visage. I had no idea if he was hung over, but I couldn't imagine anyone looking much worse.

Two more couples came in and sat in the back. The audience, of varied ages, included a few more women than men. Most were in ordinary work clothes, except for Elizabeth and two other women in velveteen blouses. The only other adults I knew by first name were Eddie, Marla, Carlton, and Abby's aide, Nina, a Shepard cousin from Old Mission. I was surprised that only two children were hanging around the meeting.

I checked out Jimmy's cheery classroom, decorated in bright retail cut-outs with a back-to-school theme: school buses, crossing guards, shiny playgrounds, professorial female teachers, and hordes of impossibly cute and happy white kids. Jimmy did have a Navajo saddle blanket and the same Window Rock poster we had in the dorm—likely Elizabeth's influence.

Hosteen uttered a couple of words in Navajo, and the few people who'd been chatting stopped. He spoke for another minute or so, looking once at Jimmy and me. He then faced Jeannie while Nina led the two children out of the room.

Checking her notes, Jeannie said, "Chairman Hosteen Shepard welcomes everyone to the meeting; he asked that the two children be escorted over to the movie. He also welcomes our two new teachers, Mr. Sean Noland and Mr. Jimmy Beale."

"Please stand, gentlemen," Hatcher said. We got up for a moment and faced a few smiles and nods. When we sat again, Hatcher stood. "Okay. For you new folks, the Council has me run these public meetings in English under Chairman Shepard's direction, all proceedings translated into Navajo or English by Miss Whitney. Since this is a special meeting, the Chairman asked to skip the last minutes until the next regular meeting." He waited for Jeannie to interpret.

"Okay," Hatcher said, "Samson Shepard has a concern he wishes to express. Oh, also Larson Charley." While Jeannie spoke in Navajo, everyone turned to the two men at the end of the other table.

"We want to make a complaint about Leonard Santos." Samson's words were low but clear. He turned to the much younger man, Larson, who nodded in agreement while Jeannie interpreted again. Both men glanced at the missionaries, who smiled in return.

"If this is a personal complaint," Hatcher said, "it is out of order at a Council meeting. It must be something that relates to his work."

As Jeannie finished, Samson nodded and Larson Charley quietly said, "*Aoó.*"

Hosteen said a blunt word in Navajo to his brother.

Samson looked down at the table. "Leonard Santos doesn't act right. He—"

"Okay," Hatcher said, "this sounds personal and should have started in my office."

"Mr. Hatcher," Leonard said from the desk next to me, "I don't want this to fester and become a big hassle. I've done nothing wrong, so please let them finish."

After Jeannie caught up in Navajo, we all looked at Samson again.

"He acts that funny way and touches the boys," he said, just audibly, staring at his hands. Jeannie interpreted over some mumbling in the audience as Mona made a smug grin. With their naïve-looking smiles, the missionaries seemed unfazed by the allegation.

His voice calm, Hosteen spoke solemnly in Navajo to Samson and Larson before Jeannie interpreted again. "Are you both saying that your boys reported this to you?"

Before she finished, Samson nodded and Larson again said, "*Aoó.*"

Hosteen responded and Jeannie immediately asked, "Which boys?"

"Peter Shepard and Larson Charley Junior," Samson said.

"What grades?" Hatcher asked; Jeannie didn't bother with Navajo.

"They're my students," Mona spoke out confidently, her drawl not as obvious as usual. "I've seen Mr. Santos acting in an unprofessional and personal manner with both boys."

Before Jeannie could finish interpreting, Felicita's face turned cross. She looked to the ceiling before letting out the first string of angry words I had heard in Navajo by an adult—in rising and falling nasal vowels with emphatic glottal stops to the consonants.

When Felicita stopped, Jeannie said, "Um—let's see if I can get this right. Mrs. Etcitty said that the accusations against Mr. Santos are, um, false. She said she knows better than anybody that when Mr. Santos touches the children—boys or girls—it isn't very often and it's always in . . . a fatherly way." Jeannie cleared her throat. "Then she said 'always' again."

"That's right," Felicita said, glancing furiously at Mona. Jon Begay nodded in agreement. This whole thing was going to come down to Hosteen.

Mona sneered at Felicita and Jon. "Say what y'all want, I know what I've seen with my own eyes from that . . . man."

As Jeannie finished, Abby stood slowly from the desk behind Leonard. "All right, that's it," she said, glaring at Samson and his crony. "First, I don't believe those boys complained to you of their own will. Please say that, Jeannie."

Abby waited for her, then turned to the other parents. "Have *any* of you ever heard this kind of complaint from your kids?" More interpretation followed. Carlton and some others shook their heads. The missionaries looked at the young couple, who remained silent, their body language neutral.

Abby nodded. "I didn't think so."

"That don't mean a thing." Mona's viciousness seemed to affect her grammar.

Hatcher looked at Elizabeth. "Miss Wilson, have you ever noticed anything like this?"

"Absolutely not," she said, a disgusted grimace on her face.

Hatcher turned to Jimmy and me. "And you two?"

"No, it's ridiculous," I said. Jimmy and Jeannie nodded, then she interpreted.

Abby faced Mona. "Miss Johnson," she said, a warning tone in her voice, "I don't care what your motives are for attacking Mr. Santos, but it's obvious that nobody agrees with you."

While Jeannie summed up in Navajo, Mona smugly tapped her pencil. Hosteen briefly raised an open hand to halt some low chatter in the audience, then he got up to speak solemnly with Felicita, Jon, and two nearby parents.

He said one emphatic sentence to all of us before Jeannie interpreted: "Chairman Shepard and the majority of the Council agree that Mr. Santos has done nothing wrong and does not even need to answer the accusation."

I thought Mona would speak up angrily, but she just smirked. Abby, who'd been whispering with Leonard, stood again. "I thank the Council for making the right decision, but there's still a problem." She glared once at Mona while Jeannie interpreted. Frowning, Abby continued. "The accusers, in my opinion, are trying to ruin Mr. Santos's reputation with their insinuations."

Before Jeannie finished, Mona jeered. "Nobody knows what y'all are blabbering about."

"Oh, I think they do," Abby said. "The irony of this is that I believe the Navajo people are, in general, more open-minded than whites about people who are supposedly different." She paused for Jeannie; I saw Elizabeth nodding. "So that we can put this nonsense behind us, Mister Santos is going to announce something. Something that's actually nobody's business."

Jeannie interpreted again, then Leonard spoke up in Navajo for several moments. His comments drew smiles from Elizabeth and most of the parents before he changed to English. "I think I said that right. We weren't going to announce this until Thanksgiving, but Mrs. McAdam and I plan to be married in Colorado just before Christmas."

I saw Hatcher's eyes widen, but nobody else seemed surprised except Mona, whose face flushed into a slow burn as Hosteen said something to wrap up the proceedings. Tongue-tied myself,

I was the last one near Leonard and Abby to reach across and offer congratulations.

)-)

When we were back in the dorm after lights out I had a chance to talk to Leonard privately. I came into the office with a file to put away while he was typing a report.

"After what Samson and Mona pulled," I said, "you must despise them." I opened a drawer of our new cabinet.

He rolled the page out and shut off the typewriter. "No, that'd be a waste of time and energy. Samson is becoming such a pariah around here that I almost pity him." Leonard heaved a rare sigh. "I do worry sometimes about those two boys when they go home."

"I doubt there's much you can do about that." I closed the drawer and rested my hip on the edge of the desk. "Why did Samson think he could get away with it?"

"I guess he considers himself a crusader after what happened last year. The Council had the five-six teacher transferred out of here for touching girls, but the FIC officially called it a 'voluntary transfer to a secondary opening.'"

"What?"

"There wasn't any actual proof. I told you the guy was mean, but he apparently was also a real creep."

"I shouldn't sound so surprised. I've seen it three or four times."

"Nobody stood up for the teacher, but Hosteen still investigated, then Samson took the credit when the FIC moved the guy." Leonard shook his head. "So Samson felt emboldened to try this, I guess, and he had Mona behind him."

"How will you be dealing with her?"

"After the meeting, we saw her in the hall, pushing Dot in the wheelchair. Dot stopped to congratulate us, but Mona just left her there—some tension between them, I guess. As far I'm concerned, Mona can just do what she does and live with it."

He shook his head. "Sean, something else." He fidgeted with an eraser. "I could tell that you were, um, attracted to Abby. I should've told you before that we were involved. I'm sorry."

"No need," I said, but I wanted to be truthful with my new friend. "Look, Abby's great, and I was attracted, but I'm learning that I'm not bad at being a loner. I was pretty dense for not picking up on how much you two care for each other. I'm the one who needs to apologize for embarrassing all of us at the potluck."

"That's nothing, Sean."

I relaxed, nodding my thanks. "So, will it be a big ceremony with all the trimmings?"

"No, thank God. It'll be at her dad's ranch on December twenty-first. I hope you can make it."

"Sounds like fun to me."

17

"**W**ake up!" Leonard shouted, and I thought he was yelling at me. Standing sluggishly near the stove in the middle of the hogan, I tried to get out of my parka but had to sit down when the shivering became an uncontrollable shudder.

"Leave the coat on, Sean." He aimed his flashlight at the moving blankets by the stove.

"Lennert?" Our star basketball player's face surfaced, a stocking cap over his ears. He squinted at the light in his face.

"Yeah, Hawthorne. I need your help."

He sat up, a blanket over his head. "Huh?"

"Mr. Noland's sick. We need a lot more wood."

That was the last sentence that connected for me, although I was still semi-conscious when I lay back on the hard ground. I shook for what felt like hours, vaguely aware of Leonard taking care of me.

When the shaking finally slowed to mild shivers, I became more aware of my environs. Lying on my side with a tarp under me and a scarf for a pillow, I saw blurry flames and glowing embers a few feet away. My vision sharpened on a rectangular opening at the end of a prone and rusted fifty-five-gallon drum. Partially blocked by a metal cover, the fire cast dim light and ghostly shadows that danced on the dark walls and ceiling of the windowless hogan.

I took a deep breath and realized I was in Leonard's down sleeping bag, encased in too-tight thermal underwear, my parka over me for a blanket. I felt a strange warmth in three places—both armpits and my crotch. The shivers had nearly stopped; I raised my head.

"No, Sean," Leonard said quietly, "take it easy." He leaned over me with a tin camping cup. "Drink some of this."

I raised my head before he put the small vessel to my lips. I sipped the warm plain water. "Thanks. Where's Hawthorne?"

"On the other side of the stove, drawing. Everything's fine."

"How long was I shaking?"

"About an hour." He held the cup to my lips again. "You had me worried." He lowered the cup. "You've gone through all the stages of hypothermia, probably the worst I've seen, but at least your heart's ticking."

Still dizzy, I laid my head back down. "Funny."

"No, it isn't. When your body temperature gets that low, your heart can stop."

"Oh." I was looking at Leonard sideways and couldn't bring him completely into focus. "What's under my arms and, uh, down below?"

"Warm water in plastic bags, to raise your temperature. Don't press on them, or we'll really have a mess."

A weak chill made me pull the parka to my chin. "Where did you come up with that?"

"Indian lore." He laughed, then stood up by the fire with a stick. "National Guard survival course."

"Did Hawthorne say anything?" I felt my eyes getting heavy.

"Not much. But he's glad we're here," he added in a whisper. "He could've taken off when he was gathering wood." Leonard checked his watch. "It's twelve-forty."

"How could that be?"

"We messed around on that hill for a long time." He poked the glowing coals.

I shook my head. "Sorry I've been such a pain in the ass."

"Forget it. It's starting to snow out there again, but we might take off after you sleep—if you're feeling up to it by then."

"I'll be fine."

"You're not there yet. Rest. I'll be quiet."

"Okay, thanks." Watching the fire, I pulled up the parka and went right to sleep.

Later, a clunking noise made me open my eyes in the dark, and I saw light and shadows flicker on the unfamiliar rounded ceiling. Then a whistling noise from the stovepipe and howls from a gale outside cleared my disorientation. Although we were sheltered from a storm in an old hogan, I felt warm in the indulgent way that tells you to stay right where you are.

I turned my head to see Leonard up and half-zipped into his snowsuit, stoking the fire while Marie slept on his bedroll. My clothes were hanging on an improvised rack made of branches near the dilapidated stove.

"Man, how long did I sleep?" I asked, removing the clammy water bags from my armpits.

"Not long enough," Leonard said just above a whisper. "It's only two-thirty. How do you feel?"

"Like a fool," I answered quietly, pushing off the parka and holding up the two bags. "I don't think I need these anymore." I felt around and found the other bag.

I laid all three bags on the ground thinking he would laugh, but Leonard kept fiddling with the fire. "Could've happened to anyone," he said seriously, his voice still low.

"I'm lucky you knew how to handle it."

With the fire blazing again, he came over and took the bags. "Yeah, all's well and all that, but to use another old bromide, we're not out of the woods yet—literally." He emptied the plastic bags into a small mess kit pan he was using to heat water on a flat metal plate that had long served as a stovetop on the drum. Leonard came back and sat by Marie on his bedroll.

"So Hawthorne's asleep?" I kept my voice down.

"Yeah, we're not going anywhere for a while." He looked up at the sibilant noises from the stovepipe at the center of the concave ceiling. "I'm not sure how chimney pipes were secured when they built these old hogans, maybe wire and hardened mud. Which puts us in a blizzard, seven miles from nowhere, relying on venerable Navajo know-how to keep from freezing."

I took a swig from a water bottle he left near me, and then laid my head down on the scarf and pulled up the parka again. "So we just wait it out?"

"That's right." He gave Marie some water in a plastic cup. After the dog slurped it up, Leonard dragged his tarp and blankets closer to me in the better light.

"You get any sleep, Leonard?"

"Not much, but we have time now."

"I feel pretty good. You can have your sleeping bag back."

"Keep it for now, but your clothes are dry, so I will take my long johns."

"More like sausage casing."

"Hm, you are feeling better."

"Sorry, that didn't sound very appreciative."

He got up, smiling, and brought over my clothes. I changed beneath my parka, and then he draped his long johns over the drying rack. Leonard came back to me with a hunk of cold fry bread and a piece of jerky. "It's not pecan pie, but Happy Thanksgiving," he murmured, crawling into his bedroll with a piece of bread in hand.

"Yeah, thanks, but I'm not very hungry."

"You should eat a little."

I chewed on the tough dough, then swallowed. "So they know by now in Raven Point that something's not right."

"Yes, I asked Marla to let Abby know if we didn't get back by the end of my shift—and if we were still gone at noon to have her call the Navajo police in Old Mission."

"That's a couple hours ago. Maybe they have a helicopter that flies through blizzards."

"Sure. Hawthorne woke up for a while, but all he said was he was ready to go. Before he went back to sleep I promised we'd leave as soon as the wind stops."

"Man," I said too loud, and then leaned closer to Leonard so we could hear each other easily. "He didn't say what he thinks is going on at the house?"

"No, he wouldn't talk about it."

I stared into the fire, watching the embers brighten from a gust that made it down the rickety chimney. "Leonard, I don't have a clue about these people."

He sat up against his pack. "That's probably a good way to look at it."

"Why?"

"I think most Navajo are accustomed to Belaganas who come out here and think they have the people all figured out. As a Belazana and outsider, I agree with you. I don't think outsiders ever know the Navajo people, and we don't know ourselves much better."

"That sounds pretty heavy."

"Not really. When we saw that coyote, I told you the Navajo taboo about turning back." His tone was still low and hoarse. "What's your take on that now?"

"It turned out to be right, a coincidence. Doesn't mean anything."

"Not to you." He got up to feed more sticks into the stove.

"Come on, you already called BS on that and regular religion."

He sat on his blanket. "I'm not a true believer, but I don't call BS on anybody's religion."

"Okay, good point. You said before that we look at this from a different perspective. Maybe you can tell me what you meant."

"You should get more rest."

"I will, after we talk. Just don't try to convert me to anything." I smiled at him.

"No, it's just my take on ideas from some big thinkers I admire."

"All right, go ahead."

He stood to stir the fire, got into the bedroll and began his muted narrative. "I'm a rationalist. I think our existence is part of a random infinity. That, of course, is in direct conflict with the major and minor religions, most aboriginal beliefs, and modern mystics—or how most people, including many scientists, deal with death and the unknown." Seeing a question on my face, he waited.

"Some would ask why you bother to live if you believe everything is random."

"Yes, that's exactly the question. People who believe our existence is fleeting often have difficulty living with that conclusion. One response is to desperately use up or take whatever you can for as long as you can. Then, just as tragic, a non-believer sometimes just checks out of life altogether, one way or another. We invent new ways to do that all the time."

His face was grave, staring at the orange-hot coals. "Those who take another path are sometimes called humanists or free-thinkers, labels that don't mean much to me. It's both hard and easy to describe, different for each person who sees a way forward without a god or gods." He got up, tossed wood on the fire, and sat again.

I glanced up at the rattling stovepipe. "Okay, let's hear the big finale."

"You might be disappointed," he said, the flames reflecting on his dark face.

"Well, you can't stop now."

"It's pretty simple. What I do is try to let my moral values guide me toward some purpose in life, literally in spite of the chaos and inhumanity."

"Some would say those values are a religion, or maybe faith."

"That's fine, but what's missing is divine power, as well as expecting some sort of payoff now or when it's all over."

The shadows on the ceiling reminded me of the jittering images inside the zoetrope in Abby's classroom. "Well, your point of view strikes me as . . . brave."

"It's a direction; I don't know how brave it is. One more thing. You might find this ironic. One of those big thinkers I mentioned was my grandmother. I listened to all her Navajo stories, and some of them influenced me. She taught me that there's no afterlife, that it's up to each Navajo to find balance in life by following the Beauty Way, which she defined as quality of character. So even as a non-believer I try to walk in beauty. First, by doing no harm, then by focusing on the love I feel for some people, and for animals and nature."

I looked right at him. "I see it in the way you live—it's not just talk."

He shrugged. "I lose my way sometimes, just like anybody else."

"Leonard, you told me all this because I asked you. Who else has heard it?"

"One of my sisters, a couple of friends, and Abby, maybe Beth someday. Yes, I told you because you asked, but also because I think you might be on a similar path."

I shook my head. "Some path—pushing fifty, divorced twice. I have no idea what I'm doing out here, and I love two people— my mom and Rebecca, who still resents me."

"You're fortunate to have your mom, and I bet your daughter will come around. Sean, look at your career. All those years you helped kids get into drama and writing. You told me you loved that work. As for what you're doing here, I can tell you—you care about these kids, and you'll give them respect, structure, and support as long as you're here."

I scoffed. "C'mon, Leonard."

"I mean it. You have a moral compass that guides your attitudes and your deeds. And you can spot others who've developed a similar quality of character." He nodded to where Hawthorne was still sleeping.

"Yeah, he's a great kid."

"And you don't give up on the ones who are floundering."

"I've given up on plenty of adults."

"That's easier to do, but I don't think you're quite the loner you say you are. Adults sometimes begin to find a moral perspective right before your eyes."

"You have any examples I might know about?"

"Sure—Dot. I've seen her begin to care more about a lot of things."

"I'll take your word for it." We watched the coals again for a few seconds. "I think I get what you're saying, Leonard. It's definitely something to think about."

"No easy answers." He let out a long breath. "Change of subject," he said finally. "Our talk reminded me of the meeting on Monday. Before we left, I spoke to a lawyer I know who sometimes works pro bono for Navajo chapters."

"Yeah, you mentioned you wanted to get some help. That'd be great. Do you really think he'll come on such short notice?"

"*She* owes me one. I just hope she was able to clear her calendar."

"Calling in the middle of the night, you must know her quite well."

"Yeah, but I need to call again as soon as we get back."

We heard rustling on the other side of the stove. "Lennert? Mr. Noland is still sick?"

I answered. "I'm fine now, Hawthorne."

"After the wind—we can go, Lennert?"

"Yes, but it could be a while. I'll let you know." Leonard got up to keep the fire going, and we settled in again, Marie next to my back because she'd figured out I had the best blanket.

"Leonard?" I kept my voice low.

"Yeah?"

"Thanks."

He just nodded. "Let's get some rest."

I snuggled in under the parka; the steady moans and whistles of the wind soon lulled me to sleep again.

We worry that Benny Yazzie
Is our five-one
Shooting guard,
Not that he's diabetic
And barely speaks English.

18

In the two weeks following the Council meeting, Raven Point settled into a routine unlike the first two eventful weeks. Hatcher was around less and less, Leonard and Felicita had the dorm running smoothly, and Elizabeth's Navajo classes went on as before. While Mona resumed her reclusive hostility, Dot no longer went out of her way to avoid the rest of us.

The business with Campbell was finally resolved. I was glad to have transportation again, no longer dependent on credit at the local store or the kindness of others to cash a check for me in town. Our agency meeting was not rescheduled, so I'd only been out once, to Old Mission to arrange for the windshield.

On my next Monday off, I drove Campbell to Window Rock. At first glance, the Navajo capital resembled the Commission-dominated towns of Tsosie and Old Mission on a larger scale, except that most of Window Rock's administrative buildings belonged to the tribe. I also got my first actual look at the iconic rock formation near the tribal council chambers. The natural sandstone bridge over the Window Rock portal was at once amazing and nerve-wracking, as if it might snap with the next strong gust.

The town's large grocery and variety store took care of my essential needs, including six gallons of water, leaving me with no inclination to visit Gallup for a while. I chatted with several friendly Navajos at the store and the Tribal Museum, where I learned more about Navajo history before I bought an argyle-patterned grey-and-black saddle blanket with bright orange fringe.

An amiable woman at the museum told me about the Tribal Zoo at the Navajo Fairgrounds. I visited the small drab attraction and found fewer than ten visible animals, including a coyote, a couple of snakes, a golden eagle, and a sleeping black bear with YOGI on its cage. Later, when I asked Leonard about the facility, he said that the bear had been left behind after the Navajo Fair and was likely from California or Oregon. He also told me that Hosteen and many other traditional Navajos opposed the caging of sacred animals at the zoo.

I was feeling good about my visit to Window Rock, technically "dry" like all of the Navajo, until I passed a café where several stumbling or passed-out drunks jolted me from my reverie. The incident with Randall and Carlton came to mind, but I tried to maintain perspective, recalling drunks of all races on the skid rows of L.A., Phoenix, Portland, and even Tucson.

Back at Raven Point, my most immediate goal was to get better acquainted with the kids as well as the non-certificated staff, who made up the majority of parents I'd met before Leonard took me on some home visits. Since my official supervision duties didn't amount to much, I made myself useful in the dorm by helping with homework and also reading stories for Abby's and Beth's library nights on Tuesdays and Thursdays.

Early on I did bring about one change after I noticed how much food Leonard was salvaging for his animals after meals, although he already had plenty of kibble donated from Albuquerque. "Why is so much of the kitchen food thrown away?" I asked him one day in late September after the kids finished lunch. Janet was working in the kitchen while her adult helper went for the broom to sweep the eating area.

"Janet follows the government menu, but the kids don't like some of the Belagana food—I hate to see it just thrown away." Leonard grabbed some wet towels from the kitchen counter and tossed one to me so we could help the kids who were already wiping off the farthest tables.

"How insistent is the FIC about the menu?"

"They come by once in a blue moon, eat a meal, and look at the menu, but the main thing they check is whether or not we use the food they send, especially federal commodities like cheese, peanut butter, flour, sugar, and canned goods."

I lowered my voice. "If Janet had more leeway, could she be more, um, creative?"

"I'm sure she could. What are you thinking?" We kept wiping.

"Maybe keep the menu items the kids usually like, and then use the rest of the food to make things they'll eat."

"That might also cut down on all the junk food they manage to find," he said quietly. "There's that meat loaf the kids hate; I bet Janet could make a beef-vegetable stew—with fry bread instead of rolls, but she'd be worried about getting in trouble."

"We'll just tell her the truth—the changes would be my responsibility. When a bureaucrat does visit, she can go back to the government menu for a day."

"Like bagging the water fountains." He gave me a look that might qualify as sly. "Good executive decision. You're learning the ropes." Janet's helper began sweeping at the other end of the room where the kids had finished wiping. We dropped our towels on the counter, waved at Janet, and walked toward the office.

"By the way," I said, "you were right about your daughter-to-be. Beth's been a different kid in P.E. and basketball—relatively happy, eager and listening."

Leonard smiled. "Good. Before we announced the engagement, I think she was just protective of all three of us. Beth and I bonded from the start over my animals. Her mother the rancher pretends to make fun of us; says we're too sentimental. So, can she play basketball?"

"Besides her height, she learns fast and can run. I think she'll be a leader, especially for the other new players. With Beth in the middle, maybe we'll even break the losing streak."

"Oh? I didn't take you for being quite so optimistic."

)·)

By the second week in October, we had gradually implemented the kitchen's new menu, with mixed results. Leonard reminded me that entrenched habits took time to change, which was equally good advice for basketball, where I also had some resistance for a while from Randall.

Since we only had a few players who could usually make a layup, I concentrated at first on defensive positioning, then layups. Randall was not pleased until I had him take the three boys who'd played before, plus Benny and George, to the "good basket," where he set up our main play on offense. Following the simple scheme that Randall and Carlton had used for years, Benny was to circle under the rim past Martin's or Calvin's screen to get open in one of the corners for a long shot. If they covered him, he would pass to Hawthorne in the high post.

Randall said that their "wing play" was how they'd scored most of their points the year before. "With Benny now, we'll score more, maybe twenty-five or thirty points," he told me as Hawthorne led the team in sprints. "But they need to practice the wing play a lot."

"So if we get twenty-five points, what would you normally expect from the other team?"

"Maybe forty. Old Mission, even more."

"Then to win, we'll also need to make layups off of some steals."

"Win?" He shook his head. "Not with three girls and five little boys."

"I'm going to try something, Randall. I think I can teach them to play a man-to-man defense that will frustrate the other teams."

"Nobody plays man-to-man. Even on men's team, man-to-man is like a zone."

"All the better. Next week, take the same five boys to work on the wing play in the second half of practice. I'll keep the rest to teach them man-to-man defense. On Thursday, we'll scrimmage for a while with a ref, then you tell me what you think."

"We'll have the play running good by then."

The next Monday, I went to Window Rock again and got back before basketball. I checked in with Abby, who was in charge at school when Hatcher and I were both gone.

As was now my habit before P.E. or basketball, I made sure the small cooler was full of water; the fountain had long been covered by one of Felicita's colorful bags. After sprints, layups and other drills, Randall and I split up the kids as planned, which left me with the tallest, Beth and Billy, and the fastest, Mary, plus plodding Winifred and the two shortest boys, Raymond and Simon. I paired off Mary with Beth, Billy and Winifred, and the two small boys.

After repeating what I'd already taught them about staying between your "man" and the basket, I demonstrated how to shadow an opponent at all times. Mary spoke right up. "When you bump them like that, isn't it a foul?"

"Sometimes, Mary, but the referees usually watch the kid with the ball. If you're covering him, you have to be more careful, but stay very close. The rest of the time, always get right on your man, hands up and in his face as much as you can. Okay, Beth, Simon, and Billy, when I call 'mid-court line,' you go touch it, Beth pretends to have the ball, then you all run back here and try to get open in the key, but remember, only three seconds in there. Raymond, Mary, and Winifred, you pick up your man and bother the heck out of him—or her."

They did that, then we switched and did it over and over again until both sides were frustrated by the pressure. "Good, now Mary, Winifred, and Raymond bring the actual ball in from mid-court. Winifred, take it out; Billy get right in her way." She managed to get the ball to Raymond, who tried to fling the ball over to Mary, but Simon intercepted it.

I blew the whistle. "Okay, everybody freeze there—good defense!" I saw Martin and George laughing at us from the other end. "You boys listen to Mr. Shepard," I shouted at them, then turned to my six players. "So, now Simon's team has an interception. The second you see that, Beth, you sprint toward the other basket, and Simon passes you the ball for a layup."

She looked worried. "But I don't make them very often."

"You will, eventually. Go on, Beth, but stop at mid-court. Throw it, Simon." He tried, but when the ball ended up rolling to her, two boys on the other end laughed until Hawthorne grumbled at them. "That's okay, Simon, good try. All right, now switch around; the other team brings it in. Mary, you're the layup person this time, but stop at mid-court."

For those three days, the six kids worked on their man-to-man defense during the second half of practice. On Thursday, Eddie Begay, one of the Old Ravens, was the referee for our scrimmage. At jump ball, Beth leaped slightly above Hawthorne and swatted the ball straight out of bounds. George and Benny went to the end line to take the ball out. The ref handed the ball to George, older but only slightly taller than Simon, who was right in his face. Since Mary had Benny well covered, George just stood there until Randall called a timeout to avoid the five-second violation. Randall turned to me. "You're gonna press?"

"That's right."

"Martin, Hawthorne," he called. Hawthorne sprinted down, Beth right with him. Martin limped all the way on his bad leg, Billy following. "Screen for him," Randall told Martin.

Eddie handed George the ball again. After Martin got in Beth's way, George was able to lob the ball up to Hawthorne, Beth covering him closely. Hawthorne dribbled the ball without much difficulty across the ten-second line, Beth still right on him. Expecting the defense to back off, the older boys hesitated, picking up the dribble to try the wing play, but Hawthorne was out of position. Benny circled around to the right corner, but Mary's defense had him smothered. Billy stayed with Martin, Winifred kept up with Calvin, and Simon was all over George. When Hawthorne tried to force a pass to Benny, Mary intercepted.

As taught, Mary ran the length of the court for a layup, but Hawthorne was there to block it and take the ball. "Get your man," I yelled, and my five players matched them right away with the full-court press.

When Billy practically enveloped Martin, the latter angrily pushed the much larger boy away and said, "Get off, dummy." Eddie blew the whistle, but before he could say anything, Hawthorne leaned over to Martin and spoke emphatically in Navajo to the boy, who looked away shamefully.

"Technical foul," Eddie said and escorted Billy to the free-throw line.

His first shot died three feet short of the basket. Mary spoke to him, and when Billy fired the next shot in a high arc, it ricocheted off the backboard and onto the rim before falling through the basket. "One to nothing!" Beth called out, pumping a fist and directing Billy back to Martin. "Get your man, everybody!"

After a few minutes against the press, Hawthorne asserted himself and swished a left-handed jump shot through Beth's flailing arms. The scrimmage was more than half over by the time Hawthorne made two free throws and another jump shot. Nobody scored over the next couple of minutes until Raymond stole the ball and passed to Mary, who ran by the panting opposition to make the layup.

"Way to go!" I yelled, also pleased with Raymond, who had subbed for Simon halfway through the scrimmage. Randall, who'd shown no favoritism for his small nephew, betrayed a hint of a grin after Raymond's steal and pass.

Benny made the last basket with a very long shot, and the final score was eight to three.

Both sides exhausted, most of the kids leaned over, hands on knees, but none of them acted openly triumphant or defeated. Randall came over to me. "Not in good enough shape," he said, which I took to mean that he was okay with the defense.

The scrimmage still on their minds the next day, the five older boys quickly picked up the full-court man-to-man defense. The Ravens first two games would be at home in the second week of November, and then the day before Thanksgiving, so we had plenty of time to get ready. The kids complained less about the constant conditioning after Randall and I started running with them. "We got to be in shape for the Old Ravens," Randall mumbled to me one day.

"Oh?" My inclusion in men's league was unexpected. Neither of us spoke more about it until mid-October, when Randall showed up at Monday practice with a black T-shirt, a white 15 screened onto the front and back. "We play the Bears in Tsosie at eight."

"Tonight?"

"You don't work, right?"

"Yeah, but don't we need to practice?"

"Just shoot around, and then win."

I found out later that Randall, one of the league's organizers, scheduled most of our away games on my days off. Leonard told me that all the kids attended the men's home games, the dorm easily covered by one aide. Besides coaching, it later became evident that I was realizing two more personal firsts. As the tallest and oldest of the Old Ravens, my job was to play center, of all things, to rebound, defend, and make an occasional layup while Randall and Carlton ran their forward-to-guard scheme. They accomplished it almost to perfection, Carlton sinking shot after shot, which led to my heady experience of playing on an undefeated team.

ꓕ-ꓕ

Halloween was a strange event in Raven Point. Dot and Mona had inculcated its celebration for years, but Elizabeth didn't make it a focus for her kids, so Jimmy wasn't about to buck that trend. According to Elizabeth, most traditional Navajos considered Halloween as some vague Belagana rite but held a modicum of cautious respect for a ritual that included witches, spirits, and evil animals. Most of the "acculturated" families, she said, were enthusiasts.

With the older kids, staff, and some parents looking on, there was a parade in the gym by the primary students, the little boys entering in orange or red mackinaws, the girls in their pink or red coats that they tossed onto the stage. The kindergartners then marched in pointy witch hats and black tissue-paper robes, while Mona's kids all filed by in skeleton costumes made of white construction paper. A carnival of sorts followed for all, including a cakewalk, musical chairs, and a basketball toss. Leonard and I added more games, using beanbags, Hula Hoops, and Frisbees.

As soon as the boarding students were in bed that night, a few costumed children of staff members came around with parents to the teachers' doors. Leonard scurried to his apartment to be home when they got there. The goblins knocked quietly, not saying "Trick-or-Treat" until they went inside, where I joined in for a moment to give out the candy bars I'd brought.

That night I asked Leonard about the coming holidays. He said that Hosteen, a U.S. Army veteran and Purple Heart recipient, would hold a school ceremony for local veterans on November 11, followed by a traditional sing at his hogan in the evening. Thanksgiving would be a popular event, the school hosting the basketball game before a community dinner. Leonard predicted that the biggest event of all would be the school's annual Christmas play, which Hosteen tolerated because most of the community enjoyed seeing their kids in the program.

)-)

On the Wednesday evening following the Veterans Day holiday, we were about to host our first basketball game against the agency's second smallest school. While both teams were changing in the dorm, I grabbed my windbreaker, went into the gym, and stopped just past the barrier. In black jeans and white blouses, our two cheerleaders waited there with Jeannie, holding homemade black and white paper pom-poms.

Most of the Raven Point kids, staff, and community were crowded onto the two stages or seated in the single row of chairs on the gym's far side. The near side had more chairs, the team benches, and a scorer's table, its front edge almost in play. Carlton ran the clock, and Leonard was in charge of the official scorebook, where Randall was writing in our line-up. Eddie Begay and another Old Raven, both in sneakers, jeans, and faded referee shirts, took some long jump shots with the game ball.

On the larger stage Dot was ensconced with her knitting well behind the Student Council concession table, where Mona and two older girls sold candy bars, chips and canned soda. Janet's coffee urn was up there filled with water along with my cooler; Jon had set up trash barrels all around. Hatcher was gone as usual, and no agency boys would be there, so I didn't uncover the water fountain. The temperature outside fell to just below freezing, but Jon had the steam on low because the crowd itself would heat up the place. A few people were already coming and going, probably for a smoke or to use the bathroom facilities in the dorm.

I waved to Randall, who left the scorer's table and joined me at the barrier. "Okay, both girls are in, like you told me," he said before we went back outside onto the boardwalk. "Can't shoot for beans, but Beth coaches them like Hawthorne," he said, as if convincing himself that Beth should be playing.

"Right, so does Mary. And you've got them all in good shape."

"Yeah. You gotta watch this coach. He could try anything."

I raised my brows, thinking he might say more, but we just walked silently to the dorm, where the Bald Rock Braves, eight boys strong, ran out in red T-shirts and shorts, but no coats. Bracing themselves against the cold, they ran past us to the gym.

Earlier, I'd met their coach in the school office; he was the other school's principal. Since I was soon to take over for Hatcher, I tried to ask the guy some FIC questions, but he just grilled me about our team. "That lefty of yours who can shoot—he must be fifteen by now," he told me.

"No, just turned thirteen. This is his last year. We do have a new five-ten center." He looked at me suspiciously and left the school hastily to join his boys.

Now the coach came out of the dorm and stopped Randall and me under a light. About my age, he was five-eight or so with receding brown hair. Coatless in slacks and a long-sleeved shirt that showed his big gut, his round pink face sweated around a confident smirk.

"Noland, I think you've been pulling my leg."

"Why would you think that?" I held a straight face.

"Your five-ten center's a girl," he said with a sneer, and then finished under his breath. "And a nigger to boot."

His abject stupidity caught me off guard, but I contained my anger. "I also forgot to tell you she can dunk and outrun all our boys." Randall and I walked on.

"I'm sure she can run—away," he called back, laughing from well behind us.

"We'll see about that," I said, and followed Randall to the door. "That tubby little shit."

"Gonna get him someday," he grumbled as we entered the dorm.

"Yeah, on the basketball floor."

In Leonard's living room, our eleven kids waited quietly in dyed black shorts and T-shirts with sewn-on white numbers. The boys stood on one side of the room, the three girls in the middle. Felicita had made sure they had on their coats.

We walked over to stand between the two groups. "All right, this is going to be fun," I said, trying to sound upbeat. "You already know our starting five, but I'll substitute with all of you, two or three at a time, so always be ready to run and get 'em—get 'em every second you're out there! If your man leaves the game, you say 'My man' when the new kid comes in. When we steal the ball, the closest one to mid-court sprints for a layup. Run the wing play on offense, and remember to screen." Most of the boys glanced at Randall, who nodded impassively.

"Circle," Hawthorne said. The girls joined the boys as their captain put out his hand. "Let's go—L-M-N-O-P-Q-R—Ravens!"

All the rest put their hands in and repeated, "L-M-N-O-P-Q-R," and then called out "Ravens!" but not very loud. They hurried out to line up at the rec room door in the warm-up order Randall had devised: first the three smallest boys, Simon, Raymond, and George—then Winifred, Billy, and Calvin followed by the five starters—Hawthorne, Benny, Martin, Beth and Mary.

"Go—give Jeannie your coats in there," Randall told them; they ran out and we walked behind. A few moments later we heard a modest cheer from the home crowd. Our team was supposed to be running a serpentine Randall had taught them. By the time he and I walked in, our kids were standing on the far court while the Braves had started layups at the "good" basket.

"Told you," Randall said through clenched teeth.

"It's okay, we're ready. Go ahead and get them moving."

Randall intentionally jogged right by their coach before starting the Ravens in a crafty layup drill he'd designed that made it look like the ball went in more often than not. Billy, Simon, Raymond, and Winifred did most of the passing, and all the starters except Beth usually made their layups. She and the second-stringers occasionally put one in followed by a big smile.

When Randall told our kids to shoot around, the boys at the other basket started free throws. Three of them were about Hawthorne's size, the rest pretty small, though they all could get the ball up to the rim. Some of their boys in line broke into laughter when they saw one of our players launch a "dying duck" that fell far short of the basket. I looked over at their bench; the coach and a boy not dressed to play were laughing at us too.

"Free throws," Randall told our kids. The starting five and Calvin lined up while the other five stayed in the lane to rebound. Hawthorne and Benny made their shots, then Martin and Mary bounced theirs off the rim. It was Beth's turn. I'd taught her that until she had more experience, the idea was never to be short, to aim for the square behind the basket. Looking determined, she shot the ball hard, but it flew over the top of the backboard.

The Braves, now shooting around, laughed again along with some tittering from the home crowd. I saw Abby smiling, but with one hand on her forehead. Beth ran back toward the line, glaring at me until Hawthorne stopped his free throw to say something to her.

After warm-ups, the starters checked in at the scorer's table and ran to their respective benches. Martin looked up at me. "They jus' wanna be mischief an' take the good basket."

"Forget it, we're used to both baskets," I told the whole team. "They're laughing at you. Does everyone know what to do about that?"

"Get 'em!" Hawthorne, Beth and Mary came back. Most of the rest nodded.

Randall spoke briefly in Navajo except for *ellemeno*, then put his hand out. We all put in our hands with his and again chanted "L-M-N-O-P-Q-R—Ravens!"—finishing louder than before.

Everyone found his or her assigned player except Beth, who lined up at center court for jump ball. She and Hawthorne exchanged signals, switching opponents without us having to tell them. Facing a boy about five-seven, Beth seemed to have grown, towering inches over him. He scowled at her, but the ref made them shake hands before tossing the ball straight up. As we'd practiced, she tapped the ball to Hawthorne, who went right in for a left-handed layup, turned around, and yelled, "Get 'em!"

With polite clapping and a couple of cheers from the crowd, our players got right after the other team, and before the coach could call a timeout, the ref made a five-second call, so it was our ball again. The kids came to the bench; the whole team gathered around as Randall told Mary to run the play—Benny to the right corner.

The kids turned to me. "As soon as they get the ball," I told them, "they might try to screen against your press. What're you gonna do?"

"Get away or call 'Switch,'" Mary said.

Hawthorne said, "L-M-N-O-P-Q-R-S—Switch!" They all repeated that and took the floor. Mary ran the play and passed out to Benny, who barely missed his shot. Most of our kids yelled, "Get 'em!" Beth directed Martin to the only boy not covered. As they tried to make a pass, Martin intercepted but fumbled it out of bounds.

"It's okay, get 'em," Hawthorne yelled to Martin, and this time the ref made a ten-second call before the Braves could get the ball to mid court. Running the wing play to the left, Mary hit Benny, who passed in to Hawthorne, but he missed a ten-footer. When our kids pressed again, the other team desperately flung a long pass that hit one of the overhead lights. Before the ref handed Mary the ball, the Braves coach called another timeout.

The five starters came over to us, all looking aggravated. "They wanna call bad names," Mary said.

"Like what?" I asked.

"They call me dwarf in Navajo, and Martin—um, like, a cripple—to make us mad."

Hawthorne glanced at Beth. "They call her *łizhinii*—the bad way—in English."

Because of Leonard's cat, I knew that *łizhinii* meant black. I looked at Beth. "They're not saying, um—"

"Yeah, they are." She turned to Hawthorne. "Don't worry about it, you guys; it just means they don't know what to do."

"She's right," I said, "but I could tell the ref."

The kids shook their heads, and Randall said, "Just play harder. Just win."

"Okay, but I'll have a little talk with that coach when I can."

After the buzzer the Ravens ran the play again, and this time Benny hit a long shot to make it 4 to 0 on the scoreboard. At the next dead ball, when I put in Calvin for Beth, George for Mary, and Billy for Martin, Randall's eyebrows went up. Hawthorne helped Billy find his man, the subs did their jobs, and the Braves were stymied again, making another turnover. The quarter went on like that, Hawthorne making a shot in the key and two free throws, so it was 8 to 0 at the buzzer.

"You guys played great," I told our kids, "but you have to keep at it with the defense. Mr. Shepard will set your offense." Randall started speaking to them in English and Navajo, then I hurried by the scorer's table to hear their coach yelling at his five boys who'd played the whole quarter. He finished as I approached, his boys panting, and drinking from water bottles.

"What do you want?" His red face was covered in sweat.

"One second, over here." I motioned away from his bench.

He followed me, grousing. "Why don't you let these kids play basketball?"

"We scored, you didn't. I have one thing to say to you. Tell your boys to stop making those slurs, or I play first string this whole quarter."

"Don't know what you're talking about."

"The hell you don't," I said, loud enough for just him to hear.

Returning to our bench, I told the starters to check back in. Beth blocked two of their best player's shots, but he forced up two others that went in. Our offense clicked as their same five boys became more exhausted, and the score at the half was 16 to 5, although Simon, Raymond and Winifred had played the last three minutes.

We met at the half in Leonard's apartment. "Any more name calling?"

Hawthorne smiled. "Coach, those boys—too tired to talk."

"Good. First string is in again for a little while."

Midway through the third quarter, we were ahead 24 to 9 when they called a timeout. We huddled with our starters, who gulped from water bottles. "Pretty good for playing on the bad basket," I said, but only Beth smiled. "All right, Benny and Haw-thorne stay in. Billy, Calvin, and George check in." Benny, always eager to keep playing, frowned this time.

After Hawthorne tipped the jump ball out of bounds, the Braves had possession, and Benny's man ran by him all the way to the other end for a layup. Then George ran the play to Haw-thorne in the post, but Benny just jogged to the wing. Haw-thorne passed the ball out to him as Benny went down on one knee. The other team intercepted and made another layup. Haw-thorne called timeout; I was already halfway over to Benny, his teammates and the refs standing around him.

"He's sick, Coach," Hawthorne said.

Damn. I'd forgotten his medical condition, playing Benny and Hawthorne every minute at full throttle. I leaned over to him. "Benny, did you eat dinner?"

He tried to stand as Felicita hurried in behind me with a hunk of chocolate she'd broken off of a candy bar. She spoke to him in Navajo; he stayed down. "Eat this, Benny," she said.

Their coach called his gawking boys over to their bench. As Benny ate the sweet, I called another timeout and faced our play-ers. "All right, you guys go over to Mr. Shepard." I turned to Fe-licita. "I'm really sorry. He's played the whole game."

"He was at dinner," she said with a frown, "but I guess he didn't eat. I'll take him back to the dorm. He'll be okay, but he shouldn't play anymore."

"Thank you, Mrs. Etcitty." I took a circuitous route back to the bench, wondering what other human element I'd ignored in my zeal to win the damn game. "All right, Raymond go in and take Benny's man. Simon go in for Hawthorne. Billy, you cover Hawthorne's man; Simon you take Billy's." Hawthorne spoke to both of them in Navajo, pointing to the other team's players as they began to leave their bench.

"What about offense?" Randall asked me.

I turned to the kids. "All right, George . . . ." After I set up the play they looked confused. "The most important thing is to keep playing defense." Randall stood back, sulking, so Hawthorne in-terpreted and again made sure everyone knew whom to cover.

Our kids brought the ball in, lost it, but covered them right away. With two minutes left in the third quarter, the Braves had scored two more baskets and Billy made a free throw, evoking the loudest cheers of the game, which he seemed to ignore. I called a timeout and put Winifred in for Calvin. By the end of the quarter, Bald Rock had only scored two more points, so it was 25 to 19.

"Great defense!" I told the kids when they came off the floor, all but Billy glaring at me. Hawthorne encouraged Raymond, while Mary and Beth glumly patted Winifred on the back. Abby was at the scorer's table, talking to Leonard, who gave me a concerned look. If the audience had been fairly quiet when we were way ahead, now they were mum. Felicita came back into the gym with Benny, who'd changed clothes. He saw the score and looked at his feet.

Yeah, yeah—I get it. "All right, everybody over here." They all gathered around, including Randall. "Okay, no more long faces. We're still ahead, and we're going to win. Billy stays in the game; Hawthorne, Martin, Beth and Mary check back in." I saw Randall's sigh of relief before he set up the offense with Martin on the wing.

The other coach finally tried his own full-court press, but Martin and Beth set screens for Hawthorne, and the Braves fouled him repeatedly. He made five out of six free throws and two baskets, then Mary added a layup, and I put in the reserves again with two minutes to go.

I thought our unexpected victory would lead to some exuberance at the final buzzer. Our players were happy but not all that excited as we walked over to shake hands with the Braves. Their coach just grumbled as he and two of his boys ignored us and hurried for the door. As for the crowd at the end of the game, there was general light applause and a shout or two. Most of them got up smiling and put on their jackets to start out into the chilly night.

19

A slobbery tongue lapped my forehead, waking me slowly from another nap that I didn't want to end. Marie whined and licked me again. "Okay, pooch." I heard no wind outside and sat up to see the outlines of Leonard and Hawthorne on their feet, eating by the dwindling fire.

"Marie and Hawthorne are ready for you and Morpheus to part company," Leonard said, probably grinning, but I couldn't tell in the dim light.

He aimed his flashlight at Hawthorne, whose face looked puzzled, maybe from the mention of "Morpheus." Already in his coat and a brown stocking cap, the boy turned to me. "Coach, we can go now?" He popped a section of orange into his mouth.

"Sure, Hawthorne." I shed the down cocoon and slipped on some dry socks that lay by my feet. "What time is it?"

"Almost four," Leonard said. "Still daylight. How do you feel?"

"I'm fine now." I pulled on my jeans and boots, then the wool sweater over my T-shirt before I stood up. There was more light by the stove, where I saw they'd used shoelaces to jury-rig dozens of sticks, crossed like five-point stars, to the bottoms of Hawthorne's boots.

Leonard zipped the top of his snowsuit, fastened his army belt, and handed me his lined windbreaker. "Start off in this again. We'll have hard going and drifts." He gave me a peeled orange. "There's a bottle of water in one pocket. Use it to stay hydrated when we stop."

"Right. Did you say it was seven miles?" I finished a section of orange.

"More or less." He was compressing his sleeping bag into its thin cover.

I began to tighten my bootlaces. "Have you checked outside?"

"Calm and pretty clear. We're completely buried on three sides—the doorway wasn't nearly as bad. For Thanksgiving, we can be thankful that hogans face the east." He chewed on fry bread as he tied the sleeping bag to his pack. Leonard handed me my flashlight then tied the parka to the top of the pack's frame.

"So how are we going to work this next leg?" I stood, putting the flashlight in my back pocket.

"Since you're doing okay, you get to break trail. I'll tramp it down with all this weight. Hawthorne goes in our tracks with his makeshift snowshoes. He should be able to keep up with your pace."

"Is that a crack about my skiing?" I ate more of the orange.

"No, but you need to find that middle ground again between working too hard and going too slow. Maybe you won't need the parka this time."

"We can go now?" Hawthorne repeated, now with a loose scarf around his neck and the wool bag hung crosswise over his shoulder. I finished my fruit as Leonard scattered the coals then inserted the last fresh batteries into his flashlight. I donned my baseball cap and scarf before he led us to the door, Hawthorne clomping along behind me. As soon as Leonard opened the door, daylight flooded in and Marie scrambled out.

We went outside to the skis, protruding from the snow by the drift-free door. The sun setting over the snow nearly blinded me as Leonard held something out. I lowered my head to see a chunk of cold charcoal that he put in my glove. He spoke in Navajo to Hawthorne, and both of them started to draw black half-moons under their eyes; I did the same.

"By the way Sean," Leonard said in his teasing tone, "you better put on extra. English teachers are known to reflect excessively."

"Ha, like physicists." I rubbed on more of the charcoal, still squinting. "Doesn't seem to help much."

"Your eyes will adjust some."

"We can go now?" Hawthorne said again.

"Yeah, we're off." I stepped onto my skis and secured them as if I'd done it a hundred times, then started for the road. After skiing a few feet, I turned to see Leonard hunch on his pack and ski off slowly, using stout sticks for poles. Behind him, Hawthorne had a bedroll cinched to his back, trying to stay on top of the snow as he made his first careful steps. He was using the other remaining ski pole and a long stick as Marie limped along next to him.

I pressed on, noticing that the worst of the drifts seemed to be around bushes or the scarce piñons that barely showed above the snow. The blizzard had left us with a washed-out blue sky, and I guessed the temperature at about twenty-five degrees. It felt almost balmy for the lack of wind or falling snow, so I didn't even pull up the scarf.

The road through the white flatlands was identifiable only by its lack of vegetation. I turned onto it and headed straight for the sunset, squinting again. After twenty feet or so, I had to slow down to ski over a massive wave of snow that had crossed and buried the road.

Slowing intermittently for the drifts, I went on for a while, and we were soon out of the piñons. The sun touched a false horizon formed by a distant flat bank of grey-and-white clouds, the kind we memorized in fifth-grade as "stratus," but I had no idea what that signified.

The glare diminished, a welcome relief for the muscles around my eyes. At a bend in the road I busted through another drift, and then turned to Leonard, who was about fifty feet back, more than I'd realized. "No more woods from here to Shepard's?" I shouted.

"And no hills, except these drifts," Leonard called back. He was standing sideways, tramping down the top of a dune for Hawthorne, who waited with Marie.

Leonard started moving again. When he was closer, I asked, "How's he doing back there?"

"Considering his equipment, he's keeping up. Maybe you can go a little slower, if it doesn't mess up your rhythm."

"Sure. I didn't think I'd ever hear that. Almost dusk, how do I know where the road is?"

"Hawthorne knows the way; we should be okay if this weather holds." He peered at the cloudbank. "For now, go west, young man—"

"Right." Reducing my pace some, I skied on, still feeling energetic until it was almost dark. I stopped and turned back. Leonard was well behind again and almost out of sight; I couldn't see Hawthorne or Marie at all. After making a careful U-turn in the deep snow, I skied back toward him in my own tracks.

"Something wrong, Sean?" Leonard called.

"I just wanted to stay in contact." I skied up to him and noticed he'd attached the flashlight to his sleeve, but it wasn't turned on.

"Okay, but you can go on; we're fine."

"All right." As Hawthorne and Marie plodded up behind Leonard, I turned around and started off again, glancing back every couple of minutes.

After another long stint of skiing and breaking through drifts, it was not only dark, but ground fog had gradually formed, ice crystals floating everywhere like very light snow. I stopped, couldn't see or hear anything, and no longer had any idea where the road was. I took my flashlight out of my back pocket, hoping it still had power. After I pushed the switch, the light wasn't real strong, but I kept it on as a guide for Leonard. I held still and listened to the silence again, remembering the predators I'd imagined before.

Leonard's beam finally materialized from the fog, waving around like a parking lot attendant's light. "Coming in," he called, and seconds later he skied up to a stop beside me and flashed his light across my face. "You're looking a little pale again, Sean."

"I'm okay." I kept my light on as a beacon for Hawthorne. "Um, I didn't tell you before," I said quietly, "that I got a little spooked when we got separated after May's."

"Easy to do out here. Let's take a short break."

I turned off my light as Hawthorne caught up with us. "Jus' only halfway," he said urgently. "Not tired."

"*We* are," Leonard said, letting his pack down slowly so it wouldn't sink in the snow.

"I'll try the pack?" Hawthorne asked as he shook powder off his improvised snowshoes.

"You've got enough to handle." Leonard opened the pack.

All of us, including Marie, had some water and fry bread. Then I tied my scarf, pulled up my flimsy hood, and put the flashlight away, leaving my hands in the windbreaker's pockets.

"Getting cold?" Leonard's hands were in his snowsuit's side pockets too.

"A little, but no shivers."

"At least the temperature isn't dropping much. We'd better get moving."

I was staring into the dark, reluctant to set off on my own again. "Um, right. You think this will turn to snow?"

"No, I'd guess ice-fog all the way to Shepard's. You did well— we're only a little way off the road. See that bush over there?" Leonard directed his lips to the left, and I realized the practicality of not removing your hand from a warm pocket in order to point at something.

"Yeah," I could barely make out the tall, round, ghostly form.

"I know the way," Hawthorne reminded us.

Leonard knelt down to lift his pack. "Let's stay right together in this soup. I'll go first; Hawthorne can call out directions."

"That way." He pointed his lips to the left of what I thought was west. Following Leonard's beam, we soon ran into more drifts, our progress still hard and slow. Hawthorne called to change our direction two or three times before we stopped. I removed the windbreaker to tie it to my waist, shuddering once for the first time since we were in the hogan.

Leonard noticed. "Starting to sweat?"

"No, but I would be if I left the windbreaker on."

"You should drink a little, Sean."

"Yeah." I reached into the coat for the bottle, then swished and took a couple swallows.

"I think you're getting the hang of it."

Before I could reply, Hawthorne said, "Maybe two miles."

"Okay, let's go." Leonard moved off into the fog with us right behind.

After what seemed like an hour of irregular skiing, Marie started whining, and I almost stumbled over the rusted frame of a car, half buried in snow. I took out my flashlight, turned it on, and aimed at Hawthorne, who was uttering low guttural words and stroking his dog to calm her. "There," he said to us, directing his lips toward what I thought was a grey silent void.

"Let's get behind the car," Leonard said, "so we can use the flashlights." Behind the derelict Chevy he put down his pack and whispered a question in Navajo to Hawthorne. The only words I picked up from the boy's long muffled answer were "Samson" three or four times, then "Ruth" and "David."

"What did he say?" I asked under my breath.

"That the doors are probably not locked," Leonard said, sotto voce. "Hawthorne thinks we should follow him to the back door and wait there."

"And then what?"

"He wants to go around and walk in the front door like it's no big deal. If there's a problem, we should be able to see or hear something from the back."

"So what's the best that can happen?"

"Hawthorne will tell him he ran away because he wanted to see Ruth, and that we caught up to him and are waiting outside. If Samson's just hung over, Hawthorne thinks he'll let us in."

"Mighty nice of him. And if he's belligerent?"

"Then we'll have a hassle of some kind, depending on how drunk he is. The good news is Samson's shotgun is busted; he only has Hawthorne's squirrel rifle."

"Long rifle shell," Hawthorne muttered as he held Marie.

"What does that mean?" I asked Leonard quietly.

He continued to whisper. "More punch than a short twenty-two shell; it can mess you up pretty good."

"Great. Well, what do you think?"

"His plan makes sense to me." Leonard took off his army belt and laid it on the pack. "If he's drunk and all of us went to the door, the surprise might set him off."

Hawthorne set his bedroll on Leonard's pack. Standing around gave me a chill, so I put the windbreaker back on over my sweater. I directed my light at Leonard, who was leaning down to remove the knife from the sheath and slip it into a narrow side pocket. He zipped up the snowsuit to his neck and took out a short leash, attaching it to Marie's collar.

"Kill your light," he told me. Still on our skis, we slid away from the dead Chevy following Hawthorne, who had Marie on the leash.

After about fifty feet, the silhouette of what looked like a government three-bedroom house appeared in the fog, a mudroom extending from the front with a steady light by its door.

"Electricity?" I whispered to Leonard.

"Yeah, telephones pretty soon."

As we moved closer, another light shone from a front window, and we saw steam or smoke billowing from a stovepipe near two aerials. A diesel engine throttled somewhere in the heavy fog.

"On Thanksgiving, out here?"

"The highway," Leonard said quietly.

Approaching the left side of the house where another outside light was on, we heard some low growling and saw two doghouses. Hawthorne made a soft smooching sound as he and Marie approached them. We caught up and saw two large chained dogs nuzzle the boy, exchange sniffs with Marie, and then settle right down.

We followed Hawthorne past a nearly new pickup with deep tire tracks in the snow behind but only an inch or so of accumulation on the cab, hood, and windshield. A beaten-down path circled the house, so Hawthorne began to untie the sticks from his feet. Leonard and I quietly removed our skis to follow Hawthorne and Marie toward the back.

After creeping past a woodpile we squatted by a large shed, watching the home's dimly lit and frosted rear windows, the screens removed for winter. All we could make out through the silent murky evening was the dark outline of a shelf indoors. After Hawthorne left us to walk around to the front, we watched a solitary tall shadow in the house move very slowly by the back windows, a rifle in his hands.

20

1-1

Hatcher informed me that he would leave Raven Point for good a week earlier than planned, the Sunday before Thanksgiving. The agency, as expected, made me acting principal up to the New Year. As if my extra assignment deserved more attention than the school's deficiencies, they offered to hire someone locally to substitute in my P.E. classes. My first thought was, *And what would I do, sit in the office all afternoon?* I suggested that we could use any excess instructional funds for a part-time classroom aide; they managed not to laugh out loud at that idea.

Jeannie told me Hatcher was having a goodbye brunch with Dot and Mona on the day he was clearing out. Before noon that

Sunday, he came by and knocked on my trailer's door for the first and last time. Wearing only a sweater against the breeze, his mass swayed my rickety porch; I invited him in out of the cold. He stepped in just far enough for a peek at my slovenly mess, then handed me his keys plus a separate ring with two padlock keys.

While Hatcher carefully backed down the steps, he said off-handedly that all I would need from the bottom drawers was the banking pouch. " . . . and ya know, Noland, you could stay in the apartment for now," he said, stepping sideways off the bottom stair.

"Thanks, I'll stay here."

"Okay, suit yourself. Good luck," he added with a smirk.

"You too," I said as he waddled away. Relieved to see him go, I was sure he had big plans to celebrate his long-awaited deliverance from the Navajo.

Enjoying my second coffee of the day minutes later, I watched Mona drive off, Hatcher just behind in a government pickup to the very end. Wondering how that vehicle would get back to Raven Point, I grabbed my jacket to go out into the inch or so of snow, which had fallen just three weeks after Jon and Eddie screwed the trailer skirting back in place.

In boots, a wool sweater under my jacket, I hurried across the road and hopped over the frozen tire tracks near the office, ready to find the water report for Leonard and see what other FIC secrets were waiting in that file cabinet.

Like any Sunday, the school was creepily quiet when I entered, then from down the hallway I heard a faint recording of chants and drums—Elizabeth in her classroom. I opened the office, plopped a notebook and my Michener novel on the principal's desk, and approached the second cabinet. After I released its lock with the regular small key, I took out the extra ring Hatcher had given me.

I opened the padlock and extracted the chain from the cabinet's frame. I opened the first of the two bottom drawers and found it about a third full—the personnel section, including applications, evaluations, and such. I started to close it but thought *What the hell*, and opened a new folder with my name freshly typed by Jeannie.

Extracting the only paper, headed OBSERVATION, I recalled that Hatcher had visited me in the gym once for five minutes of P.E. In every category but one, he checked ABOVE AVERAGE with just one comment: *Conscientious with teaching and counseling duties.* He graded me AVERAGE in STAFF RELATIONSHIPS and wrote: *Becoming a better team player.* I knew that was as negative as he could be without checking the dreaded NEEDS IMPROVEMENT, which would have required paperwork he wasn't willing to do.

I put the folder back and pushed in the drawer. "Good riddance," I said, sliding out the bottom drawer, where I found coin-roll papers, a bank pouch, and about a dozen ordinary manila folders, their labels hand printed, not typed by Jeannie. Behind two banking folders, most of the other files had something to do with the facility: blueprints, electricity, inventory, generators, maps, plumbing, septic, and so on. I saw that the last file was labeled WATER TESTING. *Okay, Mr. Hatcher, here we go.*

After pulling it out along with the plumbing file, I found the water reports, dated in May of each of the last two years. Skipping the detailed charts and graphs, I began to read some of the written content of the latest report.

> . . . samples taken: west water fountain in dormitory, tap in cafeteria, dormitory apartment "A" sink, school fountain by staff room, fountain in 3/4 classroom, kitchen sinks in school apartment #1 and in trailers 1 through 4.

And not the gym? I skipped ahead.

> . . . the shock chlorination and added filtration

to the water system has moderately reduced the relatively high levels of iron, thus remaining below recommended limits. The other hard metals, including traces of uranium, all continue to test below the standards.

Uranium? Trying to remain calm, I read more of the report, but between the technical jargon and bureaucratic obfuscation, I didn't learn much more until near the end.

> . . . as previously determined, the iron levels originate from both the natural ground water as well as apparent corrosion in the original galvanized water pipes. Although a continuing nuisance, the iron levels do not constitute a health hazard.
>
> Recommended long-term solution: Replacement of all the original pipes and plumbing, although a cost analysis still might indicate replacement of the facility.
>
> Recommended continued actions: At drinking and cooking locations, continue to run all taps and spigots wide open with cold water for one full minute after not being used for six hours or more. Warm or hot tap water could have higher hard metal levels. As initially recommended, run the cold water before heating it on a stove for cooking.

Then I skimmed the first report. From what I could tell, it was nearly the same as the new one, where they had just inserted "continue," "still," and "as before" in the appropriate places. Some of the numbers in the latest charts were a bit higher or lower, but their significance was lost on me. I checked some older material and also the plumbing file, which had the original technical information and some repair documents. None of it seemed very alarming, except for the mention of uranium. Nevertheless, I wanted Leonard to see the records right away.

The two files in hand, I left the office in my jacket and heard music from Dot and Mona's apartment. I'd started for the door when my peripheral vision picked up a slight person exiting the staff room—Elizabeth. She'd been doing some sort of art project, her old jeans and too-large flannel shirt splattered with paint.

"Hi, Elizabeth. How're you doing?"

"Fine, Sean. Figuring out all the paperwork?"

"Yes, can I ask you a question?" She nodded, her brows raised. "Last fall, how serious was Hatcher with you about running the drinking water?"

"He just told us to do it, but it wasn't really big news. I know Leonard and Abby are worried about it, but it's just iron—tastes bad and ruins your whites." She pointed at the nearby dark-orange fountain. "It would look even worse if Jon hadn't found some industrial cleaner. Even Mona runs the water, since that's official policy," she said with mild disgust.

"So Jon attaches the wires to the hall fountains on school mornings?"

"No, usually Abby. If she's gone, I do it."

"So the fountains are running out here, and in class everyone drinks from the coolers."

"Except in Mona's room, because the coolers are not policy."

"But even Hatcher didn't drink the water."

"Mona drinks pop." Elizabeth turned to go but then stopped. "You look concerned."

"Not sure." I held up the files. "I just found the latest Commission report on our water. I'm going to have Leonard take a look at it."

"Can't hurt, I guess. See you later."

"Yeah," I said as she walked away. I left for the dorm, where two missionary vans were driving off with more than a dozen kids whose parents had signed them up for Sunday services.

I found Leonard, Felicita, and Janet involved in board games with some of the remaining kids. Others were reading, drawing, or playing Foosball and ping-pong. Leonard was in a chess match against Beth and Mary, while Winifred and Calvin studiously watched the moves. The twins often visited on weekends; it occurred to me that those two very bright kids likely had minimal exposure to our drinking water.

Leonard looked up from the game. "Mr. Noland, your days off—thought you might be going into town."

"No, I need a minute to talk to you."

"Check!" his opponents called out simultaneously after Mary let go of the queen.

Leonard good-naturedly raised a warning finger. "Girls, I don't think you want to do that. All of you look it over while I talk to Mr. Noland."

The four kids huddled to quibble over the queen's placement. We walked into the office and I closed the door. "Hatcher finally left the padlock key on his way out." I held up the two folders. "The recommendations are close to what he told you, but he left out that they said the pipes or the school should eventually be replaced." I handed over the files; he opened one eagerly as I continued. "It said the other metals were okay, but you can check the numbers. Something did jump out at me—it mentions a trace of uranium."

"Pitchblende is common out here," he said, focused on his reading, "but if it's really just a trace of uranium, that's not a problem."

Before Leonard could read much more, Beth knocked on the door's glass upper half. "We've got you now," she called out confidently.

He nodded to her, then turned to me. "You play chess?"

"I know the basics." I went out to take his place, turning back to see him poring over the files. After the kids took me to a stalemate in ten minutes, I had them start a match before I went back in to Leonard and closed the door. He was slouched solemnly over the reports, tapping his head with a folder.

"That bad?" I said.

He looked up. "Worse than I could've imagined."

"The uranium?"

"No, infinitesimal. It's lead all right; they fudged it." Both his drawn face and a sigh showed Leonard's growing frustration. "They used an average of all the sites tested. Not even half the drinking fountains were included in the samples, but they used all four trailers, which have less iron and no lead at all."

"How could that be?"

"The trailers have some natural iron, but as junky as they are, they do have PVC pipes—you saw them in the summer. In here and the school, the old galvanized pipes are corroding."

"I still don't get it. There's lead in the galvanized pipes?"

"There is now. The plumbing file you brought says all the original pipe fittings were soldered with lead, which eventually breaks down if the water is corrosive. The drinking fountains are the worst—I'd guess because the water moves so slowly there. When they tested them prior to flushing, the lead levels were the same as what I found, almost ten times what they call the 'action level,' and still more than triple after they ran the water. The four trailers brought down the compound's overall average of lead just far enough."

"Jesus, why would they fudge it like that?"

"Financial priorities? Who knows?" He shrugged. "Raven Point is expendable compared to some fancy new high school on the highway that the FIC can show off to a congressman."

"Man." I was shaking my head. "At least you've cut the intake way down since last fall, but before that, the kids were—"

"Yeah, drinking it every day, but we don't know how long it's been this bad. There's no real data prior to last year. My guess is the solder has been breaking down for several years." He put both hands to his temples, his face contorted. "The larger issue is that lead contamination in the body is cumulative and the effects are irreversible, which means 'action level' is meaningless. I'm convinced that someday the lead standard will be close to zero."

"It should be zero now." I mulled over what he'd told me, then pointed at the office phone. "Is that thing working today?"

"I think so—why?"

"Hatcher was going along with somebody higher up. I just want to hear it from the horse's mouth."

"You're going to call the emergency number?"

"Damn right." I made the call, got no answer, and then tried a second time; somebody picked up right away.

"Jennings—this better be good." The assistant superintendent's voice was brusque.

"Mr. Jennings, this is Sean Noland, acting principal at Raven Point."

"Yeah, lucky you. It's Sunday morning, what the hell's wrong?"

"I just read the water reports for the facility here. The lead levels in the drinking fountains are way above the standards."

"For God's sake, didn't Hatcher tell the staff there to run the water before you use it?"

"Yes, but that doesn't take care of it."

"If you read the whole report, you'll see that the average for the compound is below the standard limits."

"Yes, I read that."

"Then what's the problem?"

"I told you, the lead in the drinking fountains is way too high."

"Did you listen to what I just said?"

I lowered the receiver and covered it with my hand. "Jerk."

Leonard whispered, "Don't rile him, Sean." I put the phone back to my ear.

"Noland, you still there, damn it?"

"I'm here. I just wanted to be sure I understood the situation."

"Is that right? Well, sometime in the next few years we're going to demolish that old school, so you'll just have to make do for now."

"What? How can you—" He'd hung up. "What a prick."

"You're on their list now. I have to shut them all off." Leonard looked out at the kids playing chess.

"*We* have to shut them off."

"Okay, but the agency will go after you more than me. You're probationary; I have five years and a little extra protection—they don't like to aggravate an enrolled Navajo who could eventually go to the tribe."

"So what do we do first?"

"The school. Most of the kids know the drill from the dorm, but some, especially younger ones, don't remember. We can't watch them in the hall all the time, although Abby tries. Then there's Mona, who lets them drink from her fountain. I should've just covered them all from the start."

"Hatcher wouldn't have let you go that far; you did what you could. Can the pipes be shut off?"

Leonard explained that the classroom sinks had shut-off valves, but the teachers needed water for projects. "Jon would know how to cut off the hall fountains under the school, but it's not fair to ask him to do something unusual that the agency hasn't approved."

"So, we cover all the fountains with pillow cases and strapping tape?"

"I guess, and we'll need good water for the hall."

"Do we have enough supply for both the school and the dorm?"

"For now. I was going to stock up at Thanksgiving. The place in Gallup where I get the water has five-gallon bottles and metal stands. I doubt they'd rent them for out here, but they do sell them."

"All right, since I'm off duty, I'll go into Gallup tonight and buy water and stands when they open in the morning. How many you think we'll need?"

"At least two for the school hallway plus one for the gym so we don't have to keep moving the coffee pot over there for basketball games. Another one for between the dorms would be much better than that little cooler we're using."

"I'll get five to be sure, and as much water as my truck can carry—might take two trips."

"Most of the staff will chip in on the cost once they hear the facts. Except Mona, of course. She'll have a fit."

"She took off today ahead of Hatcher."

"Good. She'll probably be shopping until late afternoon. Felicita and Marla will help me with the fountains before Mona gets back, and I have a small cooler for her room."

"Dot's still here; I'll explain it to her, and then try to reason with Mona later."

"Won't matter what you say, she'll blab tomorrow to Old Mission as soon as they open. One good thing is the short week. The agency office is probably half-deserted already. While you're gone, I'll tell the rest of the staff and Hosteen what's going on."

I took a key off my ring to hand to him. "That gets you into the rooms and also Fort Knox, in case you need anything. I'll see what Dot has to say."

On the way back to the school, I didn't pay much attention to a few fluttering snowflakes.

Once inside, I knocked on the apartment door. Seconds later I heard Dot call, "Isn't locked." I pulled the door open; she was waiting right there in her wheelchair, a large yellow afghan around her shoulders and over her lap. "Sorry, she'd kill me if I ask you in."

"It's okay, Dot. I need to explain something that's going on with the water."

"Oh that. I don't even use the nasty stuff. Mona thinks my camping shower is silly."

"Then she's laughing at what's probably a good idea; the water is even worse than what you were told." She listened attentively as I explained the situation and what we planned to do about it. " . . . and that includes Mona's classroom fountain."

She moved her large head back and forth, lips pursing. "So you're saying the kids been drinking like slow poison for years?"

"That's what it looks like."

"I won't tell Mona nothing when she radios, but I'll have to explain later. She'll flip after seeing the fountains. I'll tell her what you said, but she won't believe it with Leonard involved."

"Yeah. When do you expect her?"

"She's at her Holy Roller meeting, then shopping. I saw snow-flakes out my window—she won't drive if it sticks, especially after dark."

Good. "I'll let Jeannie know she might be subbing."

Dot was frowning. "This could be the last straw."

"What do you mean?"

"We been bickering a lot. I ain't gonna back her on this."

"Thanks, Dot." I left, hoping to find more snow falling, but the flakes were no longer flitting around.

Back in the dorm, I asked Leonard to tell Jeannie and Abby that their duties might have to be adjusted and to let Randall know to run basketball practice. I thanked Janet for an unexpected bagged lunch she made for me, then left to get a few things at the trailer.

It remained cloudy all the way to Window Rock, where the snow began to fall lightly. I hoped it was enough to keep Mona from returning to Raven Point for a while. Just after dark, I drove into the same run-down Gallup motel where I'd stayed in August. I checked in, glad to find a couple inches of accumulation in the parking lot.

When the businesses opened in the morning, another inch of snow had fallen, and it took me longer than expected to find, pay for, and load two-thirds of my order—three of the five water stands, eight five-gallon bottles, and two large cases of cups to ride up front with me. All that weight gave me better traction on the slick highway, and I made it back by late afternoon.

By the time Leonard, Abby, Elizabeth, and I set up the water in the hall, Mona had not made it back. Furious about the whole lead situation, Elizabeth and Abby told me they would "handle" Mona when she did show up.

I didn't sleep well that night and didn't get out of Raven Point until after ten on Tuesday morning. I returned to Gallup for the rest of the order and drove back more cautiously—the road was icier and Campbell carried less weight. It was dusk when I came to Old Mission, and I worried that those last four bottles might freeze. Not enough snow had fallen on the Raven Point road to smooth out the rough spots, so it was well after dark when I drove in. Mona had yet to brave the roads, and we set up the rest of our drinking "system" in the dorm and gym.

)·|

After another less-than-restful night I got up before ten on Wednesday morning, a few hours before our second basketball game and the big Thanksgiving dinner. I'd decided before our water fiasco that going to Tucson for the four-day holiday was too much hassle, so I called my mom to put off my visit until after Abby and Leonard's wedding. I scheduled myself in the dorm for Thursday night's graveyard shift, which freed Leonard to take Abby and Beth with him to his sister's in Albuquerque on Thanksgiving morning.

I left the trailer wearing my parka and walked carefully over the two inches or so of hardened snow to the school. Between the Demon Rum sermons on Old Mission's weak AM station, the predictions were that we'd have lower temperatures followed by more snow in a day or two.

Inside the school, the cool and empty hallway hummed from all the activity in the steam-heated classrooms, the kids excited about the game, holiday activities, and a few days off. I entered the warm office and closed the door, leaving it unlocked. The water reports were on the desk; I finally had time to read them more carefully.

Next, I put the file down and saw that Jeannie had handled the mail before she went to Mona's class. She'd also left Jon's purchase order for janitorial supplies on the desk. I signed that, put it in the mail, and decided to check the water stands while I waited for our guests from Old Mission, scheduled to arrive around eleven-thirty for the game at one. They were always the best team in the agency and also had a girls' team plus a JV team of fifth-grade boys. I'd spoken briefly with their new coach, who sounded young and friendly, a relief after the Bald Rock jerk.

The door rattled, and Jeannie entered in traditional attire—velveteen blouse, squash-blossom necklace and all. Elizabeth had asked the Navajo staff to dress up in honor of Thanksgiving. I was in my usual black jeans and open-collared dress shirt, plus a round pendant with a raven symbol crafted in tiny black beads over a white background, a gift from Felicita. When I complimented her craftwork, she told me she'd made it from Hawthorne's design.

"Good morning," Jeannie said with the usual pleasant and dimpled smile on her round face. "Oh, your new necklace looks just right."

"Thanks. Go Ravens."

She chuckled. "Did you find the purchase order I left for you, Mister Noland?"

I had given up on getting Jeannie and some others to call me Sean. "I did, Jeannie; it's already in the mail."

"My class went to Miss Wilson, but I came to tell you that Miss Mona finally got in a while ago. I heard her in the apartment on their radio."

"Well, I guess we know what she's doing."

"Yes, after she saw the fountains, she went right to Miss Dot. We could hear her start yelling, but Miss Dot wouldn't argue with her in front of the kids."

"Good for her."

She breathed an uncharacteristic sigh. "I think you and Mr. Santos are doing the right thing. Some people are mad at the agency, but most are just worried about what it all means for the kids."

"I don't blame them. I want to have a meeting about the water right after the holiday."

"Tell me what I can do to help. Which day?"

"Not sure. Leonard's asleep for night shift. I'll talk to him after he gets up for the game."

"Miss Mona's about to take her class back. Is there anything you need me to do now?"

"Just tell Mona that I'm here if she wants to talk. I'm not going to look for her."

"I don't think she'll come." Jeannie's frown showed a touch of anger before her face softened into a smile. "The girls are so excited about the game—players and cheerleaders."

I smiled back. "We'll try hard and have a good time."

"Okay, I'll be in the kitchen helping the big kids decorate."

I thanked her as she left, then straightened a few papers. I was about to leave when the phone on the desk rang. "Raven Point Boarding School."

"Noland?"

"Yes—speaking?"

"Jennings."

That didn't take long. "Yeah, hi."

"Look, Noland, I told you to let all that go with the water."

"No, I think you told me to 'make do.' That's exactly what we're doing."

"What you're doing is asking for trouble—you and that fairy Mex."

Asshole. "Oh, you mean the enrolled Navajo I work with?"

"Don't be a wise-ass. The superintendent and I will be there Monday at about three."

"I have basketball practice then. Could you come later?"

"Jesus. No, we can't come later. Just be in your office at three."

"And a Happy Thanksgiving to you."

"That attitude isn't gonna help, Noland."

"See you Monday." This time I hung up on him. "Shit," I said to the water report on the desk. I went out into the hall and checked on the water stand beside a covered fountain. Jon had set out an extra trashcan by the small table and its stacks of tiny paper cups. I filled one and took a drink of water that was as cool as the hallway. Looking at the same set-up at the other end of the school, I tossed the cup away as a large bubble gurgled to the top of the nearly full bottle.

I headed for the dorm hoping Leonard was awake so I could tell him about the call from Jennings. Before I got there, a grey panel truck like ours and a long van pulled up to the school. The Old Mission group was at least an hour early; I hurried back to greet them.

Five cheerleaders and a Navajo woman—their driver and chaperone, I assumed—climbed down from the panel in nice coats. Then at least ten near-adolescent boys, also in good winter coats, jumped down from the van. Two men got out, the first one about my age in a cowboy hat, leather jacket, and jeans; he said a few words to the boys in Navajo. I shook his hand and said my name.

He nodded, and then the second man came forward in a red ski coat, heavily padded. The young coach, about six-two with a thin dark-brown face and short natural hair, extended his hand. "Mr. Noland, I'm Hank Boston," he said amiably as we finished a firm but friendly handshake. "Sorry we're early—worried about more snow on the way."

"Not a problem, but we were hoping you could stay on for Thanksgiving dinner."

"I appreciate it, but we should just play and go."

"You don't want to camp here for the whole weekend?" I said with a grin.

"Yeah, you've got the idea."

"Tell you what, we'll get the word out in town and try to start the game early, around twelve or a little after."

"That would sure ease the pressure. Thanks, Mr. Noland."

"It's Sean." Walking behind their well-mannered entourage, we headed for the dorm, where they were to have a light brunch with our kids and a rest before the game. I reviewed the plan with Boston, then asked how he liked Old Mission.

"Still getting the hang of things," he said, and then explained that he was a beginning teacher from Phoenix. The Commission gave him his one and only teaching offer—junior high science plus coaching elementary-school basketball for the Old Mission Wolf Cubs.

"Here comes Mrs. Etcitty. She'll get you all settled in at the dorm."

"Okay, thanks again."

I asked Felicita if Janet's stew was cooked; she said the meal was ready except for the fry bread. She took over with our visitors and I went back to the school. Jeannie was still around and helped me make radio and phone contacts to spread the word that the game would start early.

Before the game, the gym filled up as before, except that people had lined up to try out the new water stand. Dot was running concessions on the stage, her aide helping out. Randall arrived near the end of layups, when Leonard also hurried in to mind the scorebook. I went over to Randall, thanked him for handling practice, and we conferred about the game. After that, Coach Boston and I met on the floor to shake hands and watch the kids finish the shoot-around.

Boston noticed my pendant. "I like your necklace."

"Yeah, team spirit and all that." We watched Hawthorne sink a jump shot. "Number 11 there designed it."

"Really? He sure knows what he's doing with that ball, and that young lady is the tallest kid I've seen out here. Are her parents on staff?"

"Her mom. She'll be some player after she gets a little experience."

"Our principal said we could bring our fifth-graders, but I heard about Bald Rock."

"Yeah, we surprised them a little. Did everything go okay at lunch? I was making calls."

"Real tasty, but not so light." He patted his stomach. "Trying to weigh us down, coach?"

"C'mon," I said with a chuckle, "our kids had the same."

"I heard you're new out here, too. What's the deal with your water?"

I told him we had some contamination but left it at that. "Okay, good luck, coach," I said as we shook hands again. "Don't run it up on us now."

"We'll try to win it, but not like that. When you come to Old Mission we'll see if we can match your hospitality. Good luck to you."

During the game we heard no derisive laughter nor any slurs from our opponents, and we definitely bothered them right away with the enthusiasm of our full-court press. Coach Boston, with the equivalent of five Hawthornes playing for him, decided to let his talented team deal with the pressure for a while without making any adjustments from the bench. Boston seemed surprised when I put in three kids from our second team, who ran the press energetically along with Hawthorne and Benny. The coach called timeout after the next dead ball and replaced three of his starters as well, but they still led at the end of the quarter, 11 to 6.

When Boston saw that our top five would begin the second quarter, he sent his starters back out. Old Mission ran a well-practiced press-breaker this time, made it into frontcourt and set screens against our defense, and soon began to take control of the game. Down 19 to 12 at half time, Hawthorne reminded his teammates during our meeting that Old Mission had been ahead by twenty-five at the half when they last played the Cubs.

The kids went out and played hard for the rest of the game and everybody got to play for both teams. Although the Ravens lost by fifteen points, they held the Cubs to their lowest total in years. Mary made a lot of steals, Beth grabbed nine rebounds, Hawthorne was perfect at the free-throw line, and tiny Raymond Shepard made a ten-foot shot that brought applause from the crowd and a smile from Carlton at the scorer's table. After his spirited defense, Billy seemed shyly pleased by congratulations from his teammates.

It wasn't snowing after the game, but the Old Mission contingent left right away for home. Thanksgiving dinner was supposed to begin at four, so Leonard started showing the first reel of *The Time Machine* to the kids and others in the boys' dorm, while Eddie and the student clean-up committee stacked chairs and straightened the gym with me.

We entered the festive rec room, draped with orange and brown streamers, each table covered with yellow butcher paper plus handmade cardstock turkeys, pilgrims, and Indians. Some kids, staff, and I helped Janet finish setting up the meal before we called for Leonard to stop the movie. Everyone came in for the feast, which included turkey provided by the teachers and classic fare that came mostly from a government can: ham, sweet potatoes, corn, cranberry sauce, and pumpkin pie.

The staff, except Mona, and a good turnout from the community enjoyed the heavy meal before some parents and children left, while the rest stayed on for the movie, which Leonard rewound for latecomers. Some other staff helped Janet while I signed out more kids to go home. It looked like nearly half of our charges would remain with us for the long weekend.

After things slowed down, I went to the boys' side, where they'd pushed the bunks to the walls and brought in folding chairs. Marla was minding both the projector and the kids; only a few adults remained. She told me Leonard was packing for his trip in the morning. I sat down in the warm room to watch Rod Taylor—for my third or fourth time—escape to the future in his Rube Goldberg contraption, while in the store window across the street from the time traveler a mannequin's frocks changed with the passing generations.

I felt a tap on my shoulder. "Mr. Noland."

"What? Oh, Leonard—is everything okay? Just resting my eyes." Some kids sitting nearby giggled.

"It's all handled here. You should go home and get some sleep."

"Uh, right, but I have a couple things to talk to you about." I got up, stretched, and walked with him to the door, yawning. "Jennings and Thurmond are coming on Monday."

"No big surprise there. What time?"

"Three. I think we should have a community meeting."

"Yes, absolutely."

"When do you want do it?"

"Let's think about it. We can start working on it Friday evening when I get back."

"Good. How early are you leaving for town?"

"Right after graveyard; Abby's driving."

"I could cover so you could go sooner."

"No, Sean, it's all set. Go home."

I wanted to tell him about the insults from Jennings but decided it could wait. I yawned again. "All right, you guys have a good trip."

"We will. See you Friday, Sean."

When I put on my parka and walked out into the brisk breeze and freezing temperatures, I felt more alert, but after I climbed the steps to the trailer and undressed, I settled right to sleep in my bed's cozy blankets. A few hours later, very early on Thanksgiving morning, the buzzer went off for some apparent problem in the dorm. I had no idea that my greatest challenges at Raven Point lie ahead.

Reformers forget
That Navajo drunks
Have crapulent cronies
On corners
Of Christian communities.

21

After a Thanksgiving that began for me around two a.m. in cold pursuit of Billy and Hawthorne by truck, on foot, and outmoded cross-country skis, it was after six that evening when Leonard and I listened to Hawthorne knock on the mudroom door on the other side of his house. A stretching spring creaked before he called out, "It's me!"

I expected some sort of hubbub after he went in, but all was quiet. A few moments later we watched through the windows as Hawthorne's silhouette gradually met the other one. The taller shadow turned the rifle sideways, handing it over to Hawthorne.

"It's okay," Leonard said. "Let's go." He took Marie into the shed and settled her in with some straw before latching the door. I followed him around to the front of the house.

The mudroom door's loud spring announced our arrival. The inner door opened and Hawthorne stood there, the simple bolt-action rifle cradled casually in his right arm, pointed down. "It's bad." he said, shaking his head.

Leonard spoke softly. "What happened?"

"Don't know." The boy added several hoarse words in Navajo.

"His aunt and sister are hurt," Leonard said as we entered the house, enveloped by the incongruous homey smell of baking pastry. We unzipped our outer layers right away in the stifling house. At first look, the living room seemed like the stage for *Father Knows Best*: burning logs in a partially open Franklin stove, a used but well-preserved set of colonial-style furniture, and a framed pastoral print on the wall, all lit by a table lamp with an ornate ruffled shade.

We stepped farther into the living room on the varnished wood floor. Instead of Robert Young smiling over this weirdly idyllic scene, Samson Shepard was passed out and snoring in a recliner, every inch of him the crapulent buccaneer Abby had once alluded to. The eyepatch almost on his nose, Samson's usually neat trousers and long-sleeved dress shirt were rumpled, and his limp hair fell over some dried mud on one cheek.

Next to a polished wooden coffee table with a three-fourths empty bottle of whiskey on top, Samson's chair faced a twenty-one-inch TV telecasting a fuzzy silent shot of the Chicago Bears going into a huddle. Samson's body was haphazardly tied several times around with clothesline to the recliner, like a pirate about to be keelhauled.

David, sitting up in an old plush chair, had apparently done the deed. The husky young man, wearing a thin blue bandana as a headband, just glared at his father and ignored the three of us standing there.

In a dining alcove near a wide portal to the kitchen, a print tablecloth with fall leaves covered a long rectangular table. Their doomed Thanksgiving dinner had progressed as far as napkins and eating utensils placed neatly before four of eight sturdy old wooden chairs.

Hawthorne said, "Over there," and led Leonard and me to the most distant of three interior doors. He leaned the rifle on the wall before he opened the door. Leonard and I followed him past a half-bathroom, and then Hawthorne flicked on a table lamp between the two beds that took up most of the small room.

Two people seemed to have been placed carefully in the larger bed, a few feet apart under barely disturbed covers. The raven-haired teenage girl on one side had a dark purplish lump on her forehead and a blackening left eye over a swollen bruised cheek. Short breaths escaped her lips, and she twitched now and then.

Next to her, a grey-haired elderly woman lay still, eyes closed—no sign of breathing at all. Leonard immediately checked her neck for a pulse. "Damn," he said, pulling back the blanket. He held her wrist for a few seconds, then laid his ear against her velveteen blouse. He straightened up moments later, sighed, and shook his head.

"Jesus," I said.

Hawthorne waited stoically near a chest of drawers, but tears welled in his eyes. Leonard moved around to the girl and checked above the knot on her forehead for fever; she only stirred slightly. "We need to ice her injuries," he whispered to us, "but I think she'll be okay."

Hawthorne wiped his face with a sleeve and switched off the lamp, then Leonard led us out to the living room, where acrid molecules of charred pastry drifted in from the kitchen. David was holding the squirrel rifle toward his semi-comatose father. Hawthorne walked over to his older brother, looked at him without speaking, and gently took the rifle again.

"Better get that oven, Hawthorne," Leonard said, "and find some ice in there or outside, whichever's quickest." Hawthorne crossed the living room and stood the rifle just inside the kitchen. Leonard put his hand softly on David's shoulder, speaking Navajo in a muted voice. The young man didn't answer, but he got up to walk to the dining table with Leonard; I followed them over there. In jeans and a flannel shirt, David was the largest Navajo I'd seen, at least six-two and maybe two hundred fifty pounds.

I sat down with them at the table, a faux-mahogany china cabinet behind the head chair. Leonard smiled at David, whose butch haircut revealed pink psoriasis from his scalp down to his square forehead. His thick black brows and dark eyes revealed little emotion, except he kept glancing suspiciously over at Samson, sprawled in the recliner.

Quietly, Leonard talked to him again, but David didn't speak until Hawthorne came back from the kitchen with a can of soda in one hand, a plastic bag of ice and a dishtowel in the other. David smiled briefly and declared, "Doctor Pecker," accepting the soda from his brother.

"Wrap the towel around the ice," Leonard told Hawthorne, "and hold it gently on the injured side of her head and face. She'll probably wake up—I think it's best if she sees you first before we try to sort all this out."

As Hawthorne left for the bedroom, David opened the can and grinned at the escaping pressure, but he paused to check Samson again. Reassured, he took a long gulp, and then turned to Leonard. He said a few more words in Navajo before pointing his lips at the bedroom and taking more soda.

Leonard spoke softly to me. "He told me that Samson hurt Ruth; he said Aunt Geraldine saw it too."

"Then he doesn't know," I whispered, "that she's—"

"He probably thinks they're both just sleeping where he left them."

"My God. And he's been guarding Samson since then."

"Not long. Enough time for the baking to burn. We'll have to wait for Ruth to explain."

Still hot, I took off the windbreaker and saw Leonard pull down the top of his snowsuit. Hawthorne came out of the bedroom with the ice pack. "Still asleep," the boy said to Leonard, "but she moved more."

"Good. Do you have any non-aspirin?"

"Don't know."

"Find whatever you have, and a glass of water."

Hawthorne went back to the kitchen and soon returned with a plastic tumbler of water and an assortment of pain medications. "Samson's," he said.

Leonard chose a small plastic bottle and handed it to me along with the water. Hawthorne set down the bottles while David took his soda to the living-room sofa. He sat as far from

Samson as he could, watching him as Leonard and I followed Hawthorne into the bedroom.

Ruth stirred a little from side to side, eyes still closed. Light rouge and eye shadow had been smudged across her pretty light-brown face and traumatized forehead. Hawthorne reached down and pulled the sheet over his aunt's face.

Leonard was shaking his head. "Good God, we don't want Ruth to wake up with Gerry."

Hawthorne removed Ruth's blanket. She was also wearing a velveteen blouse, some silver jewelry, and a long skirt. She seemed tall, at least five-eight, but so slender that when Hawthorne slid his arms beneath her he lifted her easily. She mumbled but still didn't wake up as he carried her out.

We followed them with the ice and medicine and saw that David and Samson hadn't moved. We entered a large bedroom with three sets of bunk beds jutting from walls half-covered with drawings and basketball posters. Leonard pulled back the cover from a lower bunk so Hawthorne could place Ruth carefully in the bed and cover her. Leonard handed him the ice pack and watched him apply it tenderly to her injuries. She groaned without opening her eyes.

While her brother stayed on the edge of her bed, Leonard and I sat on the nearest lower bunk, where we could only see Hawthorne's back. After I set the water and medicine bottle down on the floor, Leonard got up slowly to look at the drawings, so I joined him.

Peter's efforts were mostly coloring pages and penciled battles of warplanes versus tanks, but Hawthorne had put up basketball sketches and several charcoal and pencil renderings of rock formations, canyons, and especially animals, all of them much more life-like than the raven in the school gym. "Some of this is his best work," Leonard whispered to me.

"I'll say," I muttered. "Is that a Chinese character he uses to sign his work?"

"No, it's his jersey number, a hyphen in the middle of the eleven to also make it an *H*."

"I see—clever."

As we started to sit down, Ruth stirred, opened her eyes slowly, and mumbled her brother's name. We waited on the bunk as the siblings spoke briefly to each other in Navajo. Ruth switched to English and asked quietly about David and her aunt.

When Hawthorne told her the bad news, she just said, "No," and began to cry.

Feeling like an intruder, I went out to see if all was calm in the living room. David held his soda with two hands, vigilantly staring at Samson, who was still snoring in the recliner. I washed my hands in the kitchen for something to do, then returned to the others. When I sat by Leonard on the bunk again, Hawthorne was speaking softly to Ruth in Navajo.

"David tied him up?" she asked him in English.

"*Aoó . . .*" Hawthorne went on in Navajo, then turned aside so Ruth could see us.

She tried to smile and said, "Leonard," beckoning him with a hand to come closer. He pulled my sleeve, and we moved over and squatted near her, but I stayed back a little.

"Hi Ruthie." Leonard patted her arm. "I'm sorry you had to go through all this."

She used the edge of the towel to dry her eyes. "I'll be okay." She was sniffling as Hawthorne reapplied the ice pack.

Leonard gently touched her shoulder. "Ruthie, how much pain do you have, and where?"

"Um, my face is throbbing; I have a headache and I'm a little dizzy—that's about it."

"We have some medicine that will help." He moved aside so she could see me. "This is Mr. Noland—"

"I know. I saw the first game." She smiled weakly. "Hi."

She offered her hand; I barely grasped it. "Hello Ruth."

Leonard brought over the pill and water. After she swallowed it, Ruth looked proudly at her brother, then turned to me. "I taught him how to shoot free throws. How did you do against Old Mission?"

"We gave them a run for their money. Right, Hawthorne?"

He nodded, his face glum as he took the ice pack away from her face. Her eye, cheek and forehead were darker, but not more swollen. "You gonna rest?" Hawthorne asked her.

"Yes, little bro, as soon as I tell what happened. I'll hold that thing for a while." She took the cold compress; Hawthorne stayed on the edge of the bed and Leonard spoke again.

"Ruthie, before you put that back on, let me check your eyes." He took his flashlight out of his pocket, leaned over, and examined her pupils. "Okay, go ahead and tell us, but don't overdo it—just the basics." He squatted again, and I knelt beside him.

Ruth made a deep sigh and laid the ice pack gingerly on the side of her face. "He's been drinking for a week. Went to Gallup yesterday and got back this afternoon—don't know how he made it. So we tried to start Thanksgiving, and it was going okay because he was hung over, quiet, and watching a dumb football game. After he started on some beers, I told him he'd already had enough, then he got angry about that and over what we were cooking." She paused to remove the ice.

"Aunt Gerry wanted to have everything all Navajo, so she and I dressed up and were making a nice mutton stew instead of turkey, which really set him off. He'd already started on the hard booze he hides in his room. After Walter came by and Samson ran him off, I hoped he would just pass out and we'd have an okay day, but he came into the kitchen when we were fixing dough for fry bread. He yelled at us that the food wasn't for Hosteen and to stop cooking what he'd want.

"I tried to calm him down, telling him we had pumpkin pie made from scratch in the oven. He was stupid drunk by then and wouldn't listen, scolding us about the same old stuff, especially Gerry for speaking Navajo and teaching us some of the old ways. David heard the noise and came into the kitchen wearing the headband Gerry gave him—he'd stuck a feather in it just to be funny." Ruth sighed again and put the ice pack on.

Leonard touched her lower arm. "Take your time, Ruthie."

"I'm okay. Anyway, Samson yelled at him, calling him a damn dummy." Tears welled in Ruth's eyes. "David started to walk over to us, but Samson got in his way and slapped him on the head, knocking off the headband and feather. When he started to hit David with the back of his hand, I grabbed his arm, and he turned around and pushed me hard. All I remember after that is stumbling toward the stove. I have no idea how David tied him up or what happened to Aunt Ger—" Ruth broke down in tears, laid down the compress, and faced the wall while Hawthorne tried to comfort her.

Moments later, we heard a diesel engine that sounded closer than the highway. Leonard pulled me slowly away from the bunks. "Who could that be?" I asked him quietly.

"Larson Charley's house is between here and the road—maybe it's him. I'll ski out there later for some help if I can't get ahold of somebody on Samson's radio."

"I didn't see one."

"Probably in his bedroom."

Inhaling a long sniffle, Ruth turned to Hawthorne. He put the ice pack on her face again as we approached. She looked up at us. "I'm sorry." She wiped away a tear.

"You don't have anything to be sorry for," I told her.

Ruth mustered a half-smile and spoke to Leonard. "What did happen to Aunt Gerry?"

"Heart attack or stroke, I guess. I think she went fast."

"Thank God, but what a horrible last few seconds for her."

"Afraid so." Leonard took her hand. "Ruth, I don't want to push you, but we need to have you checked out. You might have a concussion. We have to get you to Old Mission."

Before she could respond, we heard a clamor of moving furniture in the house, then the thud of something heavy hitting the floor. "Stay with Ruth," Leonard told Hawthorne as he and I rushed out of the room to find Samson on his feet, his eye patch dislodged, clothesline hanging from his shoulders. He pointed the rifle down at David, who was sitting on the floor and holding his jaw where Samson had evidently struck him.

Leonard and I moved slowly toward Samson; he aimed the rifle at us. "Put that thing down, Samson," I said with more pluck than I felt, stopping about ten feet away.

"Shit—you two," he grumbled. His bad eye seemed normal to me before he put the patch back in place. Woozy, he struggled to focus on us while David sat up on the floor, holding his jaw and blubbering a little.

"You don't want anybody else to get hurt, Samson," Leonard said, close by me.

Samson flicked some clothesline off his shoulder and glared down at his son. "He ain't hurt—deserved it. The girl's just got a bump."

Leonard shook his head. "She probably has a concussion, and Gerry's, um, gone."

"Whaddaya mean?"

"She's dead."

"Bullshit—ol' hag just fainted."

"You want to see the body?"

"Shuddup, faggot! Whadda *you* know anyway?" His good eye winced; he opened it wide, pointing the rifle at me. "Where's Ruth an' the ol' woman?"

"In their room," I lied.

"Thought so." He seemed more alert. "What're you two even doin' here?"

"Hawthorne ran away," I said. "We were trying to find him before he got overexposed."

"Serve him right. Don't see him here, do ya?" He cackled. "Maybe you should go back out there and find the brat." He pointed the rifle toward the door, then watched David get up to sit at the dining table, still holding his jaw. "See," Samson mumbled, "the big baby's okay."

Not about to argue, Leonard said, "Our truck's broken down at May and Walter's."

"Then how'd you get here?"

"We skied."

Samson scoffed, a line of drool escaping his mouth. "Li'l brown white man—" He stopped when the diesel engine rattled even closer than before. "Who's that?"

"Maybe Larson," Leonard said.

"Not in somethin' that big."

Leonard raised his brows. "Then your guess is as good as mine."

"You're lyin'." He turned to me. "Who is it?"

"No idea, but they're close enough to see your lights."

"You're lyin' too." Samson shuffled past David to his recliner, trying to watch us as he moved. With each step Samson took, Leonard sidled closer to the mudroom door, but Samson stopped. "Hold up, half-breed, you wanna bullet in your leg?"

"You're already in trouble, Samson," Leonard said calmly, easing back to us. "You do anything else, you'll rot in jail."

"Bullshit." Samson backed up to his recliner, grabbed the whiskey bottle from the coffee table, and took a long drink, his one eye watching us. After he swallowed, Samson exhaled with satisfaction and put the bottle down. "I ain't leavin' this house for nobody."

He leaned the rifle on the plush chair nearby, and then fumbled some keys out of his pocket. He glanced at us again, then unlocked the coffee table's single drawer, taking out a large cartridge pistol that looked to me like the kind that cops use. He put an extra clip in his back pocket, and then took a quick shot of whiskey.

"Get with th' dummy," he said. "I'm gonna see Geraldine." His eye had started to droop drowsily.

Leonard and I sat near David at the dining table. Samson waved the pistol in the general direction of our legs as he headed unsteadily toward Ruth and Geraldine's room, the rifle under one arm. Outside, the diesel's rattle was steady and louder.

Staggering behind the living room furniture, Samson was about to pass the bunkroom's door, barely ajar. Hawthorne bolted out of there to tackle his father, whose gut slammed against the back of the couch, doubling him over. The pistol fell onto the sofa; the rifle hit the floor. Then Hawthorne tried to slug Samson from behind, but the blow glanced off his shoulder. Samson grabbed the fallen pistol, turned around and pointed it at the boy, whose left arm was coiled, ready to strike his father in the face. Hawthorne let his arm drop.

"G'dam li'l shit!" Samson railed, shoving him hard into the wall. As Hawthorne slid down to the floor, he called his tormentor something in Navajo. Samson laughed it off and sputtered, horse-like, through his lips. "Aaag!" he blurted, shaking his head hard as if he had wet hair, still aiming the gun at Hawthorne on the floor. Samson picked up the squirrel rifle, slid the bolt and tossed its single shell before throwing the weapon right at the boy. Hawthorne ducked; the stock hit the wall just above him, then the rifle landed several feet away.

"Don't move, punk." Samson glanced at us as he stumbled over to grab his bottle. He moved on over to the dining table, where David had his head down, sobbing. "Shut 'im up!" Samson shouted. Leonard comforted David on the shoulder, quieting him a little.

Leaning on a dining chair for support, Samson took another long slug of whiskey, then aimed the pistol straight at Leonard. "Lyin' wetback, gimme the truth."

Leonard, sighing convincingly, glanced at me before he faced Samson. "All right. Geraldine and Ruth are okay. Like he told you, I locked them in their room."

"Okay, then how'd ya really get out here?"

"We skied in from May's and found Hawthorne at the old hogan on the road. The skis are out front. Nobody's with us." Leonard held up his palms. "That's it."

Samson listened to the diesel noise, then faced me. "He tellin' the truth?"

"Yes."

"Ya were both lyin' before."

I raised my brow. "We want everybody to get out of here okay, even you."

"More bullshit. Y'r heart jus' bleeds f'r us poor Navajos." He swayed, letting the weapon down. "You an' the li'l faggot make me sick—y'r both still lyin'bout somethin'," he rambled, slurring more of his words.

"Okay, I forgot one thing," Leonard said. "Walter went to get Hosteen."

Samson gurgled down more whiskey. As the approaching diesel throttled, he turned toward it. "Good, maybe tha's th' nosey bastard outside. Si' still—nobody move." He lurched from the table closer to Hawthorne, kicking the boy's boot hard. Samson ambled unsteadily to the far end of the living room, quaffing what looked to be the end of the whiskey.

He put the bottle down and wiped condensation from the window with his sleeve. "Damn fog." He gazed outside, then staggered halfway back to the table, brandishing the pistol and grinning madly. "Road grader, prob'ly a Navajo cop, an' Hosteen's big pickup." He guffawed. "An' they're almost here."

I took a cautious step in his direction. "What're you going to do?"

He made another wicked grin. "Plug Hosteen's tire, maybe two of 'em."

"The cops will shoot back," Leonard said.

"With alla you in here? Get under the table if you're so scared." He laughed when David dropped on purpose from his chair to curl up on the floor.

Samson reeled over to the china cabinet, opened its lower section, took out a flashlight, and stuck it in his back pocket. I saw Hawthorne slowly remove his boots while his father was distracted. Samson swiped his hand over a bank of light switches to leave the living room and dining alcove as dim as the foggy evening outside. Just enough light flickered from the TV and woodstove to put everything in silhouette, much like in the old hogan a few hours before.

While Samson started back to the far window with his pistol, Leonard quietly leaned down to reassure David. Moments later I saw Leonard's knife blade glint from the firelight after he stealthily removed it from his snowsuit. Samson passed the bedroom doors just as the diesel clamored and its lights flared outside.

Samson reached the window, unlocked it, moving the sliding pane slowly until it was open a foot or so. "Ha! See 'em good now." He checked us again, then raised the pistol to the opening, resting the handle on the sill and steadying it with two hands like a TV detective. "Ha, jus' one more damn minute!" He was gleeful, almost hysterical.

I watched Hawthorne slide a few feet on the floor to pick up something before scooting back to crouch by the wall. The slowly decreasing temperature in the room set off a thermostat, then the forced-air heater kicked in, rattling the floor registers. Although it wasn't cold at all, Leonard zipped up the top of his snowsuit.

Samson gave us another suspicious glance then kept watching outside as the massive road grader inched by in the headlights of the vehicle behind. Leonard slipped under the table and began to crawl in the semi-darkness, cat-like, so his nylon snowsuit wouldn't scrape noisily along the floor. He made it beyond the front door and hid in the furniture, several feet from Hawthorne, who seemed to be extending his leg to move the rifle with his foot.

At the window, Samson lined up his shot, waited, and fired. I flinched at the explosive report, and David began crying under the table. "It's okay, David, we'll be fine," I told him quietly, hoping it was true.

Samson wheeled halfway around with the gun. "Shit, shut 'im up!"

"He's just scared," I said. "We're trying to calm him down."

"Shut 'im up or I'll give 'im somethin' to be scared about."

I got down on the floor with David and put my arm around his trembling shoulders. He resisted for a moment then relaxed as if he knew me. Samson fired again, the blast echoing in the room. I stood up briefly to watch, holding David's shuddering shoulder.

"Missed again, goddammit!" Samson groped for the bottle below, saw it was empty, and threw it against a wall; it clunked to the floor without shattering. I could barely make out that Hawthorne had shoved the rifle several feet closer to the bedroom door.

"Hol' still," Samson told the boy, who uttered a throaty word in Navajo.

Samson scoffed. "Y'r askin' for it."

"What are you doing, crazy old drunk?" It was Ruth's voice. I stood halfway up and saw her outline in the bedroom doorway, wrapped in a blanket, still holding the ice to her head.

"Well, well." Samson kept looking outside. "Y'r Uncle Hosteen's gonna lose a tire." He aimed, waited, and fired again. "Ha! Got it! Bastard ain't goin' nowhere now."

He made another hysterical laugh and took the flashlight from his back pocket to shine it on his daughter. "Y' don't look so hurt t' me."

She calmly removed the compress from her injuries. "You did this, old man,"

"So ya got pushed a little—shouldn't mess in my business." He put down the flashlight and looked outside again.

"And now you're shooting at your own brother."

"Ain't no brother a' mine." Samson continued to watch the yard.

"Same old bull," she said.

"That ol' whore raised th' bastard like he was hers—jus' like you prob'ly will someday."

"Go to hell. You shame Grandma and our whole family and you're nothing but a coward who hits his kids. I won't be quiet about it anymore. You're going to jail this time, old man."

"Stop callin' me that."

"Pickled old man. You look ten years older than Hosteen."

He faced her. "Shuddup!" Samson tried to focus elsewhere in the room, more befuddled than angry. "Tell Gerry t' come out here." He turned back to the window.

"She's dead, you fool, and it's your fault."

"Bullshit, didn't touch her. An' she ain't dead." He seemed to be aiming high out of the window. This time when he fired, I was ready for it, but David began shaking again. "Stay back, all ya bastards!" Samson shouted through the opening. He turned to where Ruth had been, but she and Hawthorne had gone into the bedroom during the last discharge.

"Get back out here, you two," he called out. "When I ain't lookin', you little shits think you're real tough." He picked up the flashlight and directed it at us. "Where's the goddam half-breed?" No less vile, he didn't sound as drunk, not slurring his words as much.

Leonard was still hiding in the furniture, too far away from Samson to approach without being seen. "He got out while you were shooting," I said. "By now he's telling them what's going on in here. You're just making this worse on yourself."

"No more damn advice—shut up," he stated more than shouted.

Except for low whimpers from David, the dusky living room was silent until the outer door creaked again.

22

The mudroom's door sprang shut, then a couple of light foot-falls pattered out there and stopped. After Samson aimed the flashlight at the doorway where Ruth had been, he appeared to put it in his pocket. He moved from the window toward the front door, his dark shape holding the pistol out front with both hands again. I could see his arms wobble as he took one unsteady step at a time past the sofa.

Impressed as I'd been by Leonard's know-how and moxie, I hoped he wouldn't attempt to use his camping knife to disarm the much larger Samson, who suddenly stopped before the door. "Lookit here. Found me a wetback," he said blandly, pointing the pistol down. "Get up. What's that, a switchblade from *War-EZZ?*"

Leonard stood silently as Samson took the knife and slid it across the floor toward the kitchen. Then he put the gun bar-rel next to Leonard's face. "Whoever ya are out there," he said toward the mudroom in a matter-of-fact tone, "touch that door an' I blow off the faggot's ear." After no response for moments, a steady clear voice called back. "Sam, it's Sergeant Nez. Let's me an' you talk."

"Got nothin' to say." Samson took out the flashlight and turned it on, directing the beam first at the bedroom, then the mudroom door.

The pistol still next to his face, Leonard's eyes were on Samson. "This could all be over, Samson, and still not be real serious," he said.

"Another word an' I'll shoot you somewhere else." Samson touched the barrel to Leonard's nose, then below his ear. The door's lock squeaked a little. Samson turned the light onto the doorknob—it revolved slowly. The hush was broken by a shot into the roof, bringing down a brief storm of plaster.

"Jesus, he did it!" I cried out, reaching for some table napkins.

"Teacher ain't lyin' *this* time!" Samson ranted, glee in his voice again.

I hurried right to Leonard, who had swerved several feet in our direction but was somehow still standing. In the faint light and with so much blood on the side of his head I couldn't tell how much of the ear was gone before I pressed the cloth to his wound.

Samson leaned on the side of the sofa. "Jus' relax, only nicked it."

The front door hadn't moved. "Sam," the cop said from the mudroom, "don't make this any worse."

"Back off," he stated dully, "or the teacher's ear is next." His adrenaline rush apparently gone, he dropped the flashlight on the sofa.

Nez called again. "Sam, listen—"

"Giddout." He stumbled to the switches and turned on the lights, the gun by his leg.

"What is it you're after, Sam? What do you want to come from all this?"

Samson stared at the bedroom. "I want you to send Hosteen in here."

"I can't do that."

"You can if I send out David an' the wetback—two for one." His tone sounded more exhausted than inebriated. "Big army hero Hosteen'll be glad to do it."

"What'll you do with him?"

Samson's sneer turned to a half-grin. "Jus' have him talk t' Ruth."

"How do I know that?"

"Because I say so. He comes in alone—no gun."

I heard the cop's footfalls, then the outer door squeaked and slammed. Samson faced the bedroom door. "You two come out or I'm comin' in," he called, his voice lacking much conviction.

"I'll shoot!" Hawthorne yelled back from the dark room, louder than I'd ever heard him.

Samson scoffed. "With one pissant bullet?"

"All I need."

"Shit. Big man." Samson stayed where he was, a few feet from the front door. I heard Ruth say something, apparently to get Hawthorne to back off.

I turned from the standoff and removed the cloth from Leonard's ear for a quick and closer look. "It isn't much worse than a nick," I told him.

"What'd you say?" Leonard pointed to his other ear.

I reapplied the dry compress and yelled into his good ear. "Not much worse than a nick!" He nodded; I lowered my voice. "But it's bleeding a lot—needs treatment."

Leonard took the cloth napkin from me, then looked at it before covering his ear again. "I'll be fine," he said, louder than he realized. "What's going on with—"

"What's wrong with him?" Samson called to me.

"He can't hear on that side."

"Damn shame. Sit down," Samson ordered. "We'll jus' wait f'r Uncle Hosteen."

"David," I said, "it's all right. Come up here and sit with us." He got up, and the three of us took our seats as if ready for Thanksgiving pie. Samson shoved a living-room chair to where he could see both doors and watch us too.

"C'mon, what's going on?" Leonard was still loud.

"He's going to let David go," I said to his unhurt ear.

"Gotta go," David mumbled, holding himself.

"Samson, David needs the bathroom." I tried to sound calm. "And I need water and ice for this bleeding." Leonard cupped his free hand behind his good ear, a quizzical look on his face.

Samson spoke groggily from his chair. "No ice. Get water in there when he's done." He waved the gun toward a door not far from the kitchen entrance. "An' leave it open."

"Go ahead, David," I said to him. "Don't close the door."

David hurried into the bathroom and took care of his business, his loud stream in the toilet seeming endless. After he finally flushed and came back to Leonard, I went over there to let cold water run in the sink. I opened the medicine cabinet.

"What're you doin'?" Samson called drowsily.

"Looking for a dressing."

"Get back out here."

I dunked a face cloth and a towel in the frigid water, then came back in with cotton, Mercurochrome and a tin of Band-Aids in one hand, the dripping linens in the other. I sat by Leonard, who put down the blood-soaked napkin. I cleaned the wound as best I could; it bled more, so I reapplied pressure with the cold towel. When David saw the blood, he whimpered to Leonard.

"Shut him up," Samson said.

"It'll be okay, David." Leonard had to reach up to pat his shoulder.

The bleeding soon slowed. "I'm going to bandage this," I told Samson.

"Okay, do it, then get away from them—up on that table."

"What?" I'd already started to apply the antiseptic to the injury.

"Yeah, up there where I can see you good."

I added cotton to the ear, taped it down with plastic strips, and then climbed up and sat on the festive tablecloth as Samson leaned back in the chair. I tried to show Leonard why I was on the table, pointing back and forth to our captor.

Before long, Samson's head began to jerk every few seconds like a driver trying to stay awake, just conscious enough to watch the doors and us.

Pass out, you old lush.

When the outside door finally squealed and shut again, Samson sat up and wiped his face with his sleeve. He got slowly to his feet, aiming the pistol at the footfalls on the other side of the door. "Who's out there?"

"Hosteen . . . ." From the rest of his sentence in Navajo, I only picked out "David."

"Stay there with your hands up," Samson said, walking close to the door.

"*Aoó.*"

Samson faced me. "Get down and bring 'em over here."

I jumped off the table and spoke to Leonard. "Help me take David out." He stood with his arm around the young man, and we started for the door.

"Ain't that sweet," Samson said, then opened the door warily, peeking into the mudroom before waving me by. I pushed the two of them through the doorway, Leonard looking back at me in surprise as Hosteen shoved them farther, all the way outside.

Samson told me to back up when Hosteen, his arms only halfway up, entered in jeans and a corduroy shirt, his sheepskin coat open over a modest silver necklace. He wore his flat black hat and a red headband, his hair, as always, in a traditional bun. As I moved back to the table, Hosteen looked at me, glum but confident. He lowered his arms and said a couple of long sentences in Navajo to his younger and taller brother. I only picked up the name "Sam."

Samson scowled, his rage building again. "English, goddammit. Yeah, I remember the ol' man singin' in the hogan. So what?"

"When you were angry, his singing sometimes helped you and . . . ." Hosteen was using more English than I'd ever heard from him " . . . need to stop all this, Samson. Nez told me I can take you to the old hogan for a while."

"I don't believe you or your shaman bullshit."

When Samson said that, I felt a brief moment of respect for his resistance to the apparent offer to rid him of evil spirits.

"*Ndaga*'," Hosteen said. "It is part of you, even if you wear the Mormon garments."

Samson's brow went up, his good eye opening wide. "I don't believe that either. It's *all* bullshit." He gestured with the pistol toward the couch. "Go stand in front of it."

Hosteen moved over there; Samson followed. Hosteen turned around and cleared his throat. "Put the gun down, Samson. I promise you we can go to my place."

"I ain't goin', bastard." He pointed the pistol at Hosteen's chest. "How many outside?"

"Nez, some new cop, Walter, and a state driver."

"You hear us in there, girl?" Samson shouted.

"I hear you," Ruth answered defiantly from the dark bedroom.

"*Uncle* Hosteen's got somethin' to tell you."

"Leave him alone, old man."

Samson raised the pistol at Hosteen. "Go on, tell her the truth—you *are* a bastard."

The proximity of the weapon didn't seem to faze Hosteen. "*Aoó*," he said, his face solemn as he added some words in Navajo.

Samson thrust the gun even closer. "Ha! Now say it in English."

"Yes, I'm a bastard," he said flatly.

"You hear that, girl?"

"So what?" Ruth called back. "He cared more about Grandma than you ever did."

Samson's bloodshot eye glowered at Hosteen. "See that? My own kids take y'r side, an' you ain't even our blood."

"*Ndaga*'," Hosteen said, then added another short phrase in Navajo.

"You liar, how are we cousins? Nobody knows where you came from."

Hosteen shook his head gravely and continued in Navajo again.

"English!"

"All right." Hosteen exhaled wearily. "Aunt May's baby didn't die; she's my birth mother. Sally and Samson took me in. That's why you have his name, not me."

Samson scoffed. "An' Walter's your father?"

"No, May met him later. She couldn't have more kids and was ashamed. May told Sally and Sam I had a better chance with them. Sam knew the right people back then to fix the papers. So I was adopted, and they kept the rest of it nobody's business."

"Still don't believe you," he said with a jeer. "Why didn't they tell me?"

"When you were ten, you heard gossip about Sally and me. Sam told you I was adopted, but that all the rest was made up. Later you began to believe the rumors about Mom. By then, you wouldn't listen to anybody in the fam—"

"None a' this changes anything. You're still a bastard."

"Yes, but we *are* cousins. Can't you believe something good about your own mother?"

"They took your side on everything, you an' all your Navajo bullshit." He jammed the pistol under his waistband and shoved Hosteen onto the sofa, knocked off his hat, and pulled the red bandana down from his forehead. Samson loosened the knot, stuffed the material into his brother's mouth, then tied it before securing Hosteen's hands behind with some clothesline.

His eye glaring wildly again, Samson retrieved the pistol and thrust its handle toward Hosteen's brow, making him flinch. "Ha! An eye for an eye! Now it's your turn."

"Stop, old man!" Ruth shouted from the bedroom doorway, the squirrel rifle trained on her father.

Samson turned to her. "Shit, I ain't gonna kill the bastard." He righted the pistol, pointing it in Ruth's general direction. "That popgun won't do you any good anyway."

The rifle barrel didn't move. "I only need one bullet to hit your eye."

"Not if I shoot first," he said unconvincingly, lowering his pistol an inch or so.

Hawthorne strode out of the bedroom, walked past Ruth to stand between his sister and Samson. "Shoot *me*, ol' man."

Ruth stepped forward to stand by her brother. She lowered the rifle, even though Samson still directed his pistol toward their legs.

"C'mon, Samson," I said quietly. "This is all over."

While he stared for moments at his kids, the only sounds were the floor registers' rattle and the diesel outside. Samson finally lowered the gun all the way. "Gerry—she's really dead?"

Ruth nodded dismally. Samson's face had metamorphosed into the hungover version of his sober self. He sat on the sofa a few feet from Hosteen. "The kids are right," he said, chin to chest, staring at the floor. "I ain't no good for anybody."

Hosteen grunted in a conciliatory tone through the gag before the outer door squeaked again. Samson looked up, trance-like at the noise. "But I ain't goin' to jail," he said calmly, raising the pistol to his own temple. Hosteen tried to shout before Hawthorne grabbed Samson's wrist as the gun went off.

The bullet struck the ceiling, causing another rain of detritus. Hawthorne took the pistol, laid it on the floor and slid it to the front door.

Two Navajo policemen burst in, their pistols at the ready. They lowered the weapons when they saw the gun on the floor and the Shepard brothers on the sofa, Samson leaning forward with bits of plaster on his shoulders, head between his knees, mumbling in Navajo.

If Anasazi pueblos
Were alive today,
The nearest hogan
Would be miles away,
And the next one
Farther than that.

23

In his stocking cap and jeans, no one would take the squat middle-aged Sergeant Nez for a policeman until he opened his coat to reveal a gun belt, badge, and cop's jersey. After I helped Nez untie Hosteen they went in to see Geraldine and check on Ruth, whom Hawthorne had taken back to the bed. The second cop, tall and young, stayed with Samson, who was cuffed and had almost passed out. The officer and I discussed the incident until his boss returned to release Samson to Hosteen, who would take him to court on Monday.

The cops, Samson, Hosteen, and I went outside, where the fog had lifted to a partly cloudy sky with stars peeking through, and it seemed colder. Leonard, David, and Walter waited in the squad car, a four-wheel-drive panel truck similar to ours. The driver of the road grader had finished changing the tire on Hosteen's pickup, which looked like a toy behind the monstrous yellow Caterpillar, its chained tires as tall as the other vehicles.

Nez had certified the death as due to natural causes, saying the coroner wouldn't need to see Geraldine's body, so he released it to Hosteen. It was after nine when we watched him drive Samson off toward the highway, the wrapped and soon-to-be-frozen corpse in his truck bed.

Hawthorne and the young cop carried Ruth on a stretcher out to their panel truck, where they settled her in the enclosed rear space usually occupied by suspects. Next to Marie and our gear, Hawthorne squatted on the floor to attend to his sister. After Leonard told Ruth to stay awake in case she had a serious concussion, he squeezed in with Walter, David and me behind the two policemen.

"Someone put a good dressing on that ear," I said loudly to him.

"Yeah, you don't have to yell. I hear better now. Cute trick you played on me. Thanks."

I smiled. "Bird in the hand. You wouldn't have gone."

Instead of taking the highway, Nez had told the state driver to plow all the way to Raven Point so he could drop off Walter and the boys and also talk to May. Grousing about the drifts we'd reported to him, the man said it would take "a hell of a long time." As he predicted, it was an hour before Nez drove slowly by the old hogan, twenty yards behind the road grader's floodlights. After the worst of the drifts, we made it up the first hill. I looked out the frosty side window in a half-hearted attempt to spot the place where I'd deliriously removed my clothes.

It was around ten when we finally made it to the Benallys' cabin, a new layer of thick snow around its puffing chimney pipe. Hawthorne got up and spoke quietly to Leonard, who then re-layed to Nez that the boy insisted on going to the hospital with his sister. After sending Walter in to give May the news about Geraldine, Nez left the idling vehicle to take David inside.

The sergeant came back soon, carrying a thermos of coffee with a tin of homemade cookies from May. We followed the grader past our forlorn panel truck and up the same radical grade that had been our downfall almost twenty hours earlier. In the next valley, the Caterpillar cleared drifts before we came into mixed woods. Nez settled his vehicle behind the grader at about fifteen miles per hour, the motor humming steadily during fairly smooth going.

Leonard looked back through the steel grating to remind Ruth to stay awake. He spoke to me under his breath. "She's do-ing okay, considering."

"After she's better," I said just above a whisper, "what happens to the four of them?"

"Social Services will be involved, but May told Sergeant Nez she'd take all the kids. Not just for now, for good."

I nodded. "Of course she did." I looked into the beams ahead at snow-laden piñons and barren cottonwoods with long rows of delicate accumulation on their branches.

"I'm pretty sure David will end up with May, Walter, and Billy." Leonard turned back to be sure the kids couldn't hear us. "Ruth's ready to take on the world. She'll be glad to have the Benallys as a home base."

"What about Hawthorne and Peter?"

"I think the social worker will look for a different placement for them, somewhere in the extended family. When their father gets out of jail, Hosteen will reach out to him, but if Samson's not much better he'll probably live out there alone."

"Are you going to file charges against him?"

"No, Nez took my statement back there. I'll testify if needed, but they have plenty to put him away for a while."

As we took a curve I stared at our headlight beams and noticed a discarded whiskey box, buckled under a mound of snow. I turned to Leonard. "This whole deal makes some of our everyday school problems seem less important."

"Except for the lead our kids have been drinking."

"Man, I haven't been thinking about that at all."

"We have a couple days; I need to call the lawyer right away. Hosteen would've been the spokesman, but he has a lot to deal with now. He probably won't start the rituals for Geraldine until midweek, but I doubt he can come. We'll just have to muddle through."

"Right. Your hearing seems a lot better now."

"Yeah, I don't need to go to Old Mission. I'll start getting ready for Monday."

Chugging along behind the grader, we entered the canyon. Over the last miles, I stared up into the sky and imagined the Anasazi out there centuries before, gazing at those same stars.

After we arrived in Raven Point, Nez dropped off Leonard and Marie. The snow on the road to Old Mission had been scraped at least twice, smoothing out the usual bumps, and we pulled into the small hospital after midnight. Nez had radioed ahead, so an orderly was waiting at Emergency with a gurney.

Not long after they admitted Ruth, one of the hospital's missionary doctors, an elderly white man, entered the small waiting room with a beatific smile, regardless of the ungodly hour. He complimented our first aid and said that Ruth apparently had a mild concussion from the two contusions. He said they would keep her at least until noon for observation. The cops left after Nez asked Hawthorne and me to come by the station later in the morning to make our statements.

Before they let Ruth sleep, a friendly nurse allowed Hawthorne a short visit. After that, we found some vending machines, and I bought soda and candy bars to take back to the empty waiting room. We took off our coats and Hawthorne opened his ever-present shoulder bag as we sat down on a long sofa.

I pulled the tab on my soda. "When Ruth is better, where do you want to go?"

"School." He took out his sketchpad, moved farther away, and began to draw solemnly with an ordinary pencil. I stretched out before two a.m. on one of the two sofas.

The waiting room had no other customers, so we slept for a few hours until a different physician came in and woke us after seven. Also elderly and white, this doctor was more abrupt than the other one. He said they were letting Ruth sleep in for a while and not to bother her. " ... her symptoms are improving. She can go home and rest there for a few days."

"She and her brother," I said, "don't really have an official home right now."

He sneered haughtily. "Mr. Shepard phoned us—he'll be here before noon."

"Oh, okay." I was surprised that Hosteen was able to come.

After another hour, a nurse let us visit Ruth in a small room that smelled like floor wax. A cold pack was taped over the left side of her face. Ice or tears had left her cheek damp, but she was alert and trying to be cheerful for Hawthorne, who glumly touched her shoulder.

I walked closer. "Hi, Ruth. The doctor says you're almost ready to go."

"Yes." Her smile faded. "Mr. Noland, do you know where I'll be staying?"

"I only heard that May wants you to come over." She began to cry a little. "Is that a problem for you, Ruth?"

"Not at all." She sniffled. "She and Gerry were so close." A tear slalomed down her face.

"Maybe you'd better get more rest before your trip. Hawthorne and I have to go make our statements to Sergeant Nez. He'll be by to take yours before you leave."

"I'm glad I don't have to tell all that to a stranger." She tried another smile. "He's a good man." Ruth patted her somber brother's hand, saying something in Navajo before we left.

Back in the waiting room, I zipped up my parka and Hawthorne put on his mackinaw and stocking cap, the woven bag over his shoulder. We walked out into a crisp, clear morning onto the snow-packed pavement and found the small town quiet the day after Thanksgiving. I bought some take-out food at the trading post, then we went next door to the storefront police station.

While they spoke to Hawthorne, I called the agency's emergency number, and Jennings barked his "Hello."

"This is Noland—I'm in Old Mission. We broke an axle on our panel truck."

"Where the hell did that happen?"

"The road from school out to Benallys."

"That's a damn trail, so what were you doing out there?"

"Going after two runaways."

"Oh," the assistant superintendent said with some contrition, probably because the FIC had recently been under pressure from the tribe and a congressman after a runaway in another agency was seriously injured. "You find them?" he asked after the long pause.

"Yes, the kids are okay, but the Navajo police were involved. That's where I am right now. There was a hostage situation. We had to—"

"Damn—is this going to involve us?"

"No, I don't think so."

"Good, I'll send a blade and a wrecker out to get the panel next week."

"We dropped Leonard Santos at school. He's going to need a vehicle, and I need some way to get back."

"Hatcher's pickup is here. I'll find someone to drive it over to the station. Probably be January before the panel gets fixed. You and the Mex can share the pickup for now."

Prick. I took what I thought was a deep silent breath.

"What, that's not good enough?"

Shit. "It's fine. We'll see you Monday."

"Yeah, you can bank on that."

After Hawthorne finished his statement, I told Nez that Hosteen was coming at noon for Ruth, so the sergeant told his partner he was leaving to get Ruth's statement.

Hawthorne had been listening. "I can go to the hospital?" he asked Nez, who looked at me, brows raised.

After I nodded, the sergeant said, "*Aoó*, let's go, son."

Hawthorne reached into his shoulder bag, took out the sketchpad and tore off a sheet. "You can have it," he said, handing me the paper before he hurried off to catch Nez.

On the way over to give my statement to the other officer, I looked at Hawthorne's stunning sketch of a hogan's interior, similar to where we'd slept two nights before. The burning stove was about the same, and somehow he'd made the firelight and shadows flicker on the walls. The two human silhouettes were not Leonard and me; one of them seemed to be a medicine man. Hawthorne's)-) was etched in the corner.

After I finished my statement, an agency maintenance guy showed up with our pickup. I dropped him at FIC housing before driving on to the hospital. At the waiting room inside, I saw Hawthorne on the sofa, drawing on his pad while his cousin Raymond watched him work. Carlton was looking down the hall through the glass wall. He turned to me, his face downcast, and just said, "Sean."

"Hi, I thought your dad was coming."

Wearing grease-stained overalls under his coat, Carlton pushed up the visor of his old green baseball cap. "No, I have his truck to take Ruth to our place for now." He glanced out at the hall. "I'll pick up Peter on the way back. My wife and I are going to keep Hawthorne and Peter."

Both the length and content of his explanation surprised me, so I just nodded, hoping that his certainty about Hawthorne and Peter was justified. "Is the nurse bringing Ruth now?"

"That's what they said."

I turned to the boys, basically the tall and short of it on our team. "Hi guys." They glanced at me. "Your drawing, Hawthorne, it's really good. Thank you."

He nodded once and went back to his current project. I faced Carlton. "Can you tell me if the ceremonies started for Geraldine?"

"Hosteen's in the old hogan with her a lot, but most of it starts next week after he gets back from Old Mission."

"I know it's a bad time, but can you tell him we have a meeting on Monday about the water?"

"Leonard told us," he said as they brought Ruth out in a wheelchair.

After we got her settled in the back seat of the dual-cab pickup, I followed them on the Raven Point road, which was so smooth by then that I had trouble keeping my eyes open. It was after two when we turned into the compound. Jeannie's car was parked at the school, so I stopped to check in. She was making radio contacts for the meeting and told me that several people already said they were coming.

I thanked her, then walked over to the dorm, where the crew cab was idling. I looked in on Hawthorne and Ruth before going into the rec room. Maybe a third of our students were assembled in the semi-darkness, laughing at an old Martin and Lewis military farce. In the office, Carlton handed the phone to Leonard, then came out.

"See you," Carlton said to me before he walked out into the audience to find Peter.

I entered the office as Leonard finished his call. His ear had a fresh but smaller dressing. "Hi, how's it going for the meeting?" I asked.

"Hi, Sean—pretty well, considering so many families aren't around. How's Ruth doing? Carlton didn't say much."

"That girl is so resilient . . . ." I gave him a short update on the events in Old Mission. "I saw Jeannie working on the contacts. Was Carlton just making one?"

"No, he was talking to Amanda, the lawyer. Carlton's going to speak in Hosteen's place."

"He is? But the lawyer's still coming, right?"

"Yes. Carlton's bringing Jon and Felicita in on Sunday to talk to Amanda about what the Council wants. Larson quit, so Hosteen and the others appointed Carlton to finish the year."

"Will anyone listen to him like they do Hosteen?" I was aware that I was sounding more anxious with each question.

"He speaks up when he wants to, just like his dad. The community will listen; the agency is another matter." He said the lawyer would arrive Sunday afternoon and stay with Abby. "Beth and her mom spent Thanksgiving making calls and worrying about us."

I felt my eyes starting to get heavy again. "I thought they knew that our fate was in the hands of a wise Navajo guide."

"Funny. Anyway, Amanda wants to study our data as soon as she arrives, before she meets with the Council. We'll see her at Abby's—we're invited for drinks in the evening."

"Good." I covered a yawn with my fist.

"Sean, we do have a lot to do, but it can wait a day. Get some sleep."

"Seems like you're always telling me that, Doc." I yawned again on cue. "See you tomorrow." I opened the door and walked to my trailer in the frigid air. I went right to bed thinking I would nod right off, but I worried about Monday and also replayed recent events in my mind for a long time before I slept.

﹀

It was still clear and cold when I walked over to see Leonard before noon on Saturday. We took the school pickup to visit contacts for the meeting, making it out to six places before dark, but we found only two families at home.

On Sunday Leonard, some kids, and I set up the gym with about fifty folding chairs, a wrestling mat, our vintage microphone, and two head tables that we put a few feet apart, one of them under the good basket. Over at school it was eerily quiet again, as Abby was the only one around. Leonard and I were reviewing the files when a Jeep wagon went by outside and drove on up to the trailers. "Good, there she is," Leonard said. "Let's take all this over to her."

"You're the expert. I'll give her my two cents worth tonight. I need to finish a couple things for next week." After he left with Abby, I did my P.E. plans and the school's paperwork.

At about eight that night, Leonard knocked, then came into the trailer with a cheese plate. After I went to the kitchen for my bottle of cheap rosé, I noticed only a Band-Aid remaining on Leonard's ear. He was snickering at my dirty kitchen and messy living room. "Maid's day off?"

"Yeah, I'll get to it one of these days." I put on my regular coat for our short walk. We went out and started up the hill on the edge of the icy narrow road.

Headlights on, Carlton was easing the crew cab downhill past Jimmy's place. Jon Begay opened the passenger window as they rolled slowly by. "See you tomorrow," Felicita called to us confidently from between the two men, smiling to suit her name.

We waved, then trudged the rest of the way up to Abby's. Beth answered the door, looking even taller in grey COLORADO sweats. She called to the kitchen, "Yeah, it's them."

Leonard and I stomped our feet and went in. Abby, alone in the kitchen, was chopping vegetables. She stopped humming and faced us. "Evening. Amanda will be right out."

"No practice tomorrow?" Beth asked me as Leonard took our offerings over to Abby.

"Not enough kids, but you can clear chairs and shoot around after the meeting."

"I'll stay until I make ten layups in a row."

"No dunks?"

"Ha-ha. Want a beer and a shot?" She was trying to sound very adult.

"Maybe one of those diet sodas for now."

"Diet soda?" a boisterous voice carried from the hallway. "Boy, this is going to be a fun evening." In sneakers, blue jeans, a neat white blouse, and a simple but colorful beaded *Yei-bi-chai* necklace, Amanda came in confidently. Built like Abby—short, sturdy but not much overweight—that was their only physical similarity. Amanda's pitchblende-black hair, cut straight across in a Dutch boy like Leonard's, shimmered in the kitchen light. With her dark brows and coppery skin plus the pendant, I judged our lawyer to be a so-called modern Navajo.

Amanda's lighthearted gruffness transformed into a winsome smile around her striking black oval eyes, small mouth, and prominent pre-Columbian nose. "I'd say this arctic weather calls for an ice-cold beer," she said to Beth, who cheerfully started for the fridge.

"Sean," Leonard beamed, "this little character is Amanda Singer Santos."

What? "Your sister?"

"I confess to being one inch shorter than my little brother," she said, a pretend sneer for Leonard as she shook my hand firmly. "So you're the other troublemaker with Darwin here?"

"I guess so." I turned to Leonard. "Why didn't you tell me?"

He had mischief on his face. "For the fun of it, and I wanted to be sure she was free."

"Free?" Amanda mocked with a smile. "In what sense? You owe *me*, Lenny."

"That depends on how you handle the FIC tomor—"

"Time out!" Abby banged a pan to interrupt the siblings' repartee. "Let's put our crappy water aside for a few minutes and relax. We even have fresh vegetables, thanks to Amanda."

Beth handed out drinks as we helped ourselves to carrot and celery sticks, Leonard's cheese, and some brownies Abby had made. Our conversation was light, as decreed, centering on Beth's new stray puppy. When Abby managed to not-so-subtly slip in my "single" status, Amanda and I caught each other rolling our eyes.

After finishing a glass of wine I had poured, I faced Amanda. "I think we can safely talk about our crappy water now. So what's the plan for tomorrow?"

She nodded gravely. "You have clear proof of FIC negligence, which we won't dwell on, although I will present the basic facts. What the agency boys want is to keep this local . . . ." For nearly an hour all of us discussed the nuts and bolts of the meeting, and then we had a nightcap as Beth went to bed.

While Abby and Leonard did the dishes, Amanda told me about a case of hers, defending a man from Acoma Pueblo in a malpractice suit. After Abby told Leonard she needed to "walk off some calories," they left, and I told Amanda how much I appreciated her brother's knowledge on our search for the boys.

She sipped her mixed drink, followed by a self-deprecating laugh. "Look, everyone we grew up with thinks I'm the tough one, that Lenny and our little sister are so, um, tender. But Abby knows how strong Leonard is in his own way."

"He saved my butt for sure." I took a swallow of my second glass of wine. "Neither of us is a fatalist, but it feels like we've been friends for years and just got around to meeting each other."

"Sounds like he told you some of his Navajo-Gandhi-Einstein zeitgeist. Don't get me wrong, I think it's interesting, but he doesn't share that with just anyone."

"I know." We chatted more about her brother until Abby and Leonard returned. I excused myself to leave, though I wanted to talk more to Amanda. Feeling a bit high, I tromped down the hill in the snow, noticing that all the teachers were back, their cars in the usual spots.

)-)

Since we were ready for the meeting and Monday was a day off for me, I slept in for a while, then decided to clean up my trailer for the first time in weeks. I checked in just after lunchtime at the school to find it busy but fairly quiet with many kids still missing, including most of those related to the Shepards. I started for the dorm and watched a few snowflakes sputter from a solitary cumulus cloud in a mostly blue sky.

In the rec room I looked down the hall and spotted Leonard outside with the pony in its new shed. Janet and two boys were cleaning up after lunch, so I asked her to tell Leonard that I was going over to the gym. I puttered around in there until a few people began to show up before three o'clock.

I'd asked Eddie Begay to meet the administrators and give them a tour of our makeshift drinking system. By a quarter after three, fewer than thirty community members, including staff, had arrived. Many still in their coats, they waited in the drafty but relatively warm gym as a handful of our older kids lounged about on the mat up front near Leonard and me. Abby, Beth, Elizabeth, and Jimmy sat in the back row; Dot and Mona weren't there. Jon, Felicita, Carlton, and Jeannie were seated at one head table, chatting with Amanda. Behind a leather briefcase, she wore a cerise business suit that complemented her bronze complexion and multicolored *yei* necklace.

Hawthorne, who came with Carlton, was the only other Shepard I could see. He'd chosen to sit alone in a chair near the gym's drinking fountain. Someone had removed its flowery cover, and Hawthorne faced the grimy porcelain fixture, sketching away on his pad.

Eddie walked in past the barrier, followed by the two men. I was disappointed that the superintendent didn't look perturbed, but it made more sense when Mona entered right behind, smug as a spoiled child with an expected new toy. She sat alone in the front row as Eddie led the men to the water stand on the stage. The administrators had passed right by Hawthorne, oblivious to both the artist and his foul subject.

At orientation I'd briefly met Thurmond, the agency's new part-Seminole superintendent. In his fifties, husky, about five-ten and fair-skinned with wavy black Elvis hair, he filled a paper cup and made a show of enjoying the water, but Jennings refused a drink. Although we'd squabbled on the phone three or four times, I'd not actually seen Jennings before. About my age and size with a blank face, the assistant superintendent looked foolish in a furry hat and coat, which he unzipped to reveal a brown suit and tie.

A notebook in one hand, Thurmond unbuttoned his lined coat. He wore dark slacks and a white business shirt with the obligatory turquoise bolo tie. I got up to greet them; Eddie took my seat next to Leonard and the kids. When I walked up, Thurmond smiled and stuck out his hand.

"Mr. Noland, you've been a busy man." His handshake was aggressive, and I didn't try to compete with him. Jennings just stayed a pace behind, glaring at me.

"Yes," I said, "we had to do something about this water."

"Of course, of course, and your runaway situation. Jennings here was worried about that, but it all turned out just fine."

Tell that to the Shepards. I watched him face the crowd with his ingratiating smile, then turn to me. "Good to see some folks out here taking an interest."

"There'd be more if the timing was better. Anyway, the Council would like to express their concerns about the water."

"Certainly, let's hear what they have to say." Thurmond turned away from the small crowd. "So the one in red must be the lawyer," he whispered to me.

Frigging Mona told them everything. "Yes."

Jennings, looking past me, finally interjected. "Not a damn word from you when this thing starts." For our own reasons, Thurmond and I acted as if we didn't hear that order.

We walked to the other table, where I presented them to the Council, then Jeannie. I'd been instructed by Amanda to use just her first two names to make her grandmother's surname more prominent. "And this is Amanda Singer—here as a friend of the Council. They've asked her to speak on their behalf." His smile unwavering, Thurmond shook her hand and Jennings nodded coldly from behind his boss.

I sat with the administrators under the basketball hoop at the other table. Neither of them removed their coats. Thurmond opened his notebook; Jennings removed the faux fur hat, showing his thin blond hair. A few late arrivals from town walked in and sat down.

At the microphone, Felicita, the acting chair, welcomed everyone and explained the purpose of the meeting in both languages. Amanda stood, stayed behind the table, and began a concise presentation of facts, pausing at times for Jeannie's interpretation in Navajo. The lawyer explained the school's water data, the known and suspected ramifications of lead poisoning, and the FIC's response.

Then Amanda called on me to describe the unofficial steps the staff had taken to reduce lead consumption. Staying seated, I did that as factually as I could. While I spoke, I noticed Jennings, his malevolent eyes darting my way. *Too damn bad, jerk.*

After Jeannie repeated my part in Navajo, Amanda called on Abby, who explained the anomalous cluster of Special Ed students in the school. She adamantly declared that lead poisoning was the only logical explanation.

Thurmond listened without comment until Jeannie finished in Navajo. "Miss Singer," he said, "wouldn't there have to be some kind of testing to prove elevated lead levels in the children?"

Jeannie interpreted, then Amanda replied. "We have some expertise here on that subject. Leonard Santos is just a year shy of his chemistry degree at UNM. Mr. Santos?"

After the translation, Leonard rose from his chair and stood sideways so he could address the tables as well as the audience. "The science is not complete on any of this," he said, projecting his voice more than I expected. "A test would only show the current levels of lead in their blood, which *should* be low because we've cut down consumption of water from the pipes since last fall."

Not as loud, he interpreted for himself, then took a planned question in Navajo from Felicita. "Mrs. Etcitty asked me if low-level blood test results would mean the kids are okay. The answer is no. As I said, a blood test is a snapshot of *recent* exposure. The effects of lead contamination are irreversible, but you can't test the students for long-term exposure. The fact is that no one knows how long the children have been ingesting lead." As Leonard switched to Navajo, Thurmond and Jennings looked confident, the former unsuccessfully masking a smirk to his sullen assistant.

Carlton stood up next and moved over to the microphone. He made sure it worked, greeting the audience in Navajo. He began speaking in low but clear English. "We don't care about proving anything for now, but the Council wants funds right away to make the temporary water system better." He interpreted for himself, then continued. "The Council wants a promise in writing from the FIC for a permanent fix to the lead problem." He added that they also needed a second Special Ed teacher and aide. When he finished in Navajo, the audience applauded with the same respectful reserve you'd hear after he hit a jump shot in a basketball game.

Amanda stood again and faced the administrators. "As you can see, Mr. Thurmond, the Council is not interested in the FIC's negligence—for now." She paused for effect. "Their priority is the children of this community, and the timely mitigation of the lead problem. That's it—the ball's in your court." Amanda pointed a forefinger and her lips at Thurmond with full bi-cultural effect.

Following Jeannie's interpretation, Thurmond stood, cleared his throat, and glanced confidently at his open notebook. "Very impressive, Miss Santos, uh, Singer." He made a sly grin. "But there's no need for all of this emotion." He nodded to the other table. "We appreciate the concerns of the Council and community, but the underlying problem will soon be moot."

He waited for Jeannie, who explained "moot" at least twice, followed by some grumbling in the crowd. "I'm pleased to announce," Thurmond said with another smile, "that the demolition of Raven Point's school building has already been moved up to this coming summer. Three portables will serve as the temporary school in the fall, and the dormitory will be replaced in a few years." After the superintendent made another condescending nod, Jeannie began in Navajo. The English speakers had already spread the word, and nearly everyone was talking, so Jeannie moved to the microphone to finish interpreting before she yielded to Thurmond.

"Thank you," he said, and everyone settled down. "As for the temporary water system, we will, of course, meet your requests. After the new principal starts here in January, we need to have a meeting with the Council and community to get your input on the new school, which will include . . . ." Now he too paused for effect, broadening his smile. " . . . an attached gymnasium."

That did it. Most of the crowd began speaking excitedly to each other, not waiting for translation. Felicita and Jon were all grins, but Carlton stared ahead. After the audience quieted,

Thurmond asked for questions while Jennings looked on, smug but still cross.

Janet asked if there would be a new kitchen; Thurmond said the old one would suffice for now. Two questions followed concerning the size and amenities of the new gym. Thurmond responded, then listened to yet another question about the gym. Eager to end on that topic, he answered briefly then stood up during translation before he thanked everyone, smirking again along with his politician's wave.

Carlton was already up and walking over to Hawthorne. The two Shepards started for the exit and passed Mona, waddling toward the superintendent, the only person moving his direction. After she shook his hand and made some effusive remarks, Amanda and Abby walked up there to confront Thurmond. Elizabeth and Leonard also approached but just stood nearby, listening.

Deciding that my two cents wouldn't influence the outcome of the debate, I walked onto the court to help Beth, Benny, Martin, and George fold up the chairs. Marla left with the rest of the kids as the delighted crowd chatted in small groups or filed out past Mona and the administrators, who stood in a face-off against Amanda and Abby.

We finished laying down all the chairs, and Leonard started over to help us, but I intercepted him. "Well, who's winning?" I asked, but he just shook his head. Eddie and some other Old Ravens showed up to help the kids, so Leonard and I walked off to talk.

"I sure didn't see that coming," he said. "Talk about changing the subject."

"Yeah, they just sat there in the catbird seat the whole damn time."

Leonard closed his eyes for a moment, then looked at me, his shoulders slumped. "I had hopes before for Thurmond, but he'll only do the minimum to defuse the situation. When Abby told him that a new dorm is more important than a gym, he laughed and said, 'Good luck with that idea.' He denied we have any health issues and said an additional teacher is out of the question. When the new principal comes, you can bet he'll just be another one of the boys."

"My God, Leonard, we must be able to do something."

"Yeah, go on with our work and watch them like a hawk. I doubt that you'll have to worry about it for very long."

"Why?"

"Remember what I told you before? You can probably expect a transfer in June to another agency, or they'll give you a positive evaluation and ask you to resign."

"Just like that?"

"That's how it works when outsiders don't play the game. If you decide to stay on the Rez, there are some state schools now where you can apply."

I watched the men carry off both tables as the kids took the last chairs. Amanda was still giving Thurmond an earful, Jennings right behind. I saw Mona interrupt, her thick arms wobbling as she made a point. Elizabeth was gone and Abby had retreated several feet back to the stage, arms crossed, glaring at the argument.

I turned to Leonard. "Well, Amanda's certainly getting her money's worth."

"You can be sure of that, but she can't do much while everybody's so excited about the new school and gym. The good thing is that Hosteen and Carlton won't be distracted by shiny objects from the FIC. Amanda will want to meet with the Council after Hosteen's back again."

"She's really something."

"Glad you think so—I wasn't sure you two would get along. By the way, I had nothing to do with Abby's little hints last night."

"I know," I said with what was probably a sheepish smile. "But I was thinking we could all get together again tonight."

He turned toward Amanda. "I don't know if she has to leave right away, but if you can break that up, we might find out. Fair warning, Sean—my sister's even more independent than you are, and she—" He exhaled audibly. "Never mind."

"Yeah, maybe I'll find out for myself."

Beth and the three boys raced for the ball box so they could shoot around at the far end of the gym. Eddie and my teammates, except the Shepard brothers, were changing shoes to get ready to cast jump shots at the good basket.

"C'mon, Leonard," I said, jesting. "I jus' wanna be mischief." He looked at me curiously before I hurried off toward his sister. I saw him join Abby at the stage as I approached Amanda, who was half-listening to Thurmond and shaking her head.

"Miss Singer," I broke in, "can we have a minute?" I tried pointing my lips—toward Abby and Leonard.

"I'm finished here, Sean." She was intentionally loud. "Eventually, I think we might see these folks in court." As we moved away I heard Mona mutter something to the two men, who cackled at our expense. At that moment, the Old Ravens fired away.

Our disillusionment began to fade as all four of us snickered at the sight of basketballs raining down on Mona and the two administrators, one ball ricocheting off Jennings's head before they all scrambled for the exit. We looked at each other again and laughed.

"Well, that was worth waiting for," I said to Abby and Amanda, who'd been holding each other in their merriment.

Finally reduced to chuckles, we got our coats and started for the door. I stopped for a moment to tell Eddie that Marla would be back later to get the kids. Following the two women and Leonard around the barrier, I watched him push the door out into a blizzard like the one we endured only days before. He slammed the door right away.

"Well, crap," Amanda said, "I'd be nuts to drive home in that."

"And we'd go nuts if you tried," Leonard told her as we began buttoning and zipping.

"That's right." Abby cinched her hood. "Ya know, none of us had much of a Thanksgiving. Let's scrounge up some eats and celebrate."

"Great idea, we can use my place," I said. "I actually cleaned it up."

Leonard nudged my arm. "Man, this *is* an occasion."

The four of us walked out and huddled together against the storm, laughing again as if we were off on a lark.

)-)

ACKNOWLEDGMENTS

Somehow, Gene Gade is still a friend since our days on the Navajo decades ago. He served there as a Conscientious Objector, then stayed on for several more years. Among other things, Gene is an author, teacher, geologist, anthropologist, whitewater guide, devoted father, and one of the founders of the Vore Buffalo Jump in Cody, Wyoming. A first reader of this book, I doubt that anyone has Gene's knowledge of both the issues and environs presented here.

A fellow graduate of the University of Arizona, Ryan Winet is the author's great-nephew and a college English teacher in Florida. He is also the illustrator of a graphic novel, *The Parish, An AmeriCorps Story* (Beating Windward Press). He designed the cover of this book and also "became" the character, Hawthorne, in order to create the six vivid illustrations inside. Ryan, another first reader, offered germane and expert comment on both content and copy.

I am also pleased to acknowledge four more first readers who offered needed criticism and encouragement: Carl Kleinschmitt (Los Angeles), Robert "RJ" Jackson (Fremont, CA), Dr. William T. Cox (Selah, WA); Lucinda Swedberg (White Cone, AZ).

My thanks to Betsy Tice White and Michelle Babb, editors, and especially to Duke Pennell, the ultimate editor of this work as well as the owner of Pen-L Publishing.

ABOUT THE AUTHOR

Born and raised in Los Angeles, Terry Winetsky has been an educator for more than four decades.

After a stint in the Peace Corps, his first teaching post was in South-Central L.A.—six classes of low-income seventh-graders. It was the spring of 1968, when Martin Luther King was assassinated. Those experiences were germane to both the setting and conflicts of his historical novel, *Los Angeles, 1968, Happy Ranch to Watts,* which is Book III in the American Teachers Series. (2014- Pen-L publishing).

After returning to college for his certification, Winetsky taught English and Spanish to students of all ages in the Southwest and Northwest. Before retiring in 1998, he was a Bilingual/Migrant Education specialist in Yakima, Washington, where he is now a part-time volunteer for La Casa Hogar, tutoring adult farmworkers.

Pen-L has also republished his previous stand-alone novels, *Grey Pine* and *María Juana's Gift,* which are now the first two books in the American Teachers Series. More information on those novels can be found at Winetsky's website below.

Winetsky's fourth novel, *Belagana-Belazana* (Book IV in the American Teachers Series), published by Pen-L in January of 2017, takes place in the Navajo Nation, where he and his spouse taught for five years.

Terry lives near Yakima with his wife of forty-seven years, Kathleen, an Early Childhood Special Education teacher.

FIND MORE AMERICAN TEACHERS SERIES BOOKS AT
WWW.PEN-L.COM/AMERICANTEACHERS.HTML

VISIT THE AUTHOR'S WEBSITE AT
WWW.TLWINETSKY.COM

Made in the USA
Monee, IL
23 July 2023

39575926R10157